RUNNING MATE

BY KATIE ASHLEY

Copyright @2017 Katie Ashley
Interior formatting by Indie Pixel Studio | www.indiepixelstudio.com
Cover Design and Interior Graphics by Lori Jackson Design

ISBN-13: 978-1544273877
ISBN-10: 1544273878

First Edition: March 01, 2017

CHAPTER ONE

ADDISON

THERE ARE SOME days you never expect to change your life. I'm not talking about a little change off course toward a new and exciting destination—I'm talking about having your entire world shift on its axis and completely restart. Days like these never start off like a Disney movie with singing birds awakening you from a restful slumber while woodland creatures prepare your breakfast and sort out your wardrobe choices.

No, life-altering days always seem to start off in the seventh ring of hell, like when your alarm doesn't go off and you're subsequently denied your morning caffeine fix as you sprint around your apartment getting ready at a manic pace. After ensuring that your skirt isn't tucked up in your pantyhose and that you indeed have a bra on, you haul ass to the bus stop just as the bus careens off. After cursing the bus driver and the universe, you then start jogging the ten blocks to work. Although a cab looks awfully inviting, you remember it's the end of the month, and you have exactly $66.54 left in your checking account. It's either eat or ride in a cab, and you enjoy food—well, wine, more precisely—way too much to give in to such extravagances.

So you soldier on while the theme to *The Jeffersons* plays in your head, because one day, the student loan debt will be paid off and you'll get to move on up to the East Side to a deluxe apartment in the sky—though in your case, it's a brownstone in Georgetown. Until then, you're pretty much screwed.

Just as you round the corner to your building, one of the heels on your Jimmy Choos gets stuck in a street grate, which causes you to pitch forward and practically eat cement. Not only has your purse gone flying, so has the hem of your skirt. It's currently circling your equator while you moon the morning rush hour crowd.

Oh yeah. Today was a day that would have made even Mother Teresa use a few choice expletives while downing a cold one.

As I was collecting myself off the pavement, my ass received a raucous welcome from the hard hat-wearing Neanderthals across the street. First it was whistles and barking like horndogs. Then they got verbal.

"Yeah, baby! I'd love to pound dat!"

"Mm, mm, mm. Let me pull that thong off with my teeth before I eat that ass!"

When I quickly jerked my skirt down over my hips, the hoots and hollers turned to booing. "Oh fuck off, jackholes!" I shouted over my shoulder before I grabbed my purse and the last shreds of my dignity off the sidewalk. My rebuff was met with howling laughter.

Rolling my eyes, I hobbled into the building with my Choos in one hand and the busted heel in the other. Thankfully, I was completely OCD, so I had a bottle of super glue in my desk drawer that I could use for a quick repair job. It wasn't like my current dire financial straits would allow for a new pair. These were my black heels—the big gun of my foot attire. At the moment, I could barely afford Payless, least of all more designer shoes. Since I'd bought the pair used off Ebay, I guess I was more of a designer poser than anything.

The elevator swooshed upward to the tenth floor, causing my empty stomach to lurch. After the doors opened, I hurried down the hallway and through the glass doors of the presidential campaign headquarters for Senator James Callahan. At twenty past nine, the place was already buzzing. After his narrow wins in the New Hampshire primary and Iowa caucus, the campaign had kicked into overdrive.

With just weeks until the convention, there wasn't a moment to waste. When someone runs for president, primary season is do or die. The more wins you rack up, the more likely you are to get the party's nomination at the summer convention. Since Senator Callahan had only beaten his opponent by five points in each event, he and his team had to put their noses to the grindstone, which in turn meant the campaign staff were working double time.

After tossing my heels and purse on my desk, I made a beeline to the coffee pot. Today wasn't the day to weaken the sweet, somewhat narcotic brew with sugar or cream. Nope—I began guzzling it down strong and black while it was still scorching hot. My eyes rolled back in my head, and I moaned in almost orgasmic bliss as the caffeine pumped through my system.

Once I'd had a good hit, I turned my attention to the boxes of donuts on the table. Sugar overload and high fat content were the staples of a campaign staffer's diet. You could count on donuts and pastries for breakfast and pizza followed by more pizza throughout the day. The campaign budget went to TV ads, signs, and banners; we weren't approved for catered-in nutritious foods. When I wasn't running late, I tried to bring salad and fruit with me. I'd only been with the campaign six months, but I'd already gained ten pounds. My older brother loved to tease me by saying the entire ten pounds had gone to my chest and ass, and after today's hard-hat appreciation of said ass, I was starting to agree with him.

I refilled my coffee, grabbed a cinnamon donut with my free hand, and then headed back to my desk. My phone was ringing when I got there. "Volunteer Services," I answered.

It was my New York attaché, Grant. "Hey Ads, we're in deep shit with the Latinos for Callahan's rally."

Groaning, I slurped on more coffee. "What do you mean?"

"The translator quit, so next weekend's borough rallies in NYC *and* the Jersey rallies are totally fucked."

I took a deep breath and collected my thoughts before I replied. "Okay. Go ahead and start fielding resumes for a new tri-city area translator. Worse comes to worst, I'll take the train up and do it myself."

"You speak Spanish?" Grant questioned incredulously.

"Si. Soy fluido en espanol, pendejo," I replied.

Grant chuckled. "Let me guess, you just used an expletive to describe me."

"I most certainly did."

"Call me crazy for doubting you, but didn't you grow up in North Carolina?"

"Yes, I did. I also spent every summer in Central America. You tend to pick things up."

"I see."

"For future reference, pendejo is asshole. I could also call you a cabrón."

"Okay, okay. I'll never doubt your skills again."

"You better not. Keep me posted on the translator."

"You got it."

"Adios pendejo."

Grant laughed. "Bye Ads."

After hanging up with Grant, I fielded a few more calls while downing my coffee and scarfing down the donut. Since my stomach was still rumbling, I decided my day from hell allowed me to throw calorie counting to the wind, so I snagged another cinnamon donut.

As I made my way back to my desk, I couldn't help feeling so very blessed that I called the Callahan campaign home. Not only was it a total coup that I'd landed the job at just twenty-seven, it couldn't have come at a better time for me both professionally and personally. I'd spent the first two years out of college working as the personal assistant to Representative Walter Gregson. While I spent my days with Walt Sr., my nights were spent with his son, Walt Jr., so yeah, you could say nepotism had landed me that job.

Walt and I met our senior year at Duke where we were both political science majors, and we started living together after just six months. Once we graduated, we moved to an apartment in Georgetown. While I started working for his father's political office, Walt took a job with a lobbying firm.

Everything seemed perfect—like *put a ring on it* perfect. Looking back now, I realize how naïve I was about all the nights I went to bed alone. Walt assured me that his long days were being forced on him by his bosses. He was the new guy and had to earn his stripes, which meant working into the wee hours of the morning.

The truth was Walt had fallen victim to what I liked to call the DC Dick Curse. Something about the air is different in DC; it fans the flames of narcissism and inflated egos. Even the most committed man who would never dream of straying can get the wandering eye. It's like they're sucked into the Bermuda Triangle of Pussy.

It wasn't just Walt's eye that did the wandering; his dick ended up wandering into the vagina of one of the office interns. I had the pleasure of discovering this one night when I went to surprise him with his favorite Thai takeout. Instead of finding him toiling away at his computer, I found him nailing the intern doggy style over his desk.

After he had chased me down to the elevators with his semi-erect dick flapping in the wind, he begged me not to leave. He did the familiar song and dance that all men who get caught cheating do. He promised he would never do it again. It was only about sex. He loved me, never meant to hurt me. He even offered up all the heavy hitters like therapy and having the intern transferred.

But, in my heart of hearts, I knew I could never trust him again, so I broke up with him. What I would soon learn is when I broke up with Walt Jr., I also broke up with his father. I was unceremoniously let go the very next day—and by unceremoniously, I mean a security guard met me at the door with a box containing the contents of my desk and told me I didn't work there anymore. Bad news obviously traveled from son to father quickly. *Bastards.*

In the span of a few days, I found myself jobless and homeless. I could have tucked my tail between my legs and gone home to my parents in North Carolina, but I was far too independent for that. My strength of character was both a blessing and a curse for my parents. They were the ones who raised me to be resilient and stand on my own two feet. During their time as missionaries in Central America, my sister, brother, and I had learned to be scrappy and resourceful, but I think now they wished I was a little less independent and self-reliant so I could take a nice job close to home and marry some youth minister at their church like my older sister, Amy, had.

Instead, I stayed with my older brother at his apartment in Arlington, Virginia, until I got the job with the Callahan campaign. After a few months with a steady paycheck, I moved into an overpriced yet extremely shitty one-bedroom apartment in the city—the very one I'd been running around in like a maniac when I woke up late that morning.

With a few free moments, I dug the super glue out of my desk drawer. As I lay the materials out on my desk, it felt like I was scrubbing up to go into surgery. Saving a beloved and necessary shoe was serious business. "Work with me, Choo. You still got life in you, bud," I cajoled. Laying my hand on the toe of the shoe, I pinched my eyes shut and channeled my best televangelist impression as I cried dramatically, "Heal your heel, Choo!"

"Miss Monroe?"

My eyes snapped open as I jerked my gaze from my shoe into the eyes of Bernard George, the head of the campaign. My boss. The big cheese.

After swallowing hard, I squeaked, "Yes sir?"

"Might I have a word?"

Oh, fuckity, fuck, fuuuuck! No one had ever had just *a word* with Mr. George. You had to get through three staffers just to wave at him. His palatial office with a view of the Potomac appeared to have more guards around it than one of the security checkpoints at the airport. This was soooo bad.

I forced a bright smile to my face. "Yes sir, of course."

After sliding on my gimpy shoe, I then proceeded to hobble off-kilter after Mr. George. The broken Choo seemed to fit what I could only anticipate was my break with the campaign, and my chin trembled as I dealt with the impending doom. You didn't come back from being fired from a campaign—

political staffers had a long memory when it came to people who fucked up. Four years down the road, there might be a new candidate, but you would forever have the word loser on your forehead like a biblical mark of the beast.

Instead of ushering me into his office, Mr. George held the glass exit door open for me. I bit down on my lip to keep from crying. I wasn't even going to get a courteous brushoff in his office. Someone was probably emptying my desk drawer right now. It would be just like my demise at Representative Gregson's office. Considering I'd been kicking ass and taking names at my job, I couldn't help but wonder what I had done that had so offended Mr. George.

He gave me a tight smile as we got onto the elevator, and we spent the ride down in awkward silence. Once we reached the ground floor, he didn't head to the front of the building. Instead, he started toward the back exit. *Jesus, talk about a walk of shame.* Instead of dissolving into hysterics, I threw my shoulders back and held my head high. There would be time for falling to pieces later. For the moment, I had to save face.

When I got outside, the sunlight momentarily blinded me, but after my eyes adjusted, I did a double take at the sight of Mr. George standing in front of a stretch limo.

"Wow, you guys really fire in style, don't you?" I mused.

Mr. George's salt and pepper brows knitted together. "Excuse me?"

"You're firing me, right?"

He chuckled. "Of course not. You're one of the best volunteer coordinators I've ever seen in all my years of running campaigns."

Suddenly I felt very stupid for overreacting; jumping to paranoid conclusions was one of my worst character traits. "I'm sorry. It's just…no one on my level ever gets to see you, least of all have a meeting with you. I couldn't help but assume I was being fired."

"No, Miss Monroe, you are definitely not being fired."

"Then what exactly is going on?"

"Senator Callahan has something he wishes to speak to you about in private."

"You're shitting me." My extreme shock had apparently rendered me foul-mouthed. Mortification rocketed through me, and my cheeks flushed. "Excuse my language. This is all very unexpected."

Mr. George just chuckled. "It's quite all right, Miss Monroe. I find my mouth runs away with me sometimes as well." It was hard to imagine Mr. George ever being less than completely straitlaced.

My knees started shaking in my Choos. I couldn't possibly imagine what Senator Callahan wanted to speak to me about. The part of me that wanted to see the glass half full imagined he wanted to promote me to a higher position in the campaign, but the pessimistic side of me was much, much bigger, especially after the morning from hell I'd had so far.

But then an icy feeling of unease crept its way up my spine. Although most days I struggled with self-esteem just like any other woman, I still knew in my heart of hearts that I was a decent-looking girl. What if Senator Callahan had seen my picture and decided he wanted to have his way with me? Even though he could easily be considered a silver fox, there was no way in hell I would ever use sex to further my career.

It was then that I quietly began humming "He Had It Coming" from the musical *Chicago*. After spending middle and high school immersed in musical theater, I often resorted to humming show tunes whenever I was nervous. Most of the time, I managed to find a tune to go with my current mood.

As the driver opened the limo door, Mr. George patted my back. "Stop worrying, Miss Monroe. Your job is safe, but better yet, *you* are safe."

At his knowing look, a relieved breath whooshed out of me. "I'm glad to hear that, sir," I replied as I dropped into the limo. I slid across the seat, leaving plenty of room for Mr. George, who eased down beside me.

Once we got on our way, Mr. George dug a mini bottle of Moet out of the mini-fridge across from us. "Would you like some champagne?" he offered.

Although it would have probably settled my out-of-control nerves, I decided I should pass. After a breakfast of champions comprised of black coffee and donuts, I wasn't sure my stomach could handle the bubbles. Besides, I needed a clear head for what was about to happen, and alcohol wasn't going to make me sharp. There was also the less than desirable fact that champagne always made me burp, and the last thing I needed was to gross Mr. George out after cursing around him.

"No, thank you," I politely declined.

With a wink, Mr. George put the champagne back and handed me a bottle of water. "Just so you know, I wasn't trying to ply you with alcohol to make a pass at you."

A flush of embarrassment tinged my cheeks since that thought had crossed my mind. "That's not what I was thinking," I lied.

"It's exactly what you were thinking, along with the fact that you didn't think drinking would calm your anxiety about your meeting with Senator Callahan."

I widened my eyes. "How could you possible know that?"

"Because the whole *limo ride to see a powerful man* thing would seem nefarious in most people's minds. Throw in the fact that you are an attractive young woman and it makes it seem even seedier."

"Well...I..."

"Since I could read your apprehension, I thought a sip or two of alcohol might calm your nerves."

"Did you also anticipate that I refused on the grounds that champagne makes me burp?" *Oh Jesus, did I actually say that out loud?*

Mr. George chuckled. "No, but I know what you mean. It gives me the worst indigestion."

I smiled. "Let me guess, you worked in profiling before you switched over to campaign work?"

"You're very good, Miss Monroe. I worked thirty years with the FBI. Becoming a campaign manager is part of my retirement."

"Doesn't seem like a very relaxing job to me."

"It keeps my mind active, which is what I wanted, and I still get time off between election years." Mr. George turned in his seat to face me directly. "Enough about me. Tell me, how familiar are you with James Callahan?"

A smirk crept across my lips. "I could probably recite his stances on foreign and domestic policies in my sleep, not to mention his voting history in the Senate."

Mr. George nodded. "I imagined as much. I'm more interested in what you know about him personally."

It was an odd inquiry, but while I rarely concerned myself with Senator Callahan's private life when I was working with volunteers, it didn't mean I was unprepared. If there was one thing I prided myself on, it was being over-prepared for any given situation. "Before interviewing for the job with the Callahan campaign, I did extensive research on his background."

Stroking his chin, Mr. George questioned, "And what did you learn?"

I furrowed my brows in confusion. "You want me to tell you what I know?"

"Yes."

Okay then, ask and you shall receive. After sucking in a breath, I began reciting what felt like a class report. "James Thornton Callahan III was born in Alexandria, Virginia. He attended military prep schools before graduating from West Point and was decorated for his service in Vietnam. After leading two tours as an Army Major, he returned home to work at The Callahan Corporation, the company his self-made grandfather had built from the ground up. His first wife, Celia, died of cancer just two years after they married. Like John F. Kennedy, he was elected to his first term in the senate as a bachelor. A decade after losing Celia, he wed his second wife, Jane Barrett, a distant cousin of the famous Vanderbilt family, and they had three children, James Thornton IV, or Thorn as he is called, Barrett, and Caroline."

When I finally paused to take another breath, Mr. George smiled at me. "Very impressive, Miss Monroe."

"Thank you, sir."

Mr. George shook his head. "Please don't call me sir. It's Bernie."

"Okay, Bernie."

As the limo came to a stop, I peered out the window to see we had arrived at the ultra-posh Jefferson Hotel. I'd only been once, when I attended a fundraiser reception for Representative Gregson there. The driver opened the door and Bernie and I stepped out. At my continued hobbling, Bernie glanced down at my broken Choo. At his puzzled look, I quickly blurted out, "It happened on the way in this morning. I was trying to fix it when you called for me."

"That's quite all right, Miss Monroe. Once we get to James's suite, you can leave the shoe with one of his staffers to repair."

"Oh, no. That won't be necessary," I argued as we stepped into the elevator.

Bernie smiled at me. "I insist."

I decided it was useless to argue anymore. Instead, I said, "Thank you. I appreciate it very much." *My Choo will live to see another day!*

After Bernie used a special key card, the elevator started climbing up to the penthouse. When the doors opened to the white and black marbled floors and sparkling chandeliers, I fought hard to keep my jaw from dropping. I couldn't imagine what it was like living with this sort of opulence on a daily basis. I mean, it was just a basecamp for the moment, but considering the wealth Senator Callahan came from, I could only imagine what his house looked like. Most likely it was more of a mansion than a house.

Although most presidential candidates set up their campaign headquarters in their hometown or home state, Senator Callahan had decided on DC for his since his home in Alexandria wasn't that far from the capital. So far, he'd only been to the headquarters twice, and I'd missed him both times because I was out of the office working events. This was the first time I was meeting him, and I couldn't help feeling like a nervous wreck.

Two men who appeared to be in their late twenties were seated in the sitting room to the left of the foyer. They briefly peered up from the laptops they were hunkered over, and with a flick of his hand, Bernie had them both shooting to their feet. "Could one of you gentlemen take Miss Monroe's shoe to have it repaired?"

For a moment, it looked like they might break into a shoving match to see who could rush over to us fast enough. The taller of the two—who was also quite a looker—dropped to his knees before me. "Oh my," I gasped.

He lifted my foot up and gently took off my broken Choo then gazed up at me through the long strands of his blond hair. "I'll have it ready ASAP."

"Thank you, Jonathan," Bernie said.

I smiled down at Jonathan while trying not to imagine tackling him to the floor for a quickie. "Yes, thank you, Jonathan.

"It's my pleasure."

Don't even go there, Addison. Just because it's been almost a year since you've had sex, that's no excuse to pervert the simplest of phrases. "Would you like me to have your other cleaned and polished?" Jonathan asked.

"Oh, um, well…I guess it couldn't hurt."

He nodded before taking my other shoe and leaving me Chooless. After rising to his feet, he headed for the elevator. As I gazed down at my feet, I sighed at how pathetic they looked, and in turn, how pathetic I looked. I was going to meet the potential future leader of the free world barefoot.

Bernie nodded for me to follow him down the hallway. When we walked into a spacious living room, I almost froze at the sight of Senator Callahan sitting at the twelve-person dining room table in the next room. There were two men sitting on either side of him, and at the sight of me, they all stood up. When Senator Callahan nodded at them, they picked up the files in front of them and headed out of the room.

I followed Bernie across the living room toward Senator Callahan. A warm, inviting smile lit up his face as he came around the side of the table and he threw out his hand for me to shake. "Miss Monroe, James Callahan. It's a pleasure to meet you."

A nervous titter of a laugh escaped my lips. "No, sir, I'm sure the pleasure is all mine."

After pumping my hand several times, Senator Callahan motioned for me to have a seat. Bernie pulled the chair out for me before sitting down next to me and once we were seated, Senator Callahan once again sat at the head of the table. Then he riffled through a few papers in front of him before handing one to me. "Before we proceed with our meeting, I need you to sign this non-disclosure agreement."

Whoa. This was some pretty serious shit. I mean, I'd barely been here five minutes and they were whipping out an NDA. I guess I should have imagined that any private meeting with the senator would entail as much. As I picked up the embossed *Callahan for President* pen in front of me, I momentarily wondered what would happen if I refused. After a quick read-through, I realized I wasn't signing over my firstborn child or anything like that. Once I had scribbled my name on the form, I handed it back to Senator Callahan.

"Thank you, Miss Monroe." After he filed the form away, Senator Callahan smiled at me. "Bernie has told me what a fantastic job you're doing as our volunteer coordinator."

My pride surged. "Thank you, sir. It's truly an honor to hear you say that. I want to do everything I can to ensure you secure the party's nomination, as well as the presidency."

Senator Callahan glanced past me to give Bernie a knowing look. "I'm very glad to hear of your strong commitment to me and my campaign. It's why I hope you will be willing to accept my proposal."

The seriousness of his tone had me squirming in my seat. "And just what is your proposal, sir?"

"Since the beginning of presidential campaigns, a contender's family life was very important to voters. A man or woman needed to exude that they could maintain a strong marriage and produce healthy and successful children. The more picture perfect the family, the more likely a prospective voter was to connect with the candidate. This is still the case today."

"I would interject to say that you do have a picture-perfect family, sir. I always mention yours and Thorn's service when setting up VFW and military volunteers. If I were to be so bold, I would add that you've also had a scandal-free, happy marriage."

"I would say you are correct on all those points." With a wink, he added, "I hope Mrs. Callahan would also agree on the happy marriage part."

I smiled. "I'm sure she would."

"While I thank you for your candor, Miss Monroe, I'm more interested in what you know about my son."

"Thorn or Barrett?"

"Barrett."

When I glanced at Bernie, he nodded his head. Once again, I prepared to give my best book report. "Barrett graduated top of his class at Yale and now works for The Callahan Corporation. He was unable to follow in your military footsteps like his older brother, Thorn, because he was deemed unfit for service due to a congenital heart defect."

"Very nice. I see you presented me with the G-rated version of my son's life."

"He does have a reputation of enjoying partying and playing the field," I added, although that was putting it politely. Barrett's handsome face was always splashed across the society section of the Washington Post, and he usually had a different girl with him in every picture—thought they always fit the same mold of being blonde stick figures. Since Barrett lived in New York City, he hadn't been by campaign headquarters yet. Even if I had been out of the office at an event, I was sure the other office girls would have let me know.

While both Callahan sons would be considered very good-looking, Barrett seemed to have hit the jackpot when it came to the hotness lottery. Both men had a muscular build, although Barrett was leaner. Thorn was blond and blue-eyed like his mother where Barrett had Senator Callahan's jet-black hair and greenish-gold eyes. It made for a winning combination. It also didn't hurt that Barrett oozed sex appeal. From the videos I'd seen of him on TMZ, he had a confident swagger when he walked, along with a megawatt cocky grin. I didn't know what it was exactly, but he just had that star quality, the it factor.

"Yes, you are correct about Barrett's extracurricular activities." He slid the manila folder in front of him over to me. "Within the contents of that file, you can read about the findings of an image consultant hired by the campaign, or I can briefly sum it up for you."

"I'm fine with hearing it in your own words, sir."

A pleased expression came over Senator Callahan's face at my declaration of trust, and I wasn't bullshitting him. I couldn't have possibly worked for his campaign if I didn't believe in his character.

For a moment, I saw a flash of Barrett in the senator's more relaxed face. "Basically it boils down to the fact that with his playboy ways, Barrett is a liability to my campaign."

I furrowed my brows at him. Talking about Barrett Callahan wasn't exactly how I'd pictured this meeting going. What could I possibly to do to help Senator Callahan with such a problem?

Then the reason I'd been brought there finally hit me. "You want me to get Barrett involved with some volunteer opportunities with the campaign to improve his image."

A curious smile curved on Senator Callahan's lips. "Actually, I was thinking of another way you could help my wayward son."

"And what's that?

"While having Barrett appear at campaign events or even charitable ones would certainly help, it wouldn't do a lot to change the public perception of him. I'm looking for something a little more drastic."

"What exactly are you thinking?"

Senator Callahan leaned forward in his chair. "What I'm about to ask you is highly unorthodox, and it is something done out of sheer desperation."

I gulped. I wasn't liking the direction the conversation was taking at all. I started wondering what would happen to my job if I suddenly made a break for the elevator. Of course, I'd have to grab the magic key card from Bernie before I bolted. "Okay," I replied in a half-whisper.

"I need you to pose as Barrett's fiancée through the remainder of the campaign."

After sitting there in stunned silence for a moment, I busted out laughing. As I replayed Senator Callahan's words over in my mind, I continued dissolving into hysterics. The idea that I had been brought here to be a potential fake fiancée was absolutely ridiculous. It was the kind of thing you'd expect from the old Ashton Kutcher show *Punked*.

But, when Bernie and Senator Callahan remained stone-faced, my laughter ceased like someone had abruptly pulled the plug. "Oh, my God. You weren't joking."

Senator Callahan shook his head. "No. I wasn't."

"You are running for the highest office in the land, and you want me to be your son's fake fiancée," I said as I desperately tried to process what was going on.

"Yes, Miss Monroe."

Slowly, I shook my head back and forth. "I liked it better when I thought you were joking."

"I'm sure, on the surface, me bringing you here today to ask this of you seems quite preposterous, but please believe me when I say how very serious I am. Presidential candidates need their family's help on the campaign trail. We cannot be in ten different places at once. Thorn cannot be called home from duty to work on my campaign, and while Caroline wants to help, she's only twenty years old and in the middle of her sophomore year at Vassar."

Senator Callahan exhaled a long breath. "As you can see, Barrett is our only choice."

"Excuse me for being ignorant, but how could something like a fake engagement even be remotely possible?"

"Everything in Washington is a matter of perception. Our city is a façade built on half-truths. It's also the very reason Jackie Kennedy worked so hard to perpetuate the myth of Camelot after John Kennedy was assassinated. Part of his mystique came from the ability of those around him to spin the perception that he was a god among men while carefully concealing his many marital indiscretions."

"And you plan to spin some sort of modern day fairytale with Barrett and me?"

"Yes, I am. With the resources I have at my disposal, I'm confident it would be a great success." At what must've been my continued look of skepticism, Senator Callahan asked, "Have you ever seen the movie *Wag the Dog?*"

I nodded; we'd watched it in my political media class along with the classics like *Mr. Smith Goes to Washington*, *All the President's Men*, and *The Manchurian Candidate*. "Yes sir, I have."

"Then you know if an entire war can be fabricated by the media, it is more than possible to fabricate a relationship."

"But that was a movie," I argued.

"A movie steeped in truths." He winked. "And half-truths."

I brought my hand up to rub my forehead, which was now aching from all the questions swarming inside it. "There's one thing I have to ask." The truth was there were a *million* things I wanted to ask, but at the moment, this was the most pressing one.

"Of course."

"Out of all the women you surely have at your disposal, how on earth did you come up with me?"

Senator Callahan smiled. "I think that is a very fair question. Obviously, we knew it couldn't be anyone of our family's personal acquaintances. It would be far too easy to poke holes in the fabricated romance and disprove the relationship. We needed someone unknown to those around us."

"That makes sense."

"Upon further consideration, I realized I needed someone close to the campaign, someone who believed in me as a person and candidate, someone I felt I could trust to protect my political interests. When we began to go through the campaign staff, you immediately jumped out. Not only were you someone who would be physically appealing to Barrett, you had many personal attributes that made you desirable to the campaign."

"Such as?" Call me cynical, but I was trying not to laugh at the idea that I would be physically appealing to Barrett.

An amused look twinkled in Senator Callahan's eyes. "First and foremost, you're single."

I laughed. "Yes, I can see where that would be important."

"You also have never been married, and although we have come a long way in this country, there is still somewhat of a stigma against divorce among some political circles."

"You're telling me that my greatest attribute is the fact that I'm a single woman? Pardon me, Senator Callahan, but that usually isn't something a girl actually feels proud of."

With a chuckle, the senator replied, "No, Miss Monroe, that was just the first thing that caught our eye. It was much more about the fact that you weren't just a pretty face. You graduated magna cum laude from Duke, and you're working in a very coveted position in a campaign. Being an intelligent, educated, self-reliant woman will appeal to the women's sector of the vote."

"Yes, I can see where that would be helpful." Tilting my head, I asked, "What else?"

A shrewd look entered Senator Callahan's golden eyes. "As of this morning, you have $66.54 in your checking account. You also owe close to one hundred thousand dollars in student loans. The apartment you rent is in a less than desirable area, and you have all secondhand furniture. Instead of a car, you own a bicycle. Basically, you have no assets of any real value."

Scorching embarrassment ricocheted throughout my body at the assessment of my dismal financial situation. I already knew it was bad, but there was something about hearing it from a man I both respected and admired like Senator Callahan that made it even worse. "Okay, so I'm flat broke. What does—" I sucked in a breath while narrowing my eyes at Senator Callahan. "Wait, how do you know how much money I have in my bank account?"

"The FBI did a very thorough background check for me."

I gasped. "You know that's a real invasion of my privacy. What's next, the CIA going through my panty drawer?"

"I apologize, Miss Monroe, but it was a necessary evil. I assure you it was only a little more in-depth than what you faced when you came to work for the campaign. If we were going to ask you to do this, we had to ensure you didn't have any personal or professional skeletons in your closet."

The word skeletons caused my stomach to twist as a face flashed before my mind. *Oh shit.* He could be trouble. "Um, I guess you didn't find anything, huh?"

Senator Callahan tilted his head at me. "You wouldn't be here if we had."

"Right." A nervous laugh bubbled from my lips. "Of course not. I mean, I'm the daughter of a minister. What craziness could I possibly have gotten into in my life?" Although Senator Callahan and Bernie chuckled along with me, it didn't ease my apprehension.

Once my laughter died down and the atmosphere grew serious, I went back to a question still plaguing me. "Let me ask again: what does me being flat broke have to do with anything?"

"I'm prepared to offer you a million dollars to do this."

Holy. Shit. My knees started shaking again, and I fought the urge to break out into humming "Climb Every Mountain" from *The Sound of Music.* I blinked rapidly at Senator Callahan. "I'm sorry, but did you just say…" I could barely bring myself to utter the words. "O-One m-million d-dollars"? I finally stammered.

Senator Callahan nodded. "Yes, Miss Monroe, I did. During the campaign, the sum will be divided into monthly paychecks, and the balance will be paid upon Election Day. All your travel expenses will be covered through the campaign. You will also be allowed to keep the wardrobe the campaign purchases for you." His eyes dropped down to my bare feet. "That includes shoes."

Oh my God. I was actually sitting barefoot in front of the potential future president of the United States. "Yeah, my Choo—it got caught in a street grate and broke. I fell…and I mooned some construction workers," I explained, just as randomly as Baby saying she carried a watermelon in *Dirty Dancing.*

Oh no. I did not just say that out loud. Please tell me I didn't just say that out loud.

The corners of Senator Callahan's lips quirked. "How unfortunate."

Oh God, I had said it aloud. *Kill me now.* I was sure both Bernie and Senator Callahan were going to start having serious doubts about my ability to perform in the campaign, considering my flakiness.

"You said a million dollars, right?"

"Yes. I realize it's a little over nine months for seven figures."

"Just playing devil's advocate here…what happens if you don't secure the nomination?"

"You'll still receive the million."

"Wow," I not-so-eloquently muttered. I couldn't even begin to imagine what it would be like to have that much money. No more living paycheck to paycheck, no more student loan debt, no more buying designer shoes off Ebay and gluing the broken heels back on. No more shitty apartment where the hot water always seemed to be running out. I could consider a place in Georgetown, which had always been my dream. Okay, so maybe it was easier than I thought to imagine having that much money.

"Excuse me for saying this, but a million dollars seems a little extravagant just to be Barrett's fiancée."

"You obviously haven't met Barrett yet," Senator Callahan quipped, causing Bernie to chuckle.

"I assume you're suggesting that, because of his reputation, it will be difficult to pretend to be his fiancée."

"In some ways, yes, but it isn't just being my son's fiancée. It's months of hard work, Miss Monroe. The campaign trail has a brutal pace, of which I know you are aware. Sometimes you're in three cities in one day. It will be asking a lot of you to go on the road." He gave me a tight smile. "But the one million also ensures your silence about this deal."

Silence about this deal—could I do that not just for the next nine months, but for the rest of my life? I wasn't known for being a blabbermouth when it came to important information, but at the same time, what if I accidentally spilled the beans in a moment of panic, like if the first time a mic was stuck in my face for an interview my mind went blank so I decided to blurt out, "It's a fake engagement! I'm a fake! We're faking it!"

"As well as the non-disclosure agreement you just signed," Bernie added.

Now I knew why they'd had me sign the NDA earlier. If I broke it, I could end up being sued, which of course was the last thing I needed—not to mention that although he seemed like a sweet, gentle person, Senator Callahan probably knew people who could make me disappear if I ratted them out. I shuddered at the thought.

When Bernie reached over to pat my back, I jumped. "Don't worry, Miss Monroe. Nothing bad is going to happen to you if you don't agree to Senator Callahan's proposal."

My mouth dropped open. "Okay, that's kinda starting to get a little creepy."

He smiled. "My wife hates it, too."

"I can imagine."

When Senator Callahan cleared his throat, I turned my attention back to him. "Bernie's right. Nothing is going to happen to you if you don't take the deal. I know if you don't take it, you'll continue working hard to ensure I get elected."

Holy shit. My job—how could I have forgotten about that? "If I do say yes—and that's a very big if—what would happen to my job?"

"You would stay on as volunteer coordinator. Because I would need you working the campaign trail, we would bring someone else into headquarters while you worked part-time from the road when time allowed. Part of the cover story would be that you and Barrett met through the campaign, and the two of you decided to keep your relationship secret for many months because you didn't want people to think you landed your job due to nepotism."

Although I hated to admit it, that sounded plausible. It was obvious that they had put a lot of thought into this whole fake fiancée charade. With their effort and resources, I wasn't sure how it could possibly fail.

While the pace of the campaign trail sounded grueling, I liked the idea of getting to travel and see different parts of the country. There was also the plus that I would be doing all that traveling at someone else's expense. Throw in a million dollars, and I didn't know how I could possibly say no. This was the type of opportunity where if you didn't take it, you'd beat yourself up over it for the rest of your life.

Sitting there at that table, I felt like Eve in the Garden of Eden with the serpent coiled around my body, whispering into my ear to offer me the forbidden fruit. *Change your life, take the deal. After all, it's only for a little while. Think of how freeing it will be to no longer be bound by financial strain.*

At the end of the day, how hard could it be to pretend to be in love with Barrett? I'd faked love tons of times over the years in the theatrical productions I'd been in. This couldn't be that different.

Then, as I glanced around the table, I realized for the first time that someone was noticeably absent: my future fake fiancée. "Why isn't Barrett here?"

Senator Callahan shifted in his leatherback chair. "He isn't aware that we're having this meeting."

My mouth dropped open so far I felt it might hit the table. "You mean you just pitched this whole scheme to me without his consent?" I huffed in outrage.

"Yes."

"That's crazy."

"At first glance, perhaps, but upon further inspection, no. I wanted to be able to present the entire picture to Barrett when I sat him down, to be able to say we had someone who had confirmed, and this is who she is." With a tight smile, Senator Callahan added, "I come from a business background, Miss Monroe. I'm all about the art of the deal, and the best way to sell a product."

"What happens if Barrett says no?"

"He won't," he replied, the strength of his voice echoing his belief.

"How can you be so sure?"

"Because I know my son."

Since I hadn't yet become a parent, I knew I couldn't argue with that statement. I had to believe, like Senator Callahan did, that Barrett would agree. "Does Mrs. Callahan share your certainty?"

"Jane is fully aware of what I'm proposing. I rarely do anything without running it by her first."

So Mrs. Callahan was in on the scheme, too. I wondered just how many insiders would know the truth about Barrett. I was sure if I asked that question, Senator Callahan would merely play it off by saying Washington is built on secrets. If the identity of Deep Throat in the Watergate scandal could stay buried for decades, I was pretty sure Barrett's and my secret was safe. Maybe there would be some kind of secret handshake to let me know who was in the know. Either way, I would need to know who knew what so I didn't accidentally talk openly with someone not in the know. *Can I really do this?*

"If you need to take some time to think it over, I will understand. I know we're asking a lot of you," Senator Callahan said, breaking the silence that had fallen over the table.

Maybe I should have taken more time. Maybe I should have stopped to weigh the emotional cons of this crazy scheme. Maybe I should have thought about what would happen if I actually fell in love with Barrett Callahan.

But I didn't.

Instead, my lips slid into a smile as I said, "I accept."

CHAPTER TWO

BARRETT

"YOU LIKE THAT?" I growled into the ear of the stacked blonde I was banging. Her bare ass was pinned against the plane window. Of course, at thirty thousand feet, it wasn't like anyone was going to pass by and get an eye-full. Standing between her legs, I held her upright with my forearms under the backs of her knees.

"Oh yeah, baby. *Hard.*"

She didn't have to tell me twice. I was more than happy to oblige her. Making a woman lose her mind during sex had so many benefits. I never understood these pricks who only thought about getting themselves off. I never came harder than I did when I had a satisfied woman screaming my name while her walls convulsed around my cock.

There's also something to be said for airplane sex. You could say I was quite the connoisseur of all types of sex. Back-seat-of-the-car sex, bathroom sex, park-bench sex, yacht sex—which could be preceded by jet-ski sex, or even ocean sex, although salt water sometimes did a number on your orifices. There was even a time I'd christened the coat room of the Plaza Hotel in New York City. I was somewhat of an expert when it came to sex outside the box, or I guess I should say sex outside the bedroom. Everybody has their specialty or sometimes their kink, and screwing a woman in an unexpected place was mine.

Of course, when I say airplane sex, I should probably clarify. I'm not referring to being crammed into the lavatory where you practically have to be a contortionist to fuck. I'm talking about jet sex, the kind you have on a private plane with leather seats to fuck on and off of as well as a king-sized bed with silk sheets. I'm sure the private jet remark makes me sound like a pretentious bastard, but hey, it's just what I'm accustomed to. It also doesn't mean I'm discriminatory and only date wealthy chicks. The truth is, I like women; it doesn't matter what race or religion or tax bracket they come from. It really only matters that they enjoy sex.

Today's initiate to the mile-high club was Evangelina Petscova, a new opera diva at the Met, AKA Metropolitan Opera House. I'm sure you're wondering what a guy like me could possibly be doing at the opera; I'm sure I impress you more as the sporting-event type. While I'm not culturally illiterate, it was a gift to the most important woman in my life—my mother.

For her birthday, I'd flown my mom up on The Callahan Corporation's private jet, the very one I was screwing on now, to see *The Marriage of Figaro*. After pulling a few strings, we got backstage to meet the cast. While my mother gushed to Evangelina about her marvelous performance as Susanna, I envisioned a more pornographic performance that Evangelina could star in. The continuous fuck-me eyes I made at her were rewarded with her giving me her number. I made sure to call her the next night, and we'd been seeing each other for the last two weeks.

Each time I hit her G-spot, Evangelina's shriek of pleasure hit a high C, one of the highest notes on the musical scale. While I enjoyed her enthusiasm for my efforts, I was beginning to go deaf from the high decibels. I had an odd thought that it might offset the cabin pressure; the last thing I needed was for my out-of-control libido to crash the plane.

Thankfully, I could feel Evangelina's walls tightening around me, so two more harsh thrusts and she was scream-singing my name. Her orgasm triggered mine, and I came with a string of expletives. I'd learned the hard way a long time ago not to ever say a girl's name if at all humanly possible. I mean, it's sorta hard to control yourself in the moment; the margin for error is just too great and could end up getting you punched.

When I took my arms away and placed Evangelina on her feet, she didn't stay upright long. She slid down the wall and pooled into a satisfied heap on the floor. "That was…" She stared quizzically up at me. "I would say amazing, but that seems trite."

"I'd agree that amazing just doesn't quite cover it. More like astounding and life-altering?"

Evangelina rolled her eyes as she pushed sweat-soaked strands of hair out of her face. "Your ego is as big as your dick."

Placing my hand over my heart, I teasingly batted my eyelashes as I replied, "What a sweet thing to say."

With a laugh, Evangelina gracefully pulled herself off the floor. "You don't mind if I take a quick shower, do you? I need to be fresh for tonight's performance."

A jerked my chin at the bathroom. "Sure. Go ahead."

She arched her blonde brows seductively. "Would you like to join me?"

"I'd rather smell like you and our fucking the rest of the day."

Desire flared in her blue eyes at my words, and her pink tongue darted out across her lips. "Mm, I really like the idea of you smelling like me."

I knew she would. Women always liked to think of you going about your day with the smell of their tits and ass on you. It was the same thing as how men wanted to blow their load on a girl. It was all about marking your territory and branding someone as yours.

The truth was I was going straight from the airport to the gym so there was no point in showering just to work up a sweat again, but I didn't need to let her know that. Women have long memories, so I knew Evangelina would remember this moment the next time we were together. It ensured that she would make it up to me—maybe with a really long blow job.

With Evanagelina in the bathroom, I threw back on the shirt and pants she'd ripped off of me an hour ago. After a quick glance in the mirror, I ran a brush through my hair to tame down the damage Evangelina had done. Once I was finished, I opened the bedroom door and went out into the main cabin.

I grabbed a bottled water from the fridge, popped it open, and gulped down a long, refreshing swig before collapsing down into one of the captain's chairs. When I met my bodyguard and best friend, Ty's, disgusted gaze, I cocked my brows at him. "What's that look for?"

"Do you seriously have to ask?"

"Are you now going to police my available pussy?"

Ty rolled his eyes. "You know I never object to pussy."

"Then what's the issue?"

"It's more about having to hear someone else getting it on while I'm on the job, not to mention the fact that we're thirty-six thousand feet up and I can't go take a walk until you're finished."

Waggling my eyebrows, I said, "Did that operatic orgasm get under your skin a little?"

Ty cleared his throat as he shifted in his chair. "Let's just say I deserve a hell of a raise for putting up with you and your fuck brigade."

The captain's voice interrupted us. "Mr. Callahan, I wanted to let you know we're now thirty minutes outside of DC and we'll landing soon."

I crinkled my brows in confusion. "Wait, did he just say DC?"

"He did."

"Why the hell would he say DC? We're supposed to be going home to New York."

"Your father phoned about twenty minutes into your operatic fuckfest to change the flight plan. He wants to meet with you ASAP."

Scrubbing my face with my hands that smelled like Evangelina, I groaned. Nothing good ever came from the last-minute meetings my father called—or *any* of his meetings. Several months ago, he had summoned me to my family's summer home on Martha's Vineyard. After ushering me and my twenty-year-old sister, Caroline, into his study, he had gotten a secure video call in from my brother, Thorn, an army captain serving in Afghanistan.

It was then he told us he had finally decided to heed the call to run for the highest office in the land. While I knew members of his party had been encouraging him for years, I still felt shocked as hell to hear the words come out of his mouth. He had just turned sixty. It was a time in a lot of men's lives with they started to slow down or even retire. Now he was thinking of taking on one of the most mentally and physically demanding jobs in the world.

Don't get me wrong—it wasn't that I didn't think he should run, or that he wouldn't be a good president. I couldn't imagine anyone doing a better job than my dad. He'd been preparing for this moment all his life. Like the Kennedys and the Bushes, the Callahans were another rising political dynasty. My grandfather, James Thornton Callahan Sr., was the son of a self-made millionaire. He had spent over forty years as a senator from New York. His brother, Charles, had been a two-term governor of New Jersey. From those two brothers, the northeast saw several Callahans in office, from mayors to representatives to senators. My dad was serving his thirtieth year in the senate.

Although he hadn't needed our blessing or our approval, he still wanted it; that was just the type of guy he was. Even though he'd been in politics all my life, he had never been an absentee father. I didn't know how he had managed to make it to so many football games of Thorn's and mine as well as Caroline's dance recitals.

Despite what misgivings we children might've had about the toll it might take on Dad, we each wished him well and vowed to do whatever we could to help him get elected. Now that he had won in two primaries, it was game on. "Guess he's putting out the bat call to summon me to make appearances on the campaign."

Ty nodded. "Have you given any thought to how you'll respond?"

"I'll have to say yes to at least a few days a week on the road. I can always work from the jet."

"If you're not fucking a member of the press corps."

I laughed. "That is true. Of course, I'll probably be spending most of my time on the Callahan Express."

The campaign had recently purchased three buses to transport my father and his entourage around the country. They had been dubbed the Niña, Pinta, and Santa María after the ships that brought Columbus here. I'd been given a tour last weekend, and I had to say, they were pretty posh. My dad would certainly be given the rock-star treatment when he was onboard. A roving campaign was like a band in a lot of ways. You needed an amazing crew to make it run smoothly, and then you also had the press that rode along to cover events. In the end, it was a giant operation to plan and execute.

Evangelina emerged looking fresh-faced and sexy as hell just as we started our descent. After we landed, I gave her an apologetic smile. "Ty and I have to get off here, but the captain will see you back to New York."

"Thank you. That's very kind." After bestowing a kiss on my lips, she said, "I don't know what I'll do without you to keep me occupied."

"You could always think about me while you get yourself off," I suggested.

"Now there's a nice thought."

"Make sure you video it for me."

Evangelina placed a finger on her chin. "On second thought, I think I'll wait. I don't want anyone making me come but you and that fabulous dick of yours."

"Don't forget my masterful tongue," I added.

"Jesus Christ," Ty grunted as he threw one of my bags over his shoulder before brushing past us to wait on the jet door to open.

Ignoring him, I gave Evangelina a long, lingering kiss along with a smack on the ass. When the jet door opened, I followed Ty down the three stairs and into the freezing February air, then gave Evangelina a final wave before the door slid back into place.

A chauffeur-driven car was waiting for us on the tarmac. After throwing my bags into the trunk, we got inside to make the thirty-minute drive from Dulles into the city. The trip flew by as I worked on fielding work emails. In the back of my mind, I couldn't ignore the growing anxiety I felt about Dad summoning me to chat. It felt as if an ominous cloud of uncertainty had overtaken me, though I had no reason to believe anything negative was about to go down.

When we arrived at the Jefferson Hotel, I inhaled a deep breath. Because of his love of all things historical, Dad adored the Jefferson. Whenever he had to stay in the city, he always preferred to stay there. Now it was doubling as his private campaign headquarters before he headed back on the road.

We were met at the elevators by one of the staffers. Dad had so many minions running around that I didn't bother trying to learn their names. I always just faked a look of familiarity while shaking their hand. A quick, "Hey, man, how's it going?" went a long way in someone's mind. Of course, when it was a female staffer, I made sure not to say 'sweetheart' or 'honey' for fear it would be construed as sexist.

After a quick ride up, we stepped into the penthouse and made our way to the dining room. My dad sat at the head of the table flanked by three of his closest advisors. If he got elected president, I was sure they would make it into his cabinet. Dad rose out of his chair. "I'm so happy to see you, son."

"I'm happy to see you, too, Dad." I wasn't blowing smoke up his ass just to suck up; it was the honest-to-God truth. While my parents might've been wealthy, I hadn't grown up like the other kids at my prep schools. My mom had help from a nanny, but she was the one who raised us kids. If Dad was elected president, Mom would probably be a cross between Jackie Kennedy and Laura Bush. She came from blue-blood roots, but she was very down to earth.

As for Dad, he really was the sitcom dad. He'd never been one of these politicians who donated some sperm so he could have a family of convenience to put on campaign posters. I admired the hell out of him.

One day, I hoped to be half the man he was. Clearly, I wasn't there yet, and at twenty-seven, I wasn't sure when my metamorphosis was going to begin. I figured I had time. After all, Dad hadn't become a father until he was in his thirties, so I still had time to screw around…in more ways than one.

After giving me a quick hug, he motioned for me to have a seat next to him. As I sat down, I nodded in acknowledgement at the staffers. The only one I recognized was Dad's campaign manager, Bernie George. "Afternoon, gentlemen."

"Good afternoon, Barrett. I'm so glad you could make it," Bernie said.

I jerked a thumb at Dad. "You keeping him in line?"

Bernie chuckled. "It's a hard job, but someone has to do it."

After a momentary lull in the conversation, I said, "Don't keep me in suspense. What was so important that you had to reroute a plane for it?"

"As you know, my victories in New Hampshire and Iowa weren't as solid as we would have liked."

"Hey, you won, didn't you? I mean, that's the most important thing, especially since historically the winner in New Hampshire gets the nomination."

"Yes, it is important, but it also means that going into Super Tuesday in a couple weeks, we have to find ways to widen my lead over my opponents if I'm to get the party's nomination." After unbuttoning his suit jacket, Dad leaned back in his chair. "We decided the best thing to do was hire an image consulting firm to help us prepare."

"But during your senate runs, you always thought those firms were a joke."

My father's grave expression told me just how very serious he was. "Since I never had such narrow victories during those races, I decided to reevaluate my stance on them."

"Spoken like a true politician."

"After they did a thorough investigation, they found one area of my personal life that desperately needs improving."

"And what was that?"

"You."

My brows popped up. "Me? What the hell could they have possibly found wrong with me?"

"Your playboy lifestyle."

"Oh please. I'm not a playboy."

Dad's gaze swept from mine over to his political best friend, Thomas Jenkins. After a nod, Thomas opened the manila envelope in front of him. "The image consultants did a survey of voters in the states with the largest electoral votes. They found the fact that you're unmarried and not in a committed relationship, with either a female or a male, to be undesirable. Throw in the fact that you run with a group of young men and women who are considered spoiled trust-fund kids, and it makes you *and* your father seem out of touch to mainstream voters."

Popping out of my chair like a jack-in-the-box, I jabbed my finger at Thomas. "I'm not some trust-fund twat flitting from one party to the next! I work fifty-hour weeks, if not more. I'm dedicated to The Callahan Corporation." I threw up my hands in exasperation. "Did they tell the voters I have an MBA, for Christ's sake?

Thomas shook his head. "They don't concern themselves with your professional accomplishments, Barrett. For them, it's about what they've read on Page Six, but most of all, it's what they've seen on the internet."

Inwardly, I groaned. I knew exactly what was out there, and it sure as hell wasn't flattering for my father's campaign. Since 2013, the media loved referring to me as *Bare* Callahan after I was recognized in some of the pictures from Prince Harry's infamous Vegas trip. At the time, it seemed totally legit to play a game of strip pool with a bevy of beauties and the guy who was fifth in line to the British throne. Of course, the copious amounts of alcohol that induced the shenanigans had clouded our judgment and made us oblivious to the possibility that some asshole would snap pics with their phone and expose us to the world.

Of course, the prince had the presence of mind to cup his royal jewels in the pictures while my junk was blowing in the wind. That led to the press's second nickname at my expense. I became Bear Callahan, or the Bare Bear, because I was apparently hung like a bear. Truthfully, I really got off on the Bear Callahan one.

When it came to Dad's kids, Thorn was a war hero, Caroline was a former deb with a squeaky-clean image, and I was the partying man-whore with no soul. Although I hated to admit it, I knew politics, and therefore knew I *was* a liability to the campaign. I sure as hell didn't like being the albatross around Dad's neck. I had this weird thing about always wanting people to like me, which was one of the reasons I was always up for going out and getting crazy. People tended to like carefree, inebriated Barrett—well, I guess only the people in my circle did, certainly not the ones in Dad's or the American people as a whole.

Grunting in frustration, I plopped back down in my chair. "Fine. Whatever I have to do to improve my image, I'll do it."

Dad's expression lit up. "You will?"

"I promised you when you first told us you were running that I would do whatever it takes to see you elected. It might not count for much, but I am a man of my word."

"I'm so glad to hear you say that, son, because what I'm about to ask of you is pretty extreme."

"Let me guess, you want me to do volunteer hours at a leper colony?" I jokingly asked.

"I want you to get engaged."

I snorted. "Good one, Dad. Now what do you really want me to do?"

Slowing down his speech, Dad carefully enunciated, "I want you to get engaged."

"Yeah, I heard you the first time."

"Then why did you question me?"

"Excuse me for stating the obvious, but the idea that you want me to get engaged to help your campaign is a little too absurd to believe."

"No, Barrett, I'm probably as serious as I'll ever be."

"Jesus," I muttered as I dragged my hand over my face.

"I know it might seem a little extreme—"

A maniacal laugh poured from my lips. "A little extreme? I'd say that's the fucking understatement of the year."

"I never said what I was going to ask of you would be easy."

"Can't I try some intense volunteering to better my image? Maybe start a foundation or something?"

"Only commitment is going to alter the public's perception of you." My father gave me a tight smile. "It's time for you to grow up in their eyes. The one way to do that is to show that you have matured and abandoned your frivolous past. Marriage is a natural progression."

"But you know as well as I do that I'm not the marriage type."

"Yes, I know that better than anyone, but people can and do change. I swore after I lost Celia that I would never give my heart to another woman. For many years, I held to that promise, and then your mother came along." A loving look came over his face, one that would have disgusted me as a teenager, but now that I was older, mystified me more than anything. I couldn't imagine ever having that look on my face—ever, couldn't imagine that there could actually be just one woman who would ever be enough. Cue all the soul mate/other half bullshit. I couldn't imagine a woman looking at me the way my mom looked at Dad, either. What they had was rare, and I couldn't see myself in their shoes. *Ever.*

Across the table from me, Bernie cleared his throat. "Barrett, I think it's important to remember that your father isn't asking you to actually get married. It's all just a façade. After the election, you can go right back to the life you had before, even sooner if he doesn't secure the nomination."

"Either way, it's a long fucking time to be tied down to someone I don't even know," I countered.

Leaning forward in his chair, Dad squeezed my arm. "Search your conscience, Barrett. If things go south and I don't win the nomination or the election, do you really want to think there might've been something you could have done?"

I whistled. "Nice guilt trip, Dad."

He smiled. "I'm a business man. I'm just pulling out all the stops."

"Yeah, well, what if I ignored my conscience saying this is the right thing to do and refused to go along with the charade?"

"Then you leave me no choice except to play hardball."

"Am I to assume your hardball would be worse than your guilt trip?"

"I'm afraid so."

"Okay, I give. What would you do?"

"Fire you from Callahan Corporation."

A horrified breath wheezed out of me. *Fuck me.* He wasn't joking about playing hardball. While I'd only been working full-time for the company for two years, I'd spent every summer since I was fifteen working there. Dad had started me in the mailroom, and I'd had to work my way up so I could understand the inner workings. Callahan Corporation was my life.

"You couldn't—no, you wouldn't dare."

"Since I do hold the majority stake in the company, I can fire anyone, even my own flesh and blood." My father gazed imploringly at me. "I would hate to resort to that, son, but if you pushed me to it, then I would."

"Jesus," I muttered. Talk about being between a rock and a fucking hard place. I once again saw the lady with the weights, and this time the *take the deal* side had plummeted to the ground.

Dad sighed. "In my heart of hearts, I know you would never force my hand. I know that because regardless of the media's perception of you, you have an exceptionally good heart."

"Don't flatter me, it just cheapens things," I grumbled.

"It isn't flattery. It's the truth."

When I looked into Dad's eyes, I knew he was being genuine. The man had been in politics for thirty years, and thankfully, it hadn't corrupted him. If I had a good heart, it was because I had inherited it from him, and from my mom too. I just didn't know if I could ever live up to how much they believed in me.

Dad smiled. "So will you do it?"

The one thing in life I hated was when I felt like a disappointment to my father. Because of the heart condition I'd had as a kid, I hadn't been able to see the pride on his face the first time he saw me in uniform. That had all been reserved for my older brother, and now Thorn's sacrifice of service was a matter of pride to the campaign whereas my less than exemplary character was a deficit—and therefore, in my eyes, a disappointment.

"Yes, I will."

With a wink, Dad said, "You bought my bluff about firing you, huh?"

Well damn. I sure wasn't expecting that. "Yeah, I bought it. Your poker face is perfection."

"Good. I'm glad to hear it." He rose out of his chair and gave me a quick man-hug—the kind of arm thrown around the shoulder pat gesture. "Thank you, Barrett. You don't know how happy this makes me."

Hearing those words from him made me very happy, but I didn't let him see that. Instead, I put up a strong front. "Look, I just said I would do it. That doesn't mean I don't think it's destined to fail."

"I think you'll find we have a very well-constructed story."

"Well, riddle me this: how does my fiancée fit into the fact that I just slept with a woman an hour ago on The Callahan Corporation jet?"

"Honestly, Barrett, our jet is for business purposes, not to use as a flying mattress!"

"I'm sorry." I thought it was best to refrain from telling him that a mattress hadn't been involved today; I didn't think he would have appreciated the clarification in his current mood.

"Anyway, we plan to announce the engagement on Monday, which gives us two weeks before Super Tuesday to help boost my image. The story we will give to the press is that the two of you dated previously in the past before breaking things off. Even though you were apart, you still had feelings for each other. After being reunited at a campaign function this weekend, the two of you decided you couldn't live without each other. You popped the question, and she happily accepted."

"That's quite a story. You know, you should start penning romance novels in your spare time."

"I've always found your mother's sarcastic wit endearing, but on you, it's quite irritating," Dad replied.

I held up my hands. "I'm sorry. I'll try to behave."

"So with the story we have come up with, you weren't engaged at the time you were screwing the opera diva."

Widening my eyes, I demanded, "Wait, how did you know—" Then I realized who I was dealing with. Dad had connections to the FBI and the CIA. Hell, he probably knew people in MI6 over in the UK when it came down to it. There wasn't anything he couldn't find out.

Dad winked at me. "Knowing you, I'm sure you haven't given this girl any reason to believe you had a future together."

With a smirk, I replied, "Actually, we are supposed to see each other again tonight when I get back to New York."

"But you won't. You'll break it off using the story I gave you."

Bernie nodded. "Should Miss Petscova become a problem, we will simply remind her of the NDA agreement she signed."

Yes, I was that much of a douchebag that I had anyone I slept with more than once sign an NDA. It was more about the fact that women who dated me might be privy to inside information about The Callahan Corporation, not to mention that if they flew on the jet, there might be the odd senatorial document left behind by my father. It was a way to keep my hands clean.

"Okay, I know you said my engagement would be announced on Monday, but I don't see how I can possibly find someone to get engaged to in forty-eight hours."

"That won't be necessary. We've already arranged your fiancée."

"Is she a stacked blonde with nymphomaniac tendencies?" I jokingly asked.

"No, Barrett, she is not," Dad replied tersely.

"Let me guess, she's the daughter of one of Mom's cronies? The ones who always want to pawn off one of their spawn on me?"

"Actually, she isn't anyone you know. She works for the campaign."

Warily, I eyed the folder. I was more than a little worried to see who had been picked for me since my parents were notoriously bad at fixing me up with women. After taking a deep breath, I flipped open the file to peer curiously at the smiling face of my fake future wife, Addison. Hmm, I had to give Dad and his minions credit—the woman was gorgeous. Considering the picture was only from the shoulders up, I couldn't tell if she had a rocking body or not.

"Color me surprised, she's stunning."

Dad shot me a disgusted look. "Addison is more than just a pretty face. She attended a top-ranking university. Her father is a minister in South Carolina, and she spent time in Central America as a child when her parents were working as missionaries so she is fluent in Spanish. She also works on my campaign, so she understands what's involved within the world of politics."

"Impressive."

"As you can see, she brings a lot to the table by covering many bases for us with the voting constituency," Dad said.

"I'd almost say she was too good to be true considering she can appeal to the women's and Hispanic vote while her parents hit the conservatives." I cocked my brows at them. "Are you sure she doesn't have something sordid in her past?"

Dad shook his head. "Her past is irreproachable, only one long-term relationship with a representative's son. As for her online persona, she has no pictures of drunken debauchery or excessive partying, and no nudes." Dad gave me a pointed look on the last one. "No scandals of any kind."

"We don't anticipate any skeletons in Miss Monroe's closet coming back to bite us in the ass," Bernie chimed in.

Great. Addison sounded like an utter and total bore. Who doesn't have at least one or two pictures of drunken shenanigans on their Facebook page?

How the hell was I supposed to survive for nine months with somebody like that? Maybe it wasn't too late for them to find someone else—someone who actually had a personality, or better yet, a pulse.

"You're absolutely sure she's the one?"

"Absolutely certain," Dad replied. His tone told me this wasn't up for negotiation.

"She willingly agreed to do this?"

"Yes. We met with her before you arrived. We felt her verbal confirmation was enough to have you go ahead and meet us here."

Stroking my chin thoughtfully, I asked, "What did you have to offer her?"

"Excuse me?"

"Come on. As a serious career woman, she doesn't impress me as the vapid type who would want to do this for her fifteen minutes of fame. If she's as smart as you say she is, she wouldn't just do this out of the kindness of her heart either. She would expect something in return for her time. I'm thinking some sort of monetary compensation."

"Yes. She is being compensated for her time." The corners of Dad's lips quirked. "The fact that she would have to pose as *your* fiancée made it quite costly."

"Very funny." I couldn't imagine any woman wanting to be paid to spend time with me considering how many willingly did it for free. Tilting my head, I asked, "Just how costly?"

"Seven figures."

My eyes bulged. "Jesus Christ, isn't that a little extreme?"

A curious smiled curved on Dad's lips. "You know, Miss Monroe said the same thing when she heard the figure. It must mean you two think alike."

"At least she didn't try negotiating for more."

"No, that thought never would've crossed her mind." The reverent expression on Dad's face told me just how much he admired this girl. She must have been special to have won him over—that or she had him completely snowed.

"When do I get to meet her?"

"If you're ready, you can right now. She just downstairs."

My stomach lurched at the prospect. Regardless of how much I wanted to put it off, it was now or never. "Sure. Let's get this freak show on the road."

Dad nodded. "Bernie, why don't you go downstairs to get Miss Monroe?"

Bernie rose out of his chair. "Be right back."

"Take your time," I joked as Bernie started out of the room.

"You know, son, you don't have to treat this like a death sentence. It's not like I picked some unfortunate-looking creature to torture you with. Addison has a great sense of humor. I think you're going to like her a lot."

I exhaled a frustrated breath. "Stop trying to sell this to me, Dad. Save it for the campaign trail. I'm just going to have to treat Addison like a task at work, like she's part of a job I have to do."

"You might surprise yourself when you get to know her."

"I doubt that."

"Just promise me you'll try to keep an open mind."

"Fine. I promise."

When the elevator dinged, announcing the arrival of my fake fiancée, I felt the figurative noose tightening around my neck. Bringing my hand to my tie, I loosened it slightly, then I rose out of my chair and prepared to meet my doom.

CHAPTER THREE

ADDISON

AFTER VERBALLY ACCEPTING my role of fake fiancée to Barrett Callahan, I wasn't exactly sure what the next step would be. Would one of the bedroom doors open for Barrett to come sweeping out of? Would I be sent back to work to pretend like my life hadn't just completely changed in the course of ten minutes?

"With Super Tuesday just two weeks away, I want you and Barrett with me on Monday for a campaign stop in Ohio. Because of that tight schedule, we need to get you outfitted in your battle attire as soon as possible."

"My battle attire?"

"Yes. We have a stylist waiting to meet with you downstairs."

"You guys move fast."

Senator Callahan laughed. "As I'm sure you're aware, everything in politics is meticulously planned with many backups. We had Everett on standby today in the hopes this would all work out."

"I see. But what about work?"

Bernie winked at me. "Considering I know your boss, I'll field any of the questions as to why you aren't returning this afternoon."

I laughed. "Okay. I trust you to handle it."

"Your absence this afternoon at work will also help corroborate the story we're preparing for the media. People will be left to assume you left to be with Barrett."

"Once again, the two of you have thought of everything," I complimented.

Senator Callahan smiled. "Don't worry yourself about your job at the campaign. You have a lot to focus on in your new role."

"Yes, sir."

Everett will not only take your measurements and get your ideas on what clothes you like to wear, but he will also go over some of the protocol of the campaign. Since he travels with us, you could consider him an expert."

"I'm sure I need all the help I can get," I lamented. I wasn't just talking about the fact that my wardrobe would need some serious overhauling to make me presentable to the public. It was also about the fact that I had no freakin' clue about campaign protocol. While I kicked ass at my job, that was something I was familiar with—something I had gone to school for. As far as I knew, there wasn't a school for shaking hands and kissing babies along the campaign trail.

"You'll do just fine, I'm sure. Bernie will take you downstairs where Everett is waiting."

"Thank you, sir," I said as I rose out of my chair.

Senator Callahan stood up and threw out his hand. "No, thank you, Miss Monroe."

After shaking his hand, I followed Bernie to the elevator. The staffer who had taken my Choos appeared when the elevator doors opened and gave me a smile as he handed them back to me. "Good as new," he mused.

"I'll say," I replied. Not only had the heel been repaired, someone had shined them so well I could practically see myself in them. "Thank you."

"No problem."

Once I slipped my born-again heels back on, I got onto the elevator with Bernie. I had to say I was much less nervous on this trip than I had been on the first. "I can't tell you how grateful I am that you've agreed to do this," Bernie said.

"I hope you'll still be saying that in a couple of months."

He laughed. "I think you're going to exceed not only our expectations, but your own as well."

"I certainly hope so."

Once we got off the elevator, I followed Bernie as we made our way through the lobby and down a hallway. With a knock, he entered one of the conference rooms. "Come in," a muffled voice called.

Bernie opened the door and motioned for me to enter first. When I got inside, a tall, lanky man came striding up to us. His blond hair reached his shoulders, and his blue eyes stared inquisitively at me.

"Addison, I'd like you to meet Everett Delaney, stylist for the Callahan campaign."

I extended my hand. "Nice to meet you."

Everett took my hand in his and then brought it to his lips. "The pleasure is all mine."

Bernie patted my back. "Since I know you're in very capable hands, I'm going to head back to the penthouse. We're about to initiate stage two of our plan."

Hmm. I knew that must mean Barrett was on his way, and the thought sent my stomach into a weird fluttering—the kind you get when you're anxious to see your crush. I wasn't sure where that was coming from since there was no way I was crushing on someone I'd never met.

"Okay," I replied.

"Once you're finished, feel free to have lunch in the hotel restaurant. I'll let them know you're coming, and you can just write 'penthouse' on the bill."

"Thank you, Bernie."

After the door closed behind him, a nervous laugh bubbled out of me. Everett's brows popped up as he asked, "Is something funny?"

"I'm sorry, I'm just nervous. I've never had a stylist before."

A smirk spread on Everett's lips. "You don't say."

I glanced down at my outfit. "Am I dressed that badly?"

"It's not horrible, but it ain't good either."

"Senator Callahan mentioned that besides helping me with clothes, you were going to fill me in on campaign protocol."

"That's right. The campaign can't afford any mistakes or faux pas on anyone's part, especially yours. You're going to be an old dog learning new tricks on how to walk, talk, and speak."

"Are you going to be the Henry Higgins to my Eliza Doolittle like in *My Fair Lady*?"

Everett tapped his chin in thought. "I like to think of it more like Hector Elizondo's character in *Pretty Woman*, but maybe that's because he's more my type than Rex Harrison."

"I already know what fork to use." I conveniently left out the part where I'd learned that tidbit from the movie.

"Good, we can mark that one off the list, but do you know what bag call is?"

"No, that one I'm not aware of."

"When you go out with the campaign, bag call comes ninety minutes before you are supposed to leave a hotel. You have to have your suitcase out in the hallway for pickup."

"An hour and a half before we leave?"

"Yep." Waggling a finger, Everett added, "But the trick comes in having a large purse to dump your makeup and hair products in. You can also toss your jammies in there."

A wave of panic washed over me. "I feel like I should be writing this down."

"Don't worry. I have everything you'll need written down in what I like to call the Campaign Bible."

I exhaled a relieved breath. "Good."

"But first and foremost, let's get back to your wardrobe." Everett crooked a finger, signaling for me to follow him. Racks full of designer clothes ran the length of the front of the conference room. "Since I was short on time, I took the liberty of guessing on your size. We can always alter them later."

Pop-up signs divided the clothes by designer. Names like Valentino, Ralph Lauren, Marc Jacobs, and Carolina Herrera popped out, and Everett noticed me eying them. "We try to wear only American designers when you're on the road, but sometimes we slip in some others." Pointing at the racks, Everett said, "Your wardrobe will be divided into everyday campaign wear, political rallies, and evening wear."

"I had no idea it would be so complicated. I'm just used to wearing business casual at work."

"Well, you're not in Kansas anymore, Dorothy. You could be experiencing up to three wardrobe changes a day."

"Wow." Three outfits a day times seven days a week...that was a hell of a lot of clothes. More importantly, it was a hell of a lot of money. I was used to stretching my dollars and pinching pennies when it came to my wardrobe. I had enough to wear for two weeks straight without repeating. Now I wouldn't even be repeating in the same day.

"Tell me about it. Guess who is in charge of keeping up with what you wear." Everett poked his chest with his index finger. "Yep, that would be me. I'm in charge of outfitting all the Callahans while out on the campaign trail, and trust me, it's no easy undertaking."

"I can't even imagine."

"First rule of the trail: you have to be careful about the fabrics you wear at political rallies. No silk, linen, or cotton."

"Oh, is it some sort of fashion faux pas to wear those?" As the child of missionaries, I'd spent a lot of time in linen and cotton. Although one might think the hem of my dresses reached the floor or I was expected to have covered arms, that wasn't the case at all, especially in the jungle climates. My dad sometimes gave sermons in shorts, and my mom, my sister, and I often wore sleeveless sundresses.

Everett pursed his lips. "No. It's more about the fact that if you wear those fabrics, you'll end up showing your bra-clad tits and thong-wearing ass under the heat of the heavy stage lights."

"Okay then. I will just be saying no to silk, linen, or cotton."

"It's not an all or nothing thing. You can still wear them, but we just have to ensure you won't be on a stage and that it's not a particularly sunny day."

"Got it."

Everett smiled. "All right. Let's get you ready to meet America."

I'D NEVER KNOWN picking out clothes could be so exhausting, but it was. Once again, I couldn't help cringing at the thought of what all of it was going to cost—probably more than my annual salary, and that was only for a wardrobe up until convention season. Then I would need a designer summer wardrobe. It seemed crazy, but *man* was I going to look totally amazing in the clothes. I almost wished I had gotten to take them with me so I could model them again back in my hotel room, but they were taken for Everett's team to do alterations and then they would be catalogued. Everett had shown me the computer program that printed the labels that would be added to the garment bags. I had never stopped to think about the process of dressing politicians and their families. It was truly intense.

After I was finished with Everett, I took Bernie's offer and went to the Jefferson's restaurant for lunch. I was halfway through my grilled chicken Caesar salad when Bernie came over and sat down with me. I already knew what the news was before he even opened his mouth; his pleased expression gave it away.

"Barrett accepted his father's offer."

"That's great. I mean, we can't do this without him, right?"

"That's right."

"He's very anxious to meet you, so as soon as you're finished, we'll head back upstairs."

The prospect of meeting Barrett sent my nerves into overdrive. There was no way I'd be able to finish eating now. "I'm ready."

"Are you sure?"

"As I'll ever be."

Bernie nodded. "Then let's go meet your new fiancé."

Now there was a statement one didn't hear every day. Having not dated for months, it certainly wasn't something I was expecting to hear, least of all today, not to mention any time in the near future. After Walt, I wasn't sure I ever wanted to be someone's fiancée or wife. I didn't want to give my heart away again and risk having it trampled and spit upon by a man who couldn't keep his pants zipped. But now, here I was, the fiancée of a man who was ten times worse than Walt when it came to being a womanizer. That was a sobering thought. *Think of your future debt-free existence. Think of the future. Think of all the brand new Choos.*

When I stood up, my legs felt unusually wobbly, and I thought I might face-plant for the second time that day. Taking a deep breath, I pushed forward to walk with Bernie out of the restaurant. It only grew worse when we got onto the elevator. My stomach clenched in anxiety, and my knees starting shaking, which caused me to stumble. Great, Bernie probably thought I'd gotten sauced during lunch.

Seriously, I didn't know what my problem was. I mean, I should've been less nervous this time. After all, I knew my job was safe, and that I myself was safe. I swiped my now sweaty palms on my skirt. *Gross.* The last thing I needed was for Barrett to be turned off when he shook my hand.

It wasn't so much that I was nervous about meeting Barrett because he was somewhat famous. I certainly didn't follow celebrities on Instagram or tune into TMZ or Entertainment Tonight for the latest gossip. I really only knew about him because of doing work for Senator Callahan's campaign.

What I was feeling was like first-date jitters amped up on meth. Of course, if you find yourself on a bad first date, you can bail, or at least know you're not stuck with the person beyond the next few hours. With Barrett, I was in it for a long haul, and since our relationship would be lived out in front of the cameras, there would be no bailing or running away.

Absently, I brought my hand to my throat, which had tightened considerably with emotion. I was fighting not only my nerves, but also an immense pressure to make my faked feelings for Barrett believable. Every event and every rally with him would be like opening night where I had to sell it to an audience. Even the most seasoned theater performer could succumb to nerves.

When the elevator opened, I remained frozen like a statue. For the life of me, I couldn't put one foot in front of the other. "Miss Monroe?" Bernie questioned.

"Um, yeah. I'm sorry. I had a momentary zone-out moment. I'm good." My brain screamed a message to my feet to pick their sorry asses up, and this time, they complied. We made our way through the foyer and around the living room to the dining room.

There he was—my future fake husband. He was even more handsome in person than in his pictures. He usually wore a relaxed, almost comical expression in his pictures, but today his jaw was taut with tension and worry. Amusement could not be found anywhere in his expression.

We stood there with a figurative gap the size of the Mississippi between us. We both just stared, not blinking and not moving. I wasn't sure what I had expected was going to happen, maybe that he was going to run to greet me with open arms like some Hollywood movie or something crazy like that. I guess I hadn't bargained on him being so unreceptive.

Senator Callahan nudged Barrett forward. After Barrett shook his head like he was shaking himself out of a trance, he closed the space between us. "You must be Addison," he said, his voice impossibly deep.

"Yes, I am." Extending my hand, I smiled. "It's nice to meet you."

My heart flip-flopped a little when Barrett returned my smile. "I'm not so sure I like the circumstances in which we're meeting, but yes, it's nice to meet you."

I tried putting myself in his shoes for a moment. I was sure the idea of marriage—even a fake one—was the last thing on his mind. There was also the fact that he hadn't gotten to choose who to do this whole faking plan with, and for a man like him, I was sure that had been hard.

"This is a pretty crazy scheme we've gotten ourselves into, isn't it?" I questioned.

Barrett laughed. "Yeah. It sure as hell is."

"I would say it would make a funny story to tell our grandchildren one day, but then there's that pesky NDA preventing that."

"Even if we could, I doubt anyone would believe us. Who in their right mind would pretend to be engaged to someone?"

I laughed. "Exactly."

"So you work for my father?"

"Yes. I'm the volunteer coordinator for the campaign."

Barrett appeared confused. "What exactly is it that you do?"

"I recruit and organize volunteers to help with campaign activities." I wrinkled my nose. "That sounds so boring, doesn't it?"

"Not at all," Barrett replied.

"She's doing an amazing job," Senator Callahan piped up. "Bernie raves about her."

"High praise indeed if Bernie is giving it," Barrett replied.

"I'm just very grateful to get to work for your dad."

Barrett winked. "Relax. You don't need to suck up to him just because he's in the room with us."

"I'm not sucking up. I mean every word," I countered good-naturedly.

After cocking his head at me, Barrett said, "Can I be honest with you for a minute?"

"Sure. I mean, honesty is the most important part of a relationship, and you are my fake fiancé."

"It's just I'm a little surprised to find you have a personality."

"I'm sorry?" That was the G-rated version of what I actually wanted to say. *What the fuck?* was more what I was inwardly thinking.

"It's just that after Dad and Bernie told me you didn't have any skeletons in your past and you didn't like to party, I couldn't help worrying you were going to be a total bore, but I can actually see myself being able to tolerate being around you."

Oh hell no. Tolerate? Did he actually have the balls to say he could tolerate *being around me?*

I pursed my lips at him. "Is that so?"

He nodded. "Not only that, but I was sweating bullets before I saw your picture. After hearing about what a potential bore you were, I couldn't help thinking you had to be a hag."

In that moment, I had a flash of a scene from the movie *Clue* where Madeline Kahn does the famous "Flames on the side of my face" line. That is exactly what I felt like in that moment after hearing Barrett's disparaging remarks—fiery rage.

"Well, I guess we should both be thankful I'm not a hag to disgrace you with," I bit out.

Barrett's brows furrowed in confusion. "I think you misunderstood me."

"No, actually, I think I understood perfectly well that a man like you has a certain standard he abides by when it comes to women, and you don't waste your time with anyone who doesn't make the cut."

"But you do make the cut."

"Lucky me."

Crossing his arms over his chest, Barrett said, "You're pissed at me, aren't you?"

"Wow, you sure cracked that code, Sherlock. I see you're putting that Ivy League education to good use, aren't you?"

"You're getting your panties in a twist just because I said I was glad you had a personality and you weren't a hag?"

"And because of the fact that you don't seem to think there's anything wrong with saying that to me."

"Uh, maybe because that's how I feel," Barrett countered.

"Maybe you shouldn't be so narrow-minded and judgmental."

Barrett scowled. "You're judging me."

"I'm just stating facts."

When Senator Callahan cleared his throat behind us, white-hot mortification pulsated through me. *Oh shit. Shit. SHIT!*

In my fury at Barrett's comments, I had gotten tunnel vision and completely forgot that Senator Callahan and Bernie were in the room with us. God, what they must think of me for going off on him. With my mouth and temper, I was sure they were regretting asking me to be Barrett's fake fiancée.

Meekly, I turned around. "I'm sorry, sir."

Senator Callahan smiled. "There's no need to apologize. I'm glad you put him in his place. He needed it."

My mouth gaped open. Okay, that was so not what I was expecting him to say, and it was safe to say my admiration for Senator Callahan continued to grow. "I appreciate that, sir, but at the same time, I'm going to have to learn to temper my emotions around Barrett, or this will never work when we're in public."

"I'm glad you're willing to work on it." He gave Barrett a pointed look. "I'm sure you're going to do the same."

"Sure," Barrett replied, although his tone didn't seem very convincing.

"Now that the two of you have met, I think it's best you sit down with my attorney so you can go over the contract," Senator Callahan said.

"Contract?" Barrett and I questioned in unison.

"Yes. It's something I had Marshall construct." At what must've been our continued expression of confusion, Senator Callahan said, "You don't enter into this type of serious deal without a contract." He shook his head at Barrett. "Honestly, you of all people should understand the importance of contracts."

With a scowl, Barrett replied, "In business, yes. Call me crazy for not anticipating my word wouldn't be good enough."

"This document not only protects the two of you legally, but it also outlines what is expected of you over the coming months."

"Sounds peachy," Barrett mused.

Senator Callahan ignored his son's comment. "I have some calls to make, so I'll leave you to it."

Marshall appeared seemingly out of nowhere, but then I realized he must've been working in one of the bedrooms. With his curly hair, short stature, and wiry glasses, he immediately reminded me of a young Richard Dreyfus. After shaking my hand, he smiled at Barrett. "Always a pleasure seeing you."

"I would agree, but I'm not so sure about it at this moment."

Marshall laughed. "Yes, it's usually you barking out the orders for me to draft. I see you're already lamenting your loss of power and control in the situation?"

"Yes, very much so."

God, he was a such a spoiled little rich boy, one who was always used to getting his way. I crossed my arms over my chest. "Well, you better get used to it, pretty boy, because I won't be controlled, and I'm certainly not putting you in charge."

Barrett grunted. "Why doesn't that surprise me?"

Marshall peered at us over the top of his glasses, and I could tell from his expression that he found our dynamic very intriguing. "Hopefully there won't be anything too heinous in the contract." He opened the folder in his hand and took out some paperwork. "Shall we?"

"If you insist," Barrett said.

"Miss Monroe, why don't you have a seat here"—he patted the chair to the right of the head of the table—" and Barrett, you can have a seat there." He motioned to the seat directly across from mine.

Barrett went around the top of the table. Before he sat down, he quirked his brows at me. "Ladies first."

Since his tone was far more condescending than gracious, I narrowed my eyes at him. When it came to manners and personality, Barrett was the polar opposite of his father. "Thank you," I muttered. Once I was seated, Barrett sat down as well.

After handing a contract to me and one to Barrett, Marshall cleared his throat to begin reading. "Paragraph one: For the duration of the campaign, whether long or short, both parties agree to cohabitate. This includes all hotel rooms while traveling, as well as apartments."

It felt as though a needle screeched across a record in my mind at the word cohabitating. *Oh. My. God.* With the shiny million being dangled over my head, I hadn't really stopped to think about the details—the fine print, as they say. This was so very, very bad. "I have to move in with him?"

"This isn't the 1950s, Miss Monroe. Most engaged couples live together prior to matrimony," Marshall replied.

"That's all well and good, but I don't really like the idea of living with a stranger, least of all him."

"I feel the same way, sweetcheeks," Barrett said.

With a roll of my eyes, I said, "Do not call me that."

"What? I was just practicing some terms of endearment for my fiancée."

"Yeah, well, I don't find 'sweetcheeks' endearing. I find it revolting."

"Fine then, snookums."

Instead of reaching across the table to strangle him, I took a few deep breaths. *You can do this, Addison. Just think of the one million dollars and all the brand new Jimmy Choos you can wear.* "Okay, if I agree to move in with him, what happens to my apartment?"

"You're more than welcome to keep the apartment, or you can let it go and find another either after the convention or after the election. Regardless of what you decide to do, you won't be seeing very much of it over the next few months."

The economical thing to do would be to just store my stuff at my brother Evan's place in Arlington until the campaign was over. Then I would have more time to devote to finding my dream place.

Oh shit. My family.

What am I going to tell them? Although my parents were several states away, we talked at least once or twice a week. Since I hadn't mentioned dating anyone, it was going to be a tough sell for them, and considering how close as I was to Evan, there was no way he would believe my sudden engagement. I supposed I could swear him to secrecy while also alluding to the fact that Senator Callahan knew people who could make him disappear.

"Speaking of apartments, what about the fact that I live in New York and Addison lives here?" Barrett asked.

"Your father has offered the guest cottage at his estate for the two of you to stay in when you're not on the road. As your fiancée, Addison should probably be seen leaving your apartment in New York a few times."

"Ugh, I hate New York," I said.

Barrett's eyes bulged. "How can you possibly say that?"

"Because it's the truth. It's overcrowded and overpriced. The only redeeming quality is Broadway."

Eyeing me with an expression of both disbelief and disgust, Barrett said, "Saying you hate New York is like saying you hate America."

I rolled my eyes. "No, it's not."

"Oh hell yeah it is."

"Maybe in your view it is, but for me, saying you hate Washington DC is way more unpatriotic."

Marshall tapped his pen loudly on the table. "Can we focus please?"

"Sorry," I said.

"Yeah, sorry," Barrett replied as he ducked his head to stare at the contract.

"So we're all good on paragraph one?"

"Yes," Barrett and I grumbled.

Marshall nodded. "Paragraph Two: During the course of the campaign, both parties agree to abstain from any physical or emotional contact with a member of the opposite sex."

Barrett whipped his head up so fast I thought he might get whiplash. "Hold up—I can't see anyone else but *her* for nine months?"

Ouch. Although I didn't want to admit it, that remark stung a little. I guess I shouldn't have been too surprised that Barrett wasn't thrilled by the prospect of monogamy with anyone, least of all me, but in the moment, it felt rather harsh.

Trying to save face, I mused, "Thanks for making me feel like a leper."

Barrett appeared momentarily apologetic. "It has nothing to do with you personally and everything to do with my dick."

Marshall grunted in frustration. "We're trying to sell the image of a happy, loving couple, Barrett."

Barrett poked the contract with his finger. "But this clause means I can't have sex with anyone."

"Not exactly. You and your hand can have a great time together," I countered with a grin.

Narrowing his eyes at me, Barrett said, "I have never gone without sex for nine days, let alone nine months."

"There's a first time for everything."

"This is bullshit."

"Of course you would make this only about you," I mumbled.

"Excuse me?"

"Listen up, pretty boy—being stuck with you isn't going to be a cakewalk for me either, but I'm prepared to do it."

"Because you're being well compensated by my father."

"You're such an asshole."

"Like I haven't heard that one before."

"Maybe instead of thinking with your dick, you should think about your father and how this is all in the best interest of him securing the party's nomination and being our next president?"

"I am thinking of my dad, or I never would've agreed to this insane idea."

"Then stop being selfish."

"Trust me, babe, you will not want to be around me if I go without sex. It's not pretty."

"Maybe you could find something more meaningful to do with your time, something that would contribute to the community."

"Oh, I contribute to the community when I have sex. It's not just me enjoying the experience."

"Gag me."

"With my size, that does tend to happen."

Once again, I fought the urge to strangle Barrett, or maybe kick him in the balls. Glaring at him, I said, "Is there any way we could add a clause to the contract that says Barrett has to speak to me in a respectful manner that isn't peppered with immature innuendo?"

"This is who I am, sweetheart. I'm not changing because a contract or you tell me to." Barrett placed his palms on the table. "So either you kiss the cool million goodbye and walk out of here, or you buckle your seatbelt and enjoy the ride."

Ugh. He made me sick. I didn't think I'd ever met a more infuriating and egotistical man.

"Can we please proceed?" Marshall questioned.

"Fine," I grumbled.

Marshall took off his glasses and rubbed his eyes. He appeared exhausted after just ten minutes of Barrett's and my bickering. "As for your previous misgivings about this clause, Barrett, it is morally bankrupt of me, but I would suggest that perhaps you find someone to satisfy your needs on the side."

Oh hell no. "Wow, you're actually advocating him cheating?" I demanded of Marshall.

"I said it would be morally bankrupt of me."

"That's putting it mildly," I huffed before crossing my arms over my chest.

Marshall adjusted his glasses. "I'm not sure how in the vast scheme of things you could take offense to this when you are about to lie to the entire American public."

Narrowing my eyes at him, I countered, "I consider what I'm doing to be for the greater good. Even if our relationship isn't real, I'm not a big fan of being made to look like fool if he's caught screwing some other woman."

"Let me finish," Marshall said. He looked from me to Barrett. "I would add that the entire purpose of having a fiancée is to show your commitment to the bonds of marriage, and as Miss Monroe has suggested, if you were discovered, the media would have a field day of epic proportions. I believe you can also understand how humiliating it would be for Miss Monroe as well."

Barrett sat in a stunned silence after Marshall's remarks. I could tell the wheels in his head were spinning, and he didn't like the inevitable answer that he was about to be forced into celibacy.

"It's shit like this that makes the evil part of me root for Dad to get defeated on Super Tuesday."

"Am I to assume your response means you agree to sign off on paragraph two?" Marshall questioned.

Barrett exhaled a painful breath. "Yeah. Whatever." *Asshole.*

"Now we come to the appearance clause in paragraph three." Marshall peered at me over his wire-rimmed glasses. "This is more directed you, Miss Monroe."

"Does this outline a specific number of events I will appear at as Barrett's fiancée?" I asked as I turned the page on the contract.

Marshall cleared his throat. "Actually, it is more about your personal appearance, how you'll look along the campaign trail."

"I'm aware Senator Callahan will be providing my clothes."

"It's more about how you'll look *in* the clothes."

"You have got to be kidding me. You're that worried about how my ass is going to look in my Donna Karan suit? Shouldn't you guys be more concerned about *Bare* keeping his clothes on?"

Barrett grunted. "Jesus. The naked pictures happened three years ago."

"I wasn't talking about the alleged pictures. I was talking more about the fact that you have a reputation for not being able to keep your pants on. I wouldn't be here if that wasn't the case."

Marshall rapped his knuckles on the table to get our attention. "I think you should read the fine print before jumping to conclusions about your attire or Barrett's, Miss Monroe."

"Fine." I ducked my head to read the one sentence under the appearance clause. I sucked in a horrified breath. "You want me to dye my hair?" I questioned incredulously. Before Marshall could answer, I turned my wrath on Barrett. "You had them put this in, didn't you?"

"I don't know how that would be possible considering I just found out about this deranged plan less than an hour ago."

"It reeks of something you would demand," I muttered.

"Well, I didn't."

"I can't believe in the vast scheme of things, Senator Callahan would give two shits about my hair's hue."

"I guess it made sense to him considering I only date blondes."

"Are you seriously that discriminatory?"

Barrett shrugged. "I just like blondes."

"Don't you think people who know me are going to find it a little suspect when I suddenly show up *blonde*?"

"Maybe they'll think you did it to keep your man happy."

Groaning, I swept my hands over my eyes. "Please tell me you didn't just say that."

"What's wrong with it?"

"Everything."

"You're going to have to be a little more specific."

"Okay, how's this: it's sexist and outdated. The very idea that any woman would do something just to make their man happy is ridiculous. Like you couldn't be happy with me as a brunette."

"I'm sorry, but I don't see anything wrong with women doing things to please men."

"As long as you can back that up with men doing things to please women."

A wicked look flashed in Barrett's eyes. "Of course. I make it my mission to please women—many times."

I rolled my eyes. "Spare me."

Marshall cleared his throat. "Miss Monroe, perhaps we can find a compromise. Maybe you can merely lighten your hair, rather than completely dyeing it?"

"Here's a thought: what if I don't do anything to my hair and we propagate the idea that Barrett likes me for me and not for my hair?"

Barrett stroked his chin. "Actually, that could work. It would make sense that as a brunette, Addison is different from the other women I've dated."

I blinked my eyes as I processed what Barrett had just said. "Did you actually just agree with me?"

"In a way, yes, but don't hold your breath waiting for me to do it again."

"Trust me, I won't."

"Okay, so I'll just make an addendum here about the hair," Marshall said as he scribbled on his paper. As we worked our way through the remainder of the contract, Barrett and I continued to bicker, and I couldn't help but feel sorry for the woman who ended up with Barrett as her real husband—that is, if the man-whore player actually ever tied the knot.

Senator Callahan emerged from the hallway just as we finished signing the contracts. "Everything go okay?"

Barrett scrubbed his face with his hands. "I don't see how this is possibly going to work."

"Considering you just met, isn't it a little early to be waving the white flag of defeat?"

I drew in a deep breath as I tried to thoughtfully weigh my words before I spoke. "With all due respect, sir, I'm afraid what originally looked good on paper might not be feasible in real life."

"And I think you just need time to work the kinks out. That's why the next step is vital to the success of this plan."

"What is it?" I asked warily.

"Trial by fire," Senator Callahan replied.

"What is that supposed to mean?" Barrett questioned.

"It means you spend the next forty-eight hours together here at the Jefferson."

"What?" I demanded as Barrett bellowed, "Oh hell no!"

Senator Callahan shook his head. "You two need to bond. We need you to be a cohesive couple to hit the campaign trail on Monday. It is essential that you two have time to get to know each other before you're thrown into the intensity of public scrutiny."

I wrinkled my nose. "But I can hardly stand being in the same room with him. Surely I can learn more than enough about Barrett simply by googling him."

With a wink, Barrett countered, "Make sure you click the dick pics. That way you can speak more knowledgeably about how good our sex life would be."

"You're seriously disgusting."

He held his hands up. "Fine, maybe you shouldn't look at them. I'd hate for you to be ruined forever by seeing what you can't have."

"I'm sure I'll manage just fine."

Crossing his arms over his chest, Barrett said, "Admit it, you're kinda curious."

"I know this will be a shocking blow to your overinflated ego, but trust me, I'm not the least bit interested."

Okay, that was a lie. I was more than a little bit interested since I'd heard he'd been nicknamed the Bear because he was hung like a bear. The three prior lovers I'd had were moderately endowed—growers not showers. I'd never had the pleasure of a well-endowed guy.

"Your loss."

"Again, I'm sure I'll manage just fine."

Marshall cleared his throat. "I'm just going to run these into the office to prepare the final versions." I wasn't sure if he actually needed to do that or if he just wanted an excuse to get away from us.

"Thank you, Marshall," Senator Callahan replied. He then turned his attention back to Barrett and me.

"Let's sit down for a moment, shall we?"

CHAPTER FOUR

ADDISON

ALTHOUGH WE DIDN'T argue, Barrett and I did stomp over to the couch like petulant toddlers before sinking down at opposite ends. When he saw what we had done, Senator Callahan gave us a disappointed look. Reluctantly, Barrett and I both started easing our way down the couch until we bumped into each other.

"I'm going to speak as freely as I can with the two of you." He narrowed his eyes at Barrett. "You have got to start respecting women as more than sex objects, but most importantly, you need to respect Addison. No more talking to her like a jock in a locker room. Be a gentleman by treating her with the respect that is her due."

Barrett started to open his mouth to argue, but then he closed it back. "Okay. I'll try."

"Addison, while you have every right to want to throttle Barrett, I need you to internalize that anger. Neither one of you can afford to be volatile when you're at a rally or fundraiser."

"Yes sir." I was sure I sounded a lot more confident than I felt, but at the same time, I did realize that going off on Barrett wasn't going to do any good. Unfortunately, he was who he was. I just had to treat this like a job and him as an infuriating coworker I had to deal with.

"I know I don't need to remind the two of you what is at stake here. Our country is in a perilous state. My opponents do not have the experience or the wherewithal to meet the needs of the American people like I do. I've spent the last thirty years of my life trying to help the people of Virginia. I've done that because it was what I was called to do. When I was fighting my way through the jungles of Vietnam, I promised God that if he got me out of there alive, I would spend the rest of my life trying to make this country a better place and in turn, the world. I know both of you are patriotic and want to see this country be the best it can be. That's why you have to band together and make this engagement work."

After he finished speaking, tears pooled in my eyes. It wasn't just the words he had said, but also the way he'd delivered them. That combination was the exact reason I'd wanted to come work for his campaign to start with, and once I had the job, it was Senator Callahan's passion and devotion to the American people that fueled me to do everything within my power to see him elected. In an odd way, being Barrett's fake fiancée was an extension of that promise—an extension I was also being well compensated for—and I never, ever wanted to fail at a job. I was too much of a perfectionist.

"So are you two in this?" Senator Callahan prompted.

Barrett turned to look at me. From his expression, I could see his father's speech had moved him also. Gone was the cocky smirk and mischievous glint in his eyes; instead, he appeared solemn. "I'm in."

"Me too."

Senator Callahan bobbed his head. "Good. Now I need to go check with Mary Anne to see if your suite is ready. I'll be right back."

After Senator Callahan left, I was alone with Barrett, and we sat in an uncomfortable silence—although, maybe for the two of us, silence was good. When I stared down at my hands, it suddenly hit me that my left hand was a little naked for a gal who was affianced.

"What about an engagement ring? Marshall didn't mention it in the contract."

"Don't worry. You'll get one."

"Do I get to pick from a briefcase full of rings like Princess Diana did, or do we see what the claw picks up from the arcade game?"

Barrett snorted as he shook his head. "Just like with everything else in this fucked up situation, Dad took care of the ring." He reached into his coat pocket to procure a black velvet box. Without any moving words or declarations of fake love, he tossed the box to me. Considering my lack of athletic ability, I of course promptly fumbled it, and the box dropped to the floor.

Although I should have been completely offended by the offhanded way he was treating our engagement ring, curiosity got the better of me, and I opened the box. I gasped as I gazed down at the gleaming emerald-cut diamond before me—the *mammoth* emerald-cut diamond.

When I finally found my voice, I asked, "Just out of curiosity, how many carats is that?"

"Five."

"And how much would a ring like this cost?"

"In today's market, well over a hundred grand."

"Holy shit," I muttered under my breath. I couldn't begin to imagine what it was going to be like wearing a hundred thousand dollars' worth of bling on my hand. Then the other part of what Barrett had said registered. "What do you mean 'in today's market'?"

"It's a vintage ring that belonged to my late maternal grandmother."

My gaze snapped up to Barrett's face. "You mean this is a family heirloom?"

"Yep."

Now I was even more paranoid about something happening to the ring. A whole litany of scenarios where I lost the ring ran through my mind, everything from accidentally knocking it down the drain to flushing it down the toilet. It would be bad enough losing it if it were a new ring with insurance, but you couldn't replace a family heirloom.

As I traced the sparkling diamond with my finger, I couldn't push aside another nagging feeling. "Why would you want to waste something like this on me?"

Barrett's forehead crinkled. "I don't think I follow you."

"By giving this ring to me in a fake engagement, it seems to taint it. Wouldn't you rather wait and use this on a real fiancée one day?"

"First of all, that's the ring from my grandmother's *third* marriage after her first two husbands died."

"Did she outlive the third?" I curiously asked.

"Actually, no."

I stared down at the ring in slight revulsion. "So this ring belonged to your grandmother, the black widow?"

Barrett chuckled. "She didn't off them or anything like that. Her first husband died in the influenza outbreak of 1919, and then my grandfather died of cancer. The last husband died at ninety-nine."

Okay, that news made me feel slightly better—I hadn't inherited a ring belonging to a society murderess. Instead, it was from a woman who had endured a lot of heartache when it came to love. I could certainly feel for her on that one. "Even if it was her third wedding ring, wouldn't you still like to give it to your future real fiancée?"

"Since I never plan on getting married, that would be a no."

"You don't really mean that."

"Yeah, actually, I do."

I blinked at him in disbelief a few times. I'd heard about men who were so commitment phobic they remained lifelong bachelors; I'd just never actually met one in real life. Usually the men came from broken or abusive homes, or they had parents who'd married and divorced many times. That certainly wasn't the case for Barrett. He had two parents who were utterly devoted to each other, so I couldn't help wondering where his negative feelings came from. "Wow. I don't know what to say."

With a shrug, Barrett replied, "There's nothing you can say. It's just how I feel."

"Never is a very strong word. I've said I would never drink again after a night of downing tequila-laced Jello shots, but I always do."

Barrett laughed. "I think binge drinking and a lifetime commitment are two very different things."

"Yes, but the gist of what I was saying is that you could change your mind. Stranger things have happened."

"I don't think so, but don't worry. Regardless of how I feel about the state of matrimony, I'll still be able to fulfill my duties to you as a fake fiancé."

"How comforting." As I slid the ring on my finger, I frowned. I didn't like the way it felt on my finger. While the large diamond was naturally heavy, there was something else about it, like a burden weighing me down.

"What's wrong?"

"Nothing," I murmured.

"I call bullshit. You seriously have to work on your poker face, Addison."

I sighed. "Fine. I was just having one of those annoying girly moments thinking that this wasn't how I pictured it would be when I got engaged."

"Well, that's because it isn't the moment you got engaged. It's the moment you slid a ring on your finger as part of a deal to be a fake fiancée."

"Way to cheapen it."

"Truth hurts, babe."

"Ugh, you don't seriously use that term with women, do you?"

"Yeah, why?"

"Because you sound like some caveman who climbed out of a glacier."

Barrett laughed. "Ah, so you're one of those feminazis."

"No, I'm a feminist."

"I'm not sure there's a difference."

"Maybe not in your misogynistic eyes."

With a shake of his head, Barrett mused, "The next few months sure are going to be fun."

I opened my mouth to say something I probably shouldn't have but was interrupted by a petite middle-aged woman teetering into the living room on impossibly high heels.

"Addison, this is Mary Anne Thompson. She's my father's personal assistant," Barrett said in introduction.

I extended my hand. "It's nice to meet you. At my previous job, I was the personal assistant to a representative."

"Ah, so you know how tortuous a task it is to wrangle political men," she said with a smile.

"Yes, I do."

Barrett chuckled behind me. "You know you love every minute you have with us Callahan men."

She winked at him. "Some days are better than others."

"Whatever," Barrett replied good-naturedly.

Mary Anne opened the folder in her hands. "First of all, I want to show you where you'll be staying for the weekend."

"We won't be staying here in the penthouse?" I asked.

"With all the craziness leading up to Super Tuesday, we've arranged a much more private suite for the two of you to use to get to know each other."

"Great," I muttered. The farther I was from the penthouse and the calming presence of Senator Callahan, the less likely it was that I'd be able to control my temper.

With a flick of her wrist, Mary Anne started for the elevator, and Barrett and I fell in step behind her. After she tapped the button for the twenty-ninth floor, I exhaled a relieved breath. We were only one floor below the penthouse. The doors opened, and we trailed behind Mary Anne as she walked purposely down the long, carpeted hallway.

She came to a stop outside a door that read *Presidential Suite*. Throwing a grin over her shoulder, she said, "I couldn't help myself when I was booking this one, like in a weird way the fact that it was available on short notice was some sort of sign."

I laughed while Barrett only grunted. Just as Mary Anne started to use the key card to open the door, her phone rang. I didn't have to guess who was calling since "Hail to the Chief" echoed through the hallway. Mary Anne really was thinking positively about the election results.

With a grimace, she handed me the key card. "Go ahead and go inside. I need to take this."

As she stepped down the hallway for some privacy, I opened the door for us, and Barrett followed me inside. Once again, opulence surrounded me. While I took everything in with wide eyes, Barrett brushed past me. With barely a fleeting glance at the spacious living room and dining area, he threw open the double doors leading into the bedroom.

Since Mary Anne was still on the phone, I followed Barrett. When I eyed the giant king-sized, canopied bed, anxiety pricked its way over my skin. I wasn't sure if my uneasiness came from the fact that I was worried about Barrett trying to put moves on me or if there was a part of me—a very small and annoying part—that might have wanted him to. In a weird way, he was like one of the sexual wonders of the world. You couldn't help being curious or wanting to mark it off your bucket list.

Barrett flopped down on the side of the bed and kicked off his shoes then pushed himself back on the mattress. Lacing his fingers behind his head, he lay back against the pillows. "Comfy."

"I'm not sleeping with you," I blurted out.

"Easy, sweetheart. That was an observation, not a come-on."

My anxious gaze spun around the room. "This is a suite, right?"

"Yeah, why?"

"Because I assumed there would be another room, and more precisely, another bed."

"I'm sure there is one, if not two more bedrooms on the other side of the suite," he replied.

I swept a hand to my heart as I exhaled a relieved breath. "Thank God."

A smirk curved on Barrett's lips. "Afraid to share a bed with me?"

"Of course not."

"Come on, you just about pissed yourself while you were panicking about where the other bedrooms were."

"That's because I'm not accustomed to sleeping with strange men."

"I think it's more about the fact that you were afraid you couldn't control yourself around me."

"Excuse me?"

Barrett licked his lips. "I've never met a woman who was able to resist me."

Oh, God. Spare me from King Narcissist. "Wow. I think you just reached a new level of disgusting with that somewhat rape-y statement."

With a roll of his eyes, Barrett replied, "Rest assured, sweetheart, if we did end up in the same bed, you would be the first woman I didn't try to seduce."

Mary Anne appeared behind me. "I see you're making yourself at home, Barrett," she said, amusement vibrating in her voice.

He grinned. "I figured if I was going to be stuck here for the next forty-eight hours, I should make sure it met my needs."

"I assume you find it satisfactory?"

"Meh, I suppose it'll have to do," he teasingly replied as he climbed off the bed.

"I'm sure you'll manage." Mary Anne then turned to me. "Senator Callahan just informed me that there's a car waiting downstairs to take you to your apartment to pack the things you'll need for the next two to three weeks.

I would advise you to pack only the necessities. You'll be living in close quarters on the bus, and most of the hotels we stay at on the road are nothing like this."

Telling a female to pack only the essentials is a contradiction in terms. *Everything* seemed essential. I was destined to fail at this task.

Flipping through her leather-bound planner, Mary Anne asked, "You don't have any pets to worry about, do you?"

"No," I replied sadly. I'd lost my Goldendoodle, Kennedy, in the breakup with Walt.

Since he'd been Walt's dog before I'd come along, it had only made sense that he kept him, but it particularly hurt because Kennedy was much closer to me. Funny that I missed Kennedy more than I did Walt. Maybe it had something to do with the fact that dogs were loyal and always happy to see you.

Mary Anne bobbed her head. "Good. You were going to need to find a place to keep them if you had."

Once again, the severity of the commitment I'd just made hit me. I wasn't used to an entirely vagabond lifestyle. Even when my parents were involved in missionary work, it was always during the summers and school holidays. We always had a home base somewhere in the States, depending on where my dad's church was.

I turned to Barrett. "I guess I better go get my things."

He flashed me a shit-eating grin. "Take your time. Don't feel like you need to rush back."

I bit my tongue to keep from saying I didn't need his encouragement. *I* was certainly in no hurry to get back to him and our imprisonment. Instead, I gave him a sickeningly sweet smile. "I'll take as long as I want, *dear*." I patted his cheek—hard. "Don't feel like you need to give me your permission."

"All right, *snookums*."

We stood there in a silent faceoff for a few moments before I finally blew him a kiss. Barrett slowly shook his head at me as if I was some mutant life form standing in front of him.

"Shall we go, Miss Monroe?" Mary Anne prompted.

I snapped my gaze from Barrett's to hers. "Yes, of course," I replied.

Without another word to Barrett, I followed Mary Anne to the door. Once we were alone in the hallway, she grinned at me. "I see Barrett's met his match in you."

"We're either going to be a tremendous help to the campaign or we'll end up killing each other," I replied as we stepped onto the elevator.

"Or you might just grow to like each other."

As the elevator doors closed, my reply came with a very unladylike snort. "Don't count on it."

CHAPTER FIVE

BARRETT

A FEW MINUTES after Addison left with Mary Anne, there was a knock at the door. When I peeked through the hole, a bewildered-looking Ty stared back at me. I unlocked the door and threw it open. "Dude, you disappoint me. No champagne to celebrate my prenuptial bliss?" I teased as I waved him inside my room.

"You're really engaged?" he questioned in a strangled voice.

"I think you mean *fake* engaged."

Ty gave a frustrated grunt. "Whatever. Answer the question."

"Yes."

"Jesus," he muttered as he dragged his hand through his hair. "I don't know what's harder to believe: that this is what your dad suggested, or that you actually said yes."

"It's not like I had much choice."

"Did he play hardball with you over your job or your inheritance?"

"Yeah, but turns out he was only bluffing."

"Then why did you say yes?"

"He put it to me this way: if he lost the nomination or the presidency, would I be able to live with myself if I hadn't done everything I could to help him to win?"

Ty winced. "Emotional blackmail is the worst."

"Tell me about it."

"Okay, so you're engaged." Ty shook his head slowly back and forth. "Damn, I never thought I'd say those two words together."

"I never thought I'd hear it either."

A curious expression replaced Ty's shocked one. "What's the future Mrs. Callahan like?"

"A total shrew," I grumbled.

Ty's brows knitted together. "They fixed you up with some unfortunate-looking chick?"

"No, it's nothing like that. She's actually hot."

"Then what's the problem?"

"She's an uptight, choirgirl priss with a mixture of feminazi thrown in."

"Damn. That's bleak."

"Yeah. It is. I'm going to have to start drinking heavily to get through the next nine months with her."

"Surely she can't be that bad."

I shuddered. "Trust me, she is, but the feeling is mutual. She pretty much loathes me

as well."

"You two have only spent an afternoon together—how can you already hate each other?"

"I don't know, man. We're just gifted that way." I rolled my neck and shoulders, trying to relieve some of the tension the day's events had caused. With the walls of the hotel room closing in on me, I knew I had to get out of there. "Listen, I gotta change and go work out."

Ty cocked his brows at me. "That's not exactly what I thought you were going to say."

"Did you think I was going to ask you to assume a fake name and leave the country with me?"

With a grin, Ty said, "No. After you just said you were going to have to drink heavily for the next few months, I figured you wanted me to take you somewhere to get crazy ass lit."

"While tempting, I'm stuck here for the weekend being tortured by getting to know my fake future wife. I don't think I'd be very good at it if I were blitzed or hungover."

"You've managed to seal the deal many times when blitzed."

I snorted with disgust. "There will be *no* sealing the deal with Addison."

"Why not? You said yourself she was hot."

"Yeah, she's hot—the kind of infuriating hot that gets under your skin like a bad rash." *The kind of hot that drives you mad because you know no matter how hard you try, you can't have her.*

"There are creams for that you know," Ty teased.

"Har fucking har." I shrugged. "Nope. It's just not happening." I refrained from adding that I was pretty sure Charles Manson had a better chance of getting Addison in bed than me.

Ty's brown eyes widened. "Holy shit. Now I know what's so wrong with her. You've finally found a woman you can't charm the panties off."

"Oh please. I could have Addison flat on her back in no time."

"I bet you ten Franklins you couldn't, and that's what is freaking you out so much."

Damn Ty and his ability to see right through my bullshit. I was totally wigged out about meeting Addison; she was a complete one-eighty from what I'd assumed she'd be like. Since I was a teenager, women had practically thrown themselves at me. I'd never met a woman who didn't warm up to me, least of all a woman who seemed utterly repulsed by the very sight of me. She hadn't just bruised my ego—she'd fucking shredded it.

I shook my head at Ty. "Look, the last thing Addison and I need in this fucked-up fake relationship is to add sex to the mix."

"You can say that now when you're only a few hours into celibacy. A few weeks down the road and you'd be willing to bang Addison even if she looked like Jabba the Hut." Ty smirked at me. "But that won't matter, will it? Addison's probably made it abundantly clear that she isn't letting the Bear anywhere near her cave."

I fought the urge to punch his smug face. "You know what? Fuck you. I'm going to work out."

Ty's laughter echoed after me as I stomped into the bedroom and slammed the door. "I'll go change and join you," he called.

"Only if you'll get off my dick about Addison," I replied.

"Fine. I'll let it go."

"Then go change."

"See ya in five."

ALTHOUGH I COULD have benefited from pumping iron, I started straight for one of the treadmills. If I couldn't literally run away, then I could at least do it figuratively. With some hardcore Jay Z in my ears, my feet started pounding out the miles.

I had just finished a 5K when the notes of "Sexy Back" began playing on my phone. Yeah, go ahead and consider me a douchebag because I have "Sexy Back" as one of my ringtones—the one for when it was a chick calling. I jerked my earbuds out and glanced down at the screen.

At my loud groan, Ty turned his head to peer curiously at me.

"Fuuuuck. It's Evangelina."

"Oh shit. What are you going to say?"

"I know what I want to say—that I'm going to hop on the next plane and be buried in her pussy as soon as possible."

Ty tsked at me. "Sorry dude, you're engaged now. No more pussy for you."

His dooming declaration felt the same as if he had punched me in the gut; my free hand swept to my abdomen and I groaned. Someone might as well have put handcuffs on me because I truly felt imprisoned by the prospect of the next nine sexless months. What if my dick never recovered? You know, like when you stop working out and your body goes to hell? *Can a cock shrivel up from lack of use?*

"Answer the phone, B."

"It hurts, man," I panted.

"It's going to hurt worse if you string her along and she comes back to bite you in the ass along the campaign trail."

Ugh. Ty was right. I had to end it ASAP, or it would be more than just myself facing the repercussions. Finally, I swiped the phone and brought it to my ear. "Callahan."

"Hey you. I just wanted to see if you were going to get back into the city tonight. I was going to have my roommate leave some wine chilling for us, and I'm going through my lingerie drawer. You still like me in pasties, don't you?"

At that moment, I didn't give a flying fuck if my dad won the party's nomination or became president. I didn't care if I lost my job at The Callahan Corporation. All I—and, more importantly, the Bear—cared about was the epic case of blue balls I was starting to get. I'd spent weeks with Evangelina, and she was so fucking sexy and up for anything. God, there was nothing about the promise I'd just made that was palatable, except for giving my dad the best shot at the role he was made to fill. *I'm so screwed.*

Ty cleared his throat. When I glanced back at him, he gave me a *get the fuck on with it* look. "Uh, yeah, er, it's not looking good on me getting back to see you tonight." *Or any other night for that matter.*

There was a pause on the line. "You sound funny, babe. Is everything all right?"

"Look, Evangelina, there's never an easy way to say this, but…it's just not going to work out between us."

"You're breaking up with me?"

"Uh, well, I'm not sure you could classify what we were doing as dating, but yeah, I guess so."

"Oh hell yes we were *dating*, you bastard! Has your feeble brain forgotten we were on a date a few hours ago?" she shrieked. She was getting close to hitting another one of those high Cs, and I fought the urge to take the phone away from my ear.

"We were screwing a few hours ago. Whether or not we were dating is a matter of linguistics."

"I hope your dick rots off, you son of a bitch." Considering I wouldn't be having sex for a very long time, Evangelina might get what she wished for.

"I really am sorry." That was the truth—at least it was for the Bear. After all, he was the one who was really going to end up missing her. It wasn't like I saw some future for Evangelina and me. I never saw a future past coming once or twice with any of the chicks I banged.

"Fuck you!" Evangelina shouted before hanging up on me.

Yep. That pretty much summed it up. Fuck me, and fuck my life.

CHAPTER SIX

BARRETT

AFTER MY WORKOUT, I headed back upstairs to grab a quick shower. Once he saw me safely inside the suite, Ty went down the hall to his room. I stripped off my gym clothes and stepped into the shower, my aching muscles protesting under the scorching hot water.

As I stood under the showerhead, my mind desperately tried to process the implications of the day. I'd gone from single and carefree to engaged and shackled by responsibility in just a few hours. Did most men experience a choking feeling and sinking dread when they decided to get married?

Closing my eyes, I envisioned Addison as she had stood before me earlier. The way she'd used her red, pouty lips to verbally annihilate me. The way she'd crossed her arms defiantly under her round, perfect tits. Damn, she was even hotter when she was angry.

Almost on autopilot, my hand slid down my abdomen to grip my cock, and then, even under the scalding water, I shivered in revulsion. I snatched my hand back and eyed it with contempt. How could I possibly think of jerking off to Addison?

With a grunt of frustration, I turned off the water and stepped out of the shower. After drying off, I threw on a clean pair of jeans and a button-down shirt I had in my luggage. Leaving my hair wet, I walked barefoot out of the bedroom and into the living room.

Although I should have been checking work emails or returning calls, I knew there was no way in hell I'd be able to concentrate. So, I flopped down on the couch and turned the television on to Sports Universe where there was a replay of an old Yankees game. Four innings later, my phone rang, interrupting a two-run homer. After throwing an apprehensive glance at the screen, fearing it might be Evangelina, I exhaled a relieved breath since it was Mary Anne.

"Can't get enough of me, can you?" I jokingly answered.

Mary Anne laughed into the phone. "It's always about business, I assure you."

"What do you want to torture me with now?"

"I'm sending down a questionnaire for you and Addison to complete together as a means of getting to know each other."

"Sounds thrilling," I replied, sarcasm lacing my voice.

There was a pause on the line before Mary Anne sighed. "You need to get your head out of your ass on this one, Barrett."

"You sound like my dad."

"I'm serious."

"Fine, fine. I can't wait to sit down with the little woman."

"You're impossible."

"I certainly try."

"Just answer the door for the messenger."

"Anything for you, Mary Anne."

I'd barely hung up with her when a knock came at the door. Once again, some nameless staffer gave me a toothy smile as he handed me a large manila envelope.

"Thanks," I replied.

After flipping open the folder and skimming the contents, I grimaced. "Oh hell," I grumbled before tossing the file on the table. I couldn't look at it for another minute without a beer.

I flipped open the fridge and smiled at the sight of my beloved Heinekens sitting on the top shelf. As I popped the top, I vowed to make sure Mary Anne got a raise. The woman was perfection when it came to taking care of not only my father, but me as well. If she were twenty years younger, I might've entertained the idea of marrying her—well, you know, if I was actually the marrying kind.

After crashing on the couch, I started flipping through the channels before settling on ESPN. I'd just drained my second beer when I heard the buzz of the keycard being activated. Since I wasn't totally without a gentlemanly side, I rose off the couch to help Addison.

She came through the door ass first as she pulled two rolling suitcases behind her. Just as I reached to help her, she whirled around, nailing my junk with her elbow. Bending over at the waist, I groaned in agony as I cupped myself.

"Fuck!" I grunted out.

"Oh my God, I'm so sorry!" Addison cried, and I jerked my head up to look at her. She mistook my mask of pain for anger because she quickly added, "I swear, I didn't know you were there."

After huffing out a few breaths, I waited for the pain to subside before I added, "I'm aware you didn't do it on purpose, but that doesn't make it hurt less."

"I can only imagine." Addison's sympathetic expression flashed over to mortification. "I mean, I can't imagine since I don't have…uh, well, you know."

I chuckled at her embarrassment. "I know what you meant."

Ducking her head, she replied, "Good."

Once I fully recovered, I had the opportunity to notice the difference in her appearance. She'd changed into a pair of black yoga pants that molded to her legs and ass, and as a red-blooded American male, I would also like to note for the record just how fine said legs and ass looked. The view I'd previously had of her rack was hidden by an oversized purple sweatshirt emblazoned with the word Duke across the chest.

Her long dark hair had been swept back into a ponytail, although a few errant strands lingered around her face. She was one of those chicks who looked beautiful no matter how she wore her hair. Hell, she'd probably still look good with a buzz cut.

Damn, it was going to be a long nine months.

Changing the subject, I asked, "What are you doing bringing your own bags up? There are bellmen for that, you know, not to mention a ton of my dad's minions."

Addison opened her mouth to respond, but then a male voice responded before she could. "I'm sorry, sir, but Miss Monroe insisted on bringing up some of the luggage herself."

After glancing past Addison, I saw one of said minions, and he was laden down with bags. I raised my brows at Addison. "Not one for packing light, are you?"

She blew a wandering strand of hair out of her face. "For your information, I'm leaving most of this here to be picked up on Monday by my brother. I assumed it made more sense to sort through what all I would need here, rather than at home." Lowering her voice so the minion couldn't hear, she added, "You know, since we're supposed to be spending time together."

I nodded. After forcing a broad smile to my face, I said, "I'm glad you didn't take too long." I paused, knowing I needed some kind of endearing phrase about missing her to make it believable for the minion. The instant the thought entered my brain, I just went with it. "Cause I miss you, baby, and I don't want to miss a thing."

Addison's brows momentarily furrowed like she knew she'd heard that exact phrasing before, and she had if she'd ever listened to Aerosmith or watched the entertaining but implausible *Armageddon*. I tried very hard to stop the eye roll at my ridiculous comment. While I was sure the minion was thinking I was a giant douche, his face remained impassive.

"I hate being away from you, too." Before we could torture ourselves any more with a forced lovefest, Addison turned to the minion. "Let's get these to the bedroom."

"Yes ma'am."

She wagged a finger at him. "Now what did I say about you calling me ma'am?"

He held up his hands in mock surrender. "I know, I know. It slipped."

As I watched their banter, I noticed that Addison was actually friendly and approachable. She had no false airs or pretentiousness about her, which I guess made sense after what Dad had told me about her upbringing.

At the thought of the file, I went over to the table and picked up the folder with our homework. I figured there was no time like the present to begin the torture. I mean, the sooner we got it over with, the sooner we could separate into our own corners in the suite.

Addison and the minion emerged from the bedroom. "Thanks again for all your help, Zane."

Minion Zane flashed Addison a wide grin. "You're more than welcome."

Returning his smile, Addison added, "I hope your daughter's cold gets better."

"I hope so, too. If we have another sleepless night, I think my wife and I will be able to audition to be zombies." Zane glanced over at me, adding, "Good afternoon, sir."

With a wave, I replied, "Same to you." After the door closed behind him, I shook my head. "You managed to learn all that in barely two hours?"

"You can learn a lot about someone in just ten minutes." She cocked her head at me.

"You know, it wouldn't hurt you to get to know some of the 'minions', as you call them. They're not just nameless faces to do your bidding—they have lives outside the Callahan campaign."

Although I wanted to tell her where she could stick her holier-than-thou attitude, I knew she had a point. She sounded like my mom. Neither of my parents talked down to staff, and they never let me or my siblings do it either. "Okay. Fine."

Addison's mouth gaped open in surprise. I knew she was shocked I hadn't come back with some smartass remark. "Well, uh, good."

"But right now the only person I'm concerned about getting to know better is you." I waved the folder in my hand. "This arrived while you were gone."

As Addison's gaze zeroed in on the folder, both apprehension and curiosity flickered in her brown eyes. "What's that?"

"Our relationship homework."

"Excuse me?"

Mimicking a game show host's voice, I replied, "It's a fun-filled packet of get-to-know-you activities to ensure we fool the public into believing we're a loving, happy couple."

Wrinkling her nose, Addison said, "Please tell me you're joking."

"I wish." I handed her the stapled packet with her name on it. Instead of sitting at the formal dining room table, I motioned for us to have a seat on the couch. A tense silence hung in the air as we began reading the instructions.

"Hmm, we're supposed to handle it like a reporter doing an interview," Addison replied.

"At least in this case, we'll know the questions beforehand so they can't stump us," I mused before draining the rest of my beer.

Addison paled slightly. "Are we going to be expected to give many off-the-cuff interviews?"

"I'm sure Dad and his people will limit them as much as possible, at least in the beginning until we have more time to spend together."

"But what if we're asked a question that's not in here?"

"I doubt that is a possibility considering Bernie's thoroughness." When Addison continued to chew on her bottom lip, I said, "We'll just have to wing it. Whatever we have to spontaneously lie about will just become the truth."

"If you say so," she murmured.

Motioning to the folder, I said, "Come on. We might as well get started."

At the top of my page was a short biography on Addison, and she had the same on me. Basically, it was like the *Personal Life* section of a Wikipedia biography—the bare essentials. After I finished reading, it was pretty clear that Addison was a badass. I mean, I sure as hell didn't know many girls who could say they could start a fire from sticks, teach English to native villagers, and graduate top of their class. I could see now why Dad and Bernie had been so impressed.

After the brief biography, the remainder of the page was filled with the Ivy League lame getting-to-know-you questions. When she saw that I was finished reading, Addison clicked her hotel pen. "Ready?"

"Go for it."

"Favorite movie?"

"*The Godfather.*"

With a smirk, Addison said, "Not surprising, but I would've also bet on it being *Scarface*—or maybe *9 ½ Weeks.*"

I laughed. "Nope. *The Godfather* is in my top ten, along with *Platoon* and *Saving Private Ryan.*"

"Are you a fan of war movies because of your dad?"

"Not really. He likes to critique them more than anything, especially the ones about Vietnam."

She nodded. "My grandfather served in Korea and refused to watch any movies that even remotely referenced war. He said he'd had his fill of killing."

"I can see his point. Well, I guess I should say I understand his point. Obviously, I can't speak from experience."

She paused in doodling a flower in the margin of her packet. "It must be hard for you having a father and brother invested in the military and not be able to share those experiences."

Damn, had this chick minored in psychology or something? How could she possibly unearth that insecurity so quickly? Trying to play it off, I shrugged. "Yeah, I guess."

Addison eyed me curiously. "If you hadn't been disqualified from service because of your heart condition, would you have gone into the military?"

"Of course."

"Because of family obligation?"

"Yes, and because military service is a noble thing to do."

"You don't impress me as the military type."

With a wink, I said, "Hey, I'd totally rock a crew cut, not to mention looking hot as hell in the uniform."

"I'm not talking about the look. I'm talking about your personality." She narrowed her eyes at me. "It's more like you lack the discipline required to take orders."

I narrowed my eyes back at her. "That's a hell of a ballsy thing to say to someone you barely know."

Instead of shrinking back, Addison replied, "I'm just calling it as I see it based on several factors."

"Such as?"

"Your internet persona for starters, not to mention what I've seen so far tonight."

"Let me set you straight—I'm one hell of a disciplined man, sweetheart. Don't forget I earned a bachelor's degree and an MBA from an Ivy

League school, not to mention taking a failing division at The Callahan Corporation and making it one of the most successful in the company."

"I stand corrected," Addison replied. Even though she seemed to be agreeing with me, I could tell she remained unimpressed. I didn't know why I gave two shits about what she thought about me, but I did. I wanted her to see that there was far more to me than the image the media portrayed of me. Huh, that was a new one. *Do I really care? She'll be a nobody to me in nine months.*

"Let's get back to the bullshit questionnaire, shall we?"

"Fine."

"Now it's your turn. What's your favorite movie?"

"*The Sound of Music.*"

I groaned. "Christ. You're one of those people, aren't you?"

"If you mean the type of people who enjoy culture through musical theater, then yes, I am one of those people."

My mother had tortured us with musicals when I was growing up, taking us on theater trips to New York City at least once a month during the fall and spring. It was hell. "There's nothing more annoying than someone belting show tunes."

A wicked look flashed in Addison's eyes. "I'll be sure to remember that."

"I'm sure you will," I grumbled as I glanced back down at the sheet. "Favorite type of music?"

"Country and pop," Addison replied.

"Rap and rock for me."

"And here I thought you were going to say classical," she teased as she scribbled my response down.

"Actually, I am a fan of the symphony."

Addison's eyes widened. "Really?"

"Yes. Really."

"Let's see if you throw me with your favorite food."

"Dim sum, preferably from Chinatown."

"Interesting. I would have thought maybe hotdogs and beer from Yankee Stadium."

"Those come in at a close second. What about you?"

"Cornbread dressing like my grandmother makes."

"I prefer stuffing."

Addison tsked at me. "And you call yourself a Southerner."

"I might've grown up in Virginia, but my home is in New York."

Since I already knew her feelings about the city, Addison moved on to another question. "What is your ideal date?"

"Fucking."

She rolled my eyes. "Besides that."

I shrugged. "I don't date a lot."

"Surely you don't meet a woman and immediately go horizontal—"

"I limit being horizontal."

Her brow creased in confusion. "Excuse me?"

"I mean, I like to fuck outside the box."

Pursing her lips at me, Addison countered, "I would assume you have to be inside the box, *so to speak*, for it to be considered fucking."

I widened my eyes at her before bursting out laughing. *Holy shit.* Had Addison actually said that? Man, I had missed the mark with this girl. She was far from some boring prude with a stick up her ass. "That's a good one, but what I meant was the positions I like and where I like to fuck are outside the box."

"Thank you so much for the clarification."

"You're welcome."

"And what I meant was there has to be some kind of lead-up before you just get to sex, like dinner or a movie."

"Yeah. I do like to buy a woman dinner first."

"How solicitous of you."

With a wink, I said, "It's more about the fact that they're going to need the nutrition to keep up with my stamina."

She slowly shook her head back and forth at me. "You know, it's amazing the way your sex-obsessed brain works. Like how is it possible you're even able to keep a job?"

"I'm very good at multitasking."

"Let me guess, there's some underlying innuendo there?"

I laughed. "Maybe."

"Typical." After flipping a page on the questionnaire, Addison's eyes suddenly bulged.

"Oh. My. God," she hissed.

"What does it say?"

"Something truly horrible and disgusting."

"What?" I questioned before peering at the sheet to see what could possibly be so repulsive.

"They suggest we practice embracing and holding hands to ensure familiarity."

With a frustrated roll of my eyes, I closed the folder and tossed it onto the table. "I can't believe you got your panties in such a twist over something as simple as holding hands and hugging."

"That's not it." She jabbed the folder with her index finger. "They want us to…" She shuddered.

"What? Sacrifice a virgin? Rob a bank?"

"Kiss."

"What's the big deal with that?"

Addison stared at me like I was a mutant. "I don't know you."

"You know more about me than most women when I kiss them."

"Unlike you, I'm far more discerning about who I kiss."

"Why? It's just a pair of lips rubbing together." I flicked my tongue suggestively back and forth. "And there's that."

"Spare me."

I winked. "I will—just this once."

"Look, I know it's probably difficult for your mind to absorb, but kissing is a very intimate action."

Crossing my arms over my chest, I cocked my head at her. "Speaking of action, you might be a hell of lot less uptight if you got more of it, and I mean kissing at the very least."

I watched with amusement as Addison's face turned from cherry red to eggplant purple. It seemed like steam might shoot out of her ears at any moment.

She jabbed a finger in my chest. "Let's get one thing straight here: whatever action I do or don't get is none of your business or concern."

"Actually, my dear fiancée, it is my concern." When I placed my right hand on her shoulder, her upper lip curled in disgust, so I removed it. "Look, you can't argue with the facts. Everyone needs a good fucking from time to time. It's a good stress reliever."

"How do you manage to twist everything to make it about sex? We were just talking about kissing, nothing remotely close to anything so physically extreme."

"Hey, I just made an observation based on your response. It's not my fault you're a tad frigid."

A growl erupted from Addison's lips, and for a moment, I thought she might lunge at me like a rabid dog out for blood. Instead, she tossed the folder down on the table before stomping over to the minibar. Color me surprised when she grabbed a bottle of Jack and a Coke. She kicked the fridge door shut and then grabbed one of the monogrammed Jefferson glasses to mix the drink. Turning around, she held my eye as she proceeded to drain the cup. After swiping the back of her hand across her mouth, she slammed the glass down. Closing her eyes, she shuddered as the alcohol reverberated through her system.

Seconds passed before she opened her eyes. "Okay. Now I think I can actually speak to you again without wanting to choke you."

"Well, choking me would involve touching, which is part of our homework."

The corners of Addison's lips twitched. "You know, I don't think I've ever met anyone like you, Barrett."

"I will take that as both an insult and a compliment."

Addison laughed. "I would expect nothing less."

"So, what should we start with?"

After pursing her lips in thought, Addison replied, "Holding hands, then hugging—that way we can work up to the kissing." She said the word kissing with the same disdain as someone would say toxic waste. Was she that repulsed by me? Or was she really the prude I thought her to be? The way she just threw back that drink... I'd never had any trouble reading women, but this one had me baffled.

Taking the initiative, I closed the remaining gap between us. Once we stood directly in front of each other, I said, "Hold your hands up."

Addison eyed me warily before complying. When I smacked them with mine like girls did on the playground in elementary school, she snorted. "Seriously?"

"Baby steps."

She must've liked my tactic because she started hitting my hands back. Just as her brows furrowed in a *Is he going to keep this bullshit up all night?* look, I stopped my hands in midair. After she did the same, I reached out to curl my fingers around hers. Just like that, we were officially joined. "Holding hands accomplished," I said with a grin.

Although I could tell it slightly pained her, Addison smiled back at me. "Okay. Now let's tackle the hugging," she suggested.

Or I could just tackle you and give you the mercy fuck you're dying for. 'Gagging for a shag' is what Ty would probably say; I decided it was best to keep that thought to myself.

We dropped our hands, and thankfully Addison didn't pull some smartass move like wiping her hands off on her pants like she was de-germing herself. With a deep breath, I stepped even closer to her than before. Even though the top of Addison's chin hit at chin level on me, I somehow felt like I was looming over her.

Slowly, I reached out to wrap my arms around Addison's back. When I drew her against me, she remained limp like a rag doll with her arms pinned at her sides. "Come on, Addie. You gotta work with me here."

She scowled up at me. "Don't call me Addie. Only my family calls me that."

"Newsflash, sweetcheeks, I'm your fiancé. Therefore, I am family."

Her huff of frustration fanned against my shirt. Reluctantly, she brought her arms up to encircle my neck. She took a quick, deep breath, as if to prepare herself.

"It's really not so bad, is it?"

"Actually no, not really."

Although I hated myself for it, I kinda liked the way Addison felt pressed against me, the way her soft curves fit against the harder angles of my body. I especially enjoyed the way her soft tits pressed against my chest. I was sure if anyone could have seen us there, locked in an embrace, they would have thought we were a real a couple. I slid one of my hands down to the small of her back.

"Okay, I think that's good," Addison murmured.

"Yeah, it does feel good."

"No, I meant that's good, like enough."

"Oh, yeah, right. Got it." I jerked my arms away. "Guess the only thing left now is the kissing thing."

She chewed her bottom lip apprehensively. "Uh, I guess."

Jabbing a finger at Addison, I said, "Don't act like you're some condemned woman on death row. I'll have you know that a large part of the female population actually likes kissing me, and an even greater portion would give their eyeteeth just to be in your shoes."

With a smirk, Addison replied, "You really are to be pitied for having such an inflated ego and delusional sense of self."

"Listen sweetheart, if anyone is to be pitied, it's you and your inability to experience the pleasures of the physical side of life." Reaching out, I grabbed her arm and yanked her to me. "But get ready, because you're about to get one hell of a pleasurable experience!"

When she opened her mouth to protest, I slammed my lips against hers. I momentarily braced myself for Addison to physically assault me for manhandling her the way I was. Instead, her reaction shocked the hell out of me. As her body melted into mine, the warmth of her tongue brushed against my lips. Opening my mouth, my tongue sought out hers.

Holy.

Fucking.

Hell.

It was meant to be the thrill of Addison's life. It was meant to prove that we could do this if needed. It was meant to be like kissing a wall for me.

It wasn't meant to be a kiss that would completely reshape my opinion of the brunette in my arms.

Fuck.

CHAPTER SEVEN

ADDISON

HOLY.

> *Shit.*

Barrett Callahan was one hell of a kisser. His lips had the combustive ability to melt your thong right off while simultaneously sending a rushing geyser between your legs—but it wasn't just his lips. It was the feel of his hard, muscled body pressing against mine, and the way his fingers tangled through the strands of my hair, slightly tugging on the ends. I loved a good hair pulling from time to time. Most of the guys I knew took a little while to work up to it, but not Barrett.

In the movies, this was when the girl would clasp the back of her hand to her forehead before swooning into a puddle on the floor. After my many manless months, I'd forgotten how incredible kissing could be, but this most definitely exceeded all expectation, not to mention blowing all my prior experiences out of the water.

I didn't know who exactly broke the kiss the first—we both seemed to just pop away from the other at the same time, like a suction cup coming unhinged. We both stood there, our bodies swaying slightly as we stared at each other. After blinking a few times, I brought my fingers to my swelling lips. "Um, I…"

Yes, ladies and gentleman, one kiss from Barrett had stripped me of all coherent thought and the ability to form sentences.

"Uh…yeah, well…" Barrett replied before clearing his throat several times. "I'm glad we took care of that."

"Me too."

"Everything in that department works fine."

"Yep."

Another awkward silence permeated the air around us. When Barrett finally spoke, I jumped. "I'm hungry," he blurted out. He cocked his brows at me. "Are you hungry?"

It took me a moment after the abrupt subject change to get my wits about me to respond. "Yeah." Considering it was almost seven, it had been a long time since my lunch in the Jefferson's restaurant. Even then, my stomach had been tied in such anxious knots that I'd ended up mostly pushing my salad around rather than eating it.

"Let's go grab some dinner."

"Can we do that?"

Barrett laughed. "I don't think they intend for us to starve during this hokey get-to-know you bullshit."

"I just assumed they meant for us to eat here in the hotel restaurant. You know, on the premises."

"It's not like they put ankle monitors on us."

I rolled my eyes. "Yes, I'm aware of that."

Cocking his head at me, Barrett said, "I wouldn't have taken you for someone afraid to break the rules."

"I'm not."

"Then let's get the hell out of here and get something to eat."

"Fine." I glanced down at my yoga pants and Duke sweatshirt. "I would need to change."

"I say we go somewhere low-key without a dress code. I'm not a big fan of highbrow shit."

"You're not?"

With a smirk, Barrett replied, "Surprising, isn't it?"

"A little. I guess I just imagined you sitting around eating caviar and drinking Cristal."

"Caviar is fucking disgusting, and while Cristal is good, I'm not a big champagne fan. Makes me burp."

I snorted. "Yeah, me too—on the champagne. I've never had caviar before."

"Trust me, you're not missing anything. It doesn't taste good, and it makes this gross popping noise in your mouth."

"Ew."

"There's a great Italian place on the corner. Do you like Italian food?"

"Adore it."

Barrett grinned. "I'll be damned, we just agreed on two things."

"Cue the halleluiah chorus, it must be a miracle," I quipped.

After shooting off a quick text and grabbing the room key, Barrett jerked his thumb at the door. "We better hurry before the moment passes." A mischievous glint burned in his eyes. "Race you to the elevator?"

"You're on."

With a squeal, I pushed past him and threw open the door. Just as I was about to dart out into the hallway, I slammed into a wall of flesh. "Oof."

Removing my face from the man's rock-hard chest, I gazed up into a gorgeous face. "Oh my," I murmured. As I continued staring at him, my nipples had the audacity to harden. I knew the reason for my extreme horniness came from Barrett getting my motor running moments earlier—the guy could have been Shrek and I still would have wanted to climb him.

"I'm sorry about that. Are you okay?" a heavy British accent questioned.

"I, uh, yeah, I-I'm fine," I stammered.

Barrett snickered behind you. "I think she's more shell-shocked from the way you look than because of the fact that she smacked into you, Ty."

Embarrassment singed my cheeks at Barrett's words. "That's not it at all," I argued feebly.

Barrett stepped out into the hallway. "Addison, this is Ty Frasier. He's my bodyguard."

Refusing to look at Ty, I held my hand out to shake his. "Nice to meet you."

"It's nice meeting you, too, Miss Monroe. Now that you and Barrett are together, I won't just be his bodyguard, I'll be yours as well."

Oh man, that accent. It wasn't fair to women anywhere that someone so good-looking should also have a sexy accent. Add in the fact that he was there to protect me, and *holy freakin' swoon*. With both Ty and Barrett around, I thought I should probably check with Everett to see if he could order me some Shamwow-strength panties to wear.

"Ty tends to take his job a little too seriously," Barrett remarked.

"Oh?" I questioned as I glanced between the two of them.

Barrett nodded. "He likes to stick to me like a wet shirt."

I licked my lips at the thought of Ty in a wet shirt—the way it would stretch across what I imagined was a perfect six-pack. I wondered if he was one of those guys who had the perma-hard nipples. There was something about a man with diamond hard nipples that made me weak-kneed and wet-thonged. Earlier, when I had been rubbing myself against Barrett's chest, I had begun to feel his nipples. We won't even begin to comment on what state mine had been in.

Get a grip, Addison, and not on Barrett or Ty's cock. You're acting like some vapid sorority girl whose only major goal in life is pinging from one hot guy to another.

I cleared my suddenly dry throat. "It's nice that he takes such good care of you."

"You have my word that I'll take just as good care of you."

Trying to ignore the blatant innuendo racing through my mind, I plastered a smile on my face. "I appreciate that very much."

Ty's gaze zeroed in on Barrett. "Are you two going somewhere?"

"Just down the street for some Italian."

"Okay, I'll come along."

Barrett rolled his eyes. "Ty, I think the greatest danger awaiting me at Russo's is gluttony or heartburn."

"I'm still coming," Ty insisted.

"Fine. Have it your way. I'm not paying for your pizza or beer though," Barrett replied with a grin.

Ty laughed. "We'll see about that."

The three of us headed down the hallway and then onto the elevator. It was probably the first time in my life I'd ever been alone in an elevator with two so impossibly good-looking men. I was pretty sure the scenario qualified for some porn fantasy.

When the doors opened on the ground floor, Ty hopped off first, I supposed to shield us from any nut-jobs. Barrett and I trailed behind him through the hotel lobby and I started for the revolving doors, but Ty stopped me. "Go through the regular door."

"Let me guess—like Barrett, your favorite movie is *The Godfather*?"

Ty's brows scrunched in confusion. "No. Why?"

"Oh, I just thought you didn't want me to go through the revolving doors because of that part where the guy gets trapped and shot."

Ty held open the door for me. "While it has nothing to do with a movie, you're right that it is a safety precaution."

"Ah, I see."

Once we got outside, Barrett took my hand in his. "Do we really have to do this now?" I asked.

"Take it from me and my vast experience, you never know when and where a lens will be. What better way to sell our relationship than if the first picture taken of us has us holding hands?"

I sighed. "Good point."

With Ty walking a discreet few steps behind us, we made our way across the crosswalk. Glancing over my shoulder at him, I observed how Ty's gaze swept back and forth like he was always on alert for someone to come tackle Barrett. It was both bizarre and comforting.

"Have you always had a bodyguard?" I asked.

"Not one personally, but my family has always had one, mainly when we went on vacations. When I started becoming well-known outside of my family, I would occasionally bring someone out with me when I was partying, but I didn't warrant anyone full-time until Dad announced his candidacy."

"And since you're always surrounded by attractive people, you had to go and hire Thor?"

Barrett laughed. "Ty's looks had nothing to do with it."

"Mmmhmm."

"For your information, we've been friends since prep school. After he was wounded and discharged from the army, he started working in security." Holding the door to Russo's open, Barrett questioned, "Besides, if I was truly that superficial, wouldn't I have hired someone unattractive who wouldn't take any women away from me?"

"You do have a point."

As I started to the counter to order, Barrett grinned at Ty. "She thinks you look like Thor."

While I threw a death glare at Barrett, Ty had the decency not to gloat. "Thank you, Miss Monroe. I've gotten the Hemsworth comparison a few times before. It's always nice to hear."

"Uh, well, you're welcome," I mumbled before focusing on the menu above me.

When Ty leaned forward, I fought the urge to back away—though I feared if I didn't, I might throw my arms around him. *Why must he smell so good too?* "Just ignore Barrett. He hasn't quite achieved emotional maturity yet."

A laugh erupted from my lips. "I'll keep that in mind."

Barrett scowled at Ty, but he didn't argue. Instead, he motioned for me to give the cashier my order. The growling of my stomach outweighed my rational mind, and I ended up ordering a Caesar salad, lasagna, and a chocolate chip cannoli.

Part of me expected Barrett to make some asinine remark about me not watching my figure. After all, he usually dated willowy girls, ones my petty side would have called stick-figures-with-no-souls, but he didn't even blink an eye.

After our order was ready, we took it over to a somewhat secluded booth in the corner, and I couldn't hide my surprise when Ty bypassed us for a table next to the door. "Does he always do that when you're out with women?"

Barrett nodded as he sat down. "He's being paid to protect me, not throw a cold one back."

"I know. It just seems odd considering you're friends."

With a shrug, Barrett replied, "It's just the way we do things." After taking a bite of pizza, an amused look twinkled in his eyes. "You sure are concerned about Ty. Am I going to have to worry about you hitting on him behind my back?"

"Of course not! Why would you even suggest that?"

"Cause I can tell you're hot for him."

With a roll of my eyes, I began cutting up my salad a little more forcefully than necessary. "Just because I think he is an attractive man, that doesn't mean I want to screw his brains out." Okay, so maybe that was a tiny white lie. "Besides, not only am I a woman of my word, I just signed a binding contract to be your tried and true fiancée."

"I believe you. More than that, I know Ty, and you aren't his type."

My eyes bulged. "Excuse me?"

"Easy there. There's no need to get your panties in a twist because you think I'm insulting you physically, because I'm not."

"Do enlighten me then."

"Ty's a protector. It's why he entered the military and why he went into security. He isn't drawn to strong, independent women like you. He wants to find someone he can save."

"That's very commendable of him."

"He's a good guy."

"And very profound of you to be able to see."

Barrett grinned at me over his beer mug. "I can be very deep."

"Don't ruin the moment."

"Okay. Fine. Tell me something."

"As long as it isn't sexual."

Barrett snickered. "Not this time." After swiping his mouth with a napkin, he asked, "How exactly does someone who has been raised in the jungles decide to become a political science major?

"I wasn't raised in the jungles, as you say. Sure, I spent my summers in foreign countries, but the rest of the year was here in the States. And we weren't always out in the jungle."

"I stand corrected, but still, it certainly had to shape who you were and what you wanted to do."

I nodded. "We saw a lot a poverty both here and in other countries. I wanted to find a way to help them. Since I get nauseous at the sight of blood, I knew I couldn't be a doctor or a nurse. Then, freshman year, there was a political rally on campus for one of the candidates running for governor. Standing there watching all the people, I knew I'd found a way to help people. I could put my support behind the politicians who would help them."

"You haven't ever gotten disillusioned?"

I shrugged. "Sometimes. In the end, I just try to focus on the good that has been done, rather than what hasn't."

"And that's how you ended up as the volunteer coordinator for my dad's campaign?"

"Actually, that happened because I desperately needed a job."

With a frown, Barrett said, "That's it?"

"Well, it's a long and somewhat seedy story that led me to your dad's campaign."

His blue eyes lit up. "I've got all night."

I laughed. "Only because you like the idea of something sordid."

"You already know me so well."

After drawing in a deep breath, I unburdened myself of the story of Walt and his father. When I finished, Barrett slowly shook his head. "What a douchebag, or I guess I should say douchebags."

"That's interesting coming from you."

"Hey, I'll have you know I've never cheated on a woman," he protested.

"Is that out of moral responsibility or the fact that you never date one long enough to cheat?"

"Touché," Barrett murmured with a smile.

I pushed my half-empty lasagna plate aside and moved my cannoli in front of me. "That looks good," Barrett remarked.

"Yeah, it does," I murmured before taking a bite. At his continued covetous stare at the dessert, I laughed. "Would you like some?"

"Yeah."

"*Yeah?* That the kind of manners your prep school taught you?" I teasingly asked.

Barrett glowered at me. "Please?"

"Much better." After cutting off another bite, I brought my fork across the table to Barrett's waiting mouth.

"Man, that's good." He barely finished chewing before he rose out of his seat.

"Where are you going?"

"To get us a dozen."

I laughed. "Do you really think we need that many?"

"Maybe you can share some with Ty."

I rolled my eyes when Barrett made kissy noises at me and polished off the rest of my cannoli before he returned. "Want another?" he asked, dipping into the box.

"I'm pretty stuffed."

He made quick work of the one in his hand. "Ready to head back?"

"Sure."

I'd barely gotten out of my chair when Ty arrived at my side. "Are we going straight to the hotel, or will there be any other stops?"

"To the hotel."

Ty nodded before heading out the front door. When he deemed it safe, he waved us on outside. Once again, he fell in step behind us. We'd barely made it up the street when Barrett's phone dinged, and he reached into his pocket to dig it out.

"I'll be damned."

"What?"

"We're already on TMZ."

I froze on the sidewalk. "Like the gossip site TMZ?"

"Yeah."

"How is that even possible? Did your dad go ahead and make the announcement?"

"No. He would have let us know."

Nibbling on my bottom lip, I watched Barrett staring intently at the screen. "What are they saying?"

"See for yourself." Barrett handed me his phone, and I gasped at the sight of several grainy pictures of our dinner at Russo's. The one of me feeding Barrett my cannoli was the largest. It also had the caption, *Bare Callahan caught out on the town in DC sampling an unknown brunette's delights. This news will certainly have his latest flame, opera diva Evangelina Petscova, singing a different tune. The two were seen just yesterday boarding a private plane in Los Angeles.*

Suddenly, the fact that I was on TMZ in my ratty Duke sweatshirt paled in comparison to the fact that I was being painted as the other woman. "You were with another woman yesterday?" I asked. I hoped it was all a lie; TMZ was a gossip site after all.

Barrett winced. "Actually, I was with her today."

I shoved his phone back at him. "I can't believe this."

"Give me a break. Until eight hours ago, I didn't even know you existed. I didn't know Dad was going to spring this marriage business on me today any more than you did."

"Surely you understand what I'm worried about here, Barrett. My first mention in the press is as the homewrecking other woman!"

"Not with the story the campaign is putting out about us. Evangelina was just a side piece while I was pining for you."

"Yeah, excuse me for having a conscience about humiliating another woman," I spat. There was that, and the fact that there was no way anyone would believe Barrett had been pining over me when he had Evangelina.

Ty stepped between us. "Guys, you have to take this discussion out of the streets. We need to get you guys back to the Jefferson," Ty said. At what must've been our sullen faces, Ty added, "If TMZ has broken the story, other media outlets are picking it up. You have to sell the relationship now more than ever."

Barrett and I didn't argue. Instead, I allowed him to take my hand as we started back.

Turning to Barrett, I forced a smile to my face even though the question I was about to ask didn't warrant one. "Did you care about Evangelina?"

"Not like you're worried about."

"What does that mean?"

"She was fun to hang out with."

"'Hang out with' being code for sex?"

"Yes."

"You're such a disgusting pig."

Barrett brought my hand to his lips to bestow a tender kiss. "Thank you for the judgmental compliment, sweetheart, especially since you don't know any of the particulars."

"Such as?"

Through a smile, Barrett replied, "Women know what they're getting into when they're with me. One google search eliminates any of the mystery. The content of my character is clearly laid out in all the stories about me. If they get hurt, they really only have themselves to blame."

"Just when I think you can't possibly out asshole yourself, you go and say something like that."

"Hey, I'm honest and forthright with every woman I date. Wouldn't it be worse if I was leading them on just to get them into bed?"

"It's all equally sickening."

"Whatever."

When we turned the corner toward the Jefferson, I saw a gaggle of reporters waiting outside the front entrance. "Fuck," Barrett muttered.

"Side door?" Ty suggested.

That would have worked if we hadn't been spotted. The photographers descended on us like a swarm of locusts, and when I shielded my eyes from the flashbulbs, a murmur of shock rippled through the crowd. "She's wearing an engagement ring!" someone shouted.

"Is Bare, the eternal bachelor, tying the knot?" a reporter questioned before sticking a microphone in Barrett's face.

"How did you meet?"

"Do you think he's going to be faithful?"

As we were peppered with questions, I fought to breathe. Even though I was supposed to have had the weekend to prepare, I wasn't sure anything could have adequately prepared me for the onslaught. While my panicked gaze searched for an escape, Barrett squeezed my hand almost reassuringly. "Could you guys just back off for a minute? I will explain, but not until I know Addison is comfortable."

Since I never expected them to actually respect Barrett's wishes, I couldn't believe it when it became deathly silent around us except for the clicking of cameras. My heart beat a little faster not just out of fear, but also because of the care Barrett was showing for me.

Clearing his throat, he then gazed out at the sea of cameras. "Yes, I just got engaged this afternoon." He then repeated the story his father and Bernie had come up with. Of course, there was a wrench in the plan considering we were supposed to have the weekend to get acquainted, but damn if Barrett couldn't perform on demand.

"After seeing Addison at a political function recently, I impulsively asked my father for my late grandmother's ring. I carried it around with me, hoping I would run into her again. As fate would have it, I saw her today." He smiled lovingly at me. "So, I popped the question, and she said yes."

To seal the validity of our engagement for the virtual world, Barrett dipped his head to kiss me. Instead of a quick peck on the lips, Barrett was all about selling it. Even though reporters were shouting our names and flashbulbs were going off all around us, the world melted away. It was just the two of us. Two mouths fusing together. Two bodies molded against each other.

In the end, we were just one.

When Barrett finally pulled away, I remained as shell-shocked as after our first kiss. Bizarre didn't even begin to describe what it was like making out with a strange guy who you sorta hated in front of an audience, but it wasn't just the faking-the-relationship aspect. It seemed like everyone was way too close to me, like I was trapped by a wall of bodies. The circuits in my brain became so overwhelmed that they practically shut down. If I didn't get out of there soon, I was going to lose it.

Sensing my panic, Barrett tightened his arm around me. He then flashed a megawatt smile at the reporters and photographers. "I hope that clears up the confusion. That's all the questions we're going to take tonight. You can contact my PR rep for any further interviews." He then began leading me through the crowd to the front entrance of the hotel. The two bellmen at the front door were overwhelmed, and the crowd pushed past them to follow us.

Thankfully, an elevator was waiting, and Barrett rushed us inside. Ty and a member of the hotel's security blocked the press from getting on with us. When the doors closed, my thin veil of composure snapped, and I sagged against one of the walls. I started gasping for air as a full-on panic attack enveloped me—at least I assumed it was a panic attack. I'd never really had one before.

"Take some deep breaths, and don't lock your knees," Barrett ordered.

After inhaling and exhaling several times, my anxiety slowly began dissipating. When I pulled my gaze from the floor, I found Barrett staring expectantly at me. "Better?"

"Yes. Thank you. The cameras and the questions…it was too intense." I shook my head sheepishly. "I'm sorry for freaking out like that."

"Don't apologize. It was your first time. Everyone freaks out the first time."

"Even you?"

He grinned. "I was five years old when I had my first paparazzi onslaught.

"I guess it isn't quite the same."

"Actually, you did far better than me."

"But you were a kid."

"I was a brat. Mom had just had Caroline, and Dad was taking me and Thorn into the hospital to see them. It was mostly local media and I stuck my tongue out before kicking one of the photographers in the shin when he asked me to smile."

"You didn't."

"Oh yeah I did."

I laughed. "What did your dad do?"

"He made me stay at home with my grandparents while he took Thorn to a Yankees game."

"Ouch." From our getting-to-know-you homework, I had learned what a huge baseball fan Barrett was, and more importantly, how his blood bled blue and white for the Yankees.

"Yeah, it would have been easier on me if he'd beaten the crap out of me."

The elevator dinged on our floor. When the doors opened, James and Bernie stood waiting for us. "Guess you saw the news?" Barrett questioned as we stepped into the hallway.

"Yes we did." James placed a hand on my shoulder. "Are you okay?"

"I'm fine, Senator Callahan."

"Please call me James."

I nodded. "I just hope my first foray in front of the media wasn't a total failure."

"Now you just put that thought right out of your mind. You performed wonderfully given the circumstances."

"Thank you."

As he glanced between Barrett and me, James's expression turned from one of comfort to frustration. "I do believe you both were instructed to stay here for the duration of the weekend, yet within a few hours, you already—"

"It was just dinner. It wasn't like we were caught coming out of a bar, wasted at two in the morning," Barrett protested.

"Something you're more than familiar with from past experiences," James bit back.

With a smirk, Barrett said, "Nice one, Dad."

"Thankfully, it worked to our advantage this time, but I hope you both can now better comprehend the importance of following my instructions to the letter."

"Yes sir, I do," I replied while Barrett merely nodded.

The corners of James's lips curved into a smile. "Now go to your room, and don't come out until I tell you to."

Barrett laughed. "Come on. I haven't heard that line from you since I turned eighteen. Besides, the press already knows about us. What can it possibly hurt?"

"While I was just giving you two a hard time, I would like to be notified should you leave again, and make sure you do not go anywhere without Ty."

"Got it," Barrett replied.

"Now if you'll excuse us, we have damage control for your premature engagement announcement to attend to," James said. He and Bernie then got onto one of the waiting elevators. I hated the feeling that I had already disappointed Senator Callahan. Technically, it had been Barrett's idea, but I wasn't five. I was fully capable of saying no.

As we started to our hotel room, I smacked Barrett's arm. "Hey, what was that for?" he demanded.

I scowled at him. "Being a bad influence. I told you it wasn't a good idea to go out."

"Oh, I'm so sorry for corrupting you, Miss Goody Two-Shoes," Barrett replied playfully.

"I'm not a goody two-shoes. I just hate letting your father down."

"Hmm, I guess that would make you a suck-up or brownnoser."

"Excuse me for wanting to do the right thing for your father's campaign."

Barrett took the key card out of his pocket. "You are by agreeing to be my ball and chain for the next nine months."

"The feeling is mutual."

He grinned, which actually broke the ice a little. What I'd just experienced had been quite terrifying, to be honest. "What do you say we turn on the television and see what they're saying about us? Considering that epic on-the-spot performance I gave, I'm dying to see an instant replay."

I snatched the bag of cannolis from him, which had somehow miraculously made it back with us. "I think I'm going to need a few more of these to make it through seeing that."

CHAPTER EIGHT

ADDISON

ON MONDAY MORNING, I woke up for the last time in the Jefferson, and my wake-up call came at the ungodly hour of five AM. It was even more ungodly because of the fact that I had just gotten to sleep around two AM— I'd been too nervous about my first day on the campaign trail to sleep. The what-ifs had plagued me, my mind bombarding me with the most paranoid of scenarios.

After my trial by fire with the media, the rest of the weekend had been pretty inconsequential. I had been really worried about being called a homewrecker, but somehow, that hadn't even been an issue. We studied the answers to our relationship homework so we wouldn't have any slipups at future interviews. While I went through the stuff I needed to take with me verses the extra stuff I didn't need to take with me, Barrett caught up on emails and paperwork. I had to give him credit that he really did take his work seriously, to a level of extreme perfectionism. *That* I could actually admire.

We even managed to break out on Saturday afternoon to go to the movies. Of course, the moment we exited the hotel, the cameras came out in full force. Although Barrett always instructed me to act natural, the moment a lens became trained on me, I overthought every move I made. "Hey, Mr. Roboto, think you could lighten up a bit?" Barrett had joked.

"I'm sorry. You seem to forget that while you've had cameras on you since you were a child, this is still new to me," I had countered.

By Sunday when we went out for brunch, I had begun to look less like the Tin Man. I even managed to smile at the reporters who called my name while peppering Barrett and me with questions. Regardless of my worries, James set me at ease by texting me to say he was loving all the positive stories already floating around in the media.

After my shower, I came out of the bathroom in my new designer robe, compliments of Everett. Actually, it was one of three new robes I now had. I wasn't sure how robes translated into campaign wear, but I wasn't going to argue with him. The luxurious fabric put the sad, ratty bathrobe I had at home to shame.

A knock sounded at the door. While I hoped it would be room service with breakfast, I figured it was Saundra, the makeup artist and hair stylist who had been assigned to Barrett and me. She had come to the hotel yesterday to do a practice run with me, and she would be traveling around the country with us to do Barrett's and my hair, along with my makeup. Yes, it seemed a little ridiculous that Barrett needed someone to do his hair, but apparently, it was part of the political campaign territory.

Once I'd checked the peephole, I opened the door. "Good morning, Saundra."

"Good morning to you as well, Miss Monroe."

Wrinkling my nose at her formality, I said, "Please, call me Addison."

She smiled. "Okay then. Good morning to you, Addison."

After returning her smile, I said, "Are you ready to transform me?"

"I'm ready if you are."

"As ready as I'll ever be."

While Saundra set up in the bathroom, I slipped into the red suit Everett had picked out for me to wear. At first, I had balked when he mentioned me wearing suits. To me, that sounded way too matronly, but thankfully, he had shown me a lot of power suits that didn't look like I'd stepped off the set of *Dynasty* with killer shoulder pads and giant buttons.

The first day's ensemble had a very youthful look. Whenever I turned left and right, the bottom of the skirt flared around my knees, giving the suit an overall fun, flirty feel. I soon became way too amused by watching my floating hemline.

"Good morning."

As I jumped out of my skin, my hand flew to my chest to still my erratically beating heart. "You scared the hell out of me!" I threw a murderous glance at Barrett over my shoulder. "Did you ever hear of knocking?"

"I did knock, but you were too busy twirling to hear it."

"I was not twirling."

"Yeah, you were."

"Whatever," I muttered, refusing to acknowledge that he was right.

Barrett sported a crisp navy suit, a white shirt underneath, and crimson red tie. As much as I hated to admit it, he exuded a decidedly suit-porn vibe. What was it about a suit that made men look so damn delectable?

After giving me a onceover, Barrett said, "I see Everett's gotten to you."

"Are you trying to say I was some fashion-less hack before?"

"Easy now, it was just an observation."

"A snarky one."

He grinned. "I've never been accused of being *snarky* before."

"Well, it's the truth."

"Look, I'm sorry if I sounded *snarky*, as you say. It really was just an observation. All the women in my family have had the Everett overhaul."

"He is a very gifted stylist."

"That he is."

I sighed. "I'm sorry for sniping at you. I'm really nervous about today."

"Don't be."

"Easy for you to say."

"Hey now, this is my first presidential campaign, too."

"But you have all the experiences from the senatorial races," I countered.

"You're going to do fine, Addison."

I was surprised by the sincerity in Barrett's eyes. "Thank you. I hope you're right."

Saundra stuck her head out of the bathroom door. "I'm ready for you now."

With a nod, I headed into the bathroom. I'd never known so much could go into making someone camera-ready. I'd always been a girly-girl who loved makeup and doing my hair, but I never spent more than half an hour getting ready. It took Saundra an hour to do my hair and makeup—of course, I'd never been into highlighting or contouring or any of that.

Once she was finished, I couldn't help doing a double take at my reflection. "You are so talented," I murmured.

"Thank you. It helps when you have something gorgeous to work with."

When I came out into the main suite, Barrett and Ty awaited me, and their eyes bulged. "You look beautiful, Addison," Ty said with a warm smile. Have I mentioned the man's smile? It made me a little weak…and that fact made me a cheap hussy. After all, I was a fake-engaged woman.

"Thank you, but it's all Saundra's magic."

Saundra shook her head. "Like I said before, with your features, I don't have to do anything magical."

Although Barrett continued staring at me, he hadn't complimented me like the others. After Ty nudged him in the back, Barrett said, "Yeah. You look nice."

Nice?

That was the best he could come up with? *You look nice* is what you say to a dressed-up teenage girl going through her awkward face with braces and acne, but what could I expect? I knew the women he was attracted to, and I wasn't them.

Interrupting the awkward silence, Saundra said, "I'm ready for you, Barrett."

As Barrett and Saundra headed back into the bathroom, I sat down at the table that overflowed with room service goodies. Ty took a seat across from me. "He's spinning right now," he stated as I slathered cream cheese across a bagel.

"Excuse me?"

"Barrett is spinning with you as his fiancée."

"Ah, so your definition of 'spinning' is when someone has emotional whiplash and says rude things?" I countered.

Ty smiled. "I'm not condoning his behavior, Addison. I'm just trying to explain some of it to you. The idea of engagement itself is extremely confining to him, not to mention the fact that he doesn't know what it's like to have a woman not fall at his feet."

"Yeah, that's certainly not going to happen."

"And that fact is driving him crazy. He can't compliment you too much because then that gives you the upper hand."

I rolled my eyes. "That is so immature."

"That is so Barrett, at least with women."

I munched thoughtfully on my bagel. After swallowing, I asked, "With as much time as you spend with Barrett, how is it possible that none of your good attributes have rubbed off on him?"

With a laugh, Ty countered, "Don't put me on a pedestal I don't deserve."

"You seem pretty genuine to me."

"I appreciate the praise, but just like anyone else, I'm a work in progress."

With a smile, I said, "It's good work though."

"Thank you." I hadn't expected Ty to be so forthcoming. He knew Barrett's taste in women, and surely he knew it would never be me, but it was still nice of him to try to smooth over Barrett's inability to compliment me.

I'd managed to polish off my bagel and a cup of berries when Barrett emerged from having his hair done. While it didn't look that different to me, I supposed Saundra had some special product that kept it in place in windy situations or what have you.

Ty's phone buzzed. After glancing at it, he said, "The car is here. It's time to go."

My stomach instantly cramped at the thought of leaving the safety and security of the suite. The next three weeks would thrust me not only into the spotlight, but into a whole new world of being on the road. Even during my parents' missionary days, it was only our summers that were somewhat rootless, and in most cases, we spent the entire two months in one country or area. From the schedule I'd been given, some days I'd wake up in one state, have lunch in another, and go to bed in yet another, pinging from north to south to east to west. It was overwhelming.

Even so, I pulled my shoulders back and took a deep breath to steady my nerves. Like a good soldier, I marched out of the suite with my head held high, and I kept it that way the entire elevator ride down to the lobby and out to the car. A small throng of reporters waited outside on the curb, and both embarrassment and pride filled me when some of them whistled at me. "Lookin' good, Addison!"

"Hey uptown girl."

"You're a lucky guy, Bare," another called. Of course, they would still call him by his nickname, which I was sure irked Barrett.

Ty put us into the car before taking the front seat on the passenger side. When we got to Dulles, the car pulled us around to a special airfield for small planes. As I peered through my window, I saw a sleek jet with *The Callahan Corporation* in blue on the side. "Wow," I murmured.

"Ever been on a jet before?" Barrett asked.

I gave him side-eye. "Although I've been on noncommercial planes, I'd hardly call the rickety four-seaters we rode into the jungle *jets*."

"I'd have to say it took balls of steel to ride those things."

I laughed. "I was a kid at the time. It felt more like being on a ride at the fair."

"Is a fair like Disney World?"

"Uh, yeah, I guess." Tilting my head at him, I asked, "Wait, have you never actually been to a fair?"

"Nope."

"You've really missed out."

"Maybe we can find one along the campaign route and you can enlighten me as to its wonders."

I smiled. "That sounds good."

We pulled up alongside another sleek black Lincoln sedan and I didn't have to wonder for long who was inside it because James and his wife, Jane, exited a moment later. I started to fumble with the door handle before it was opened for me by the driver.

I stepped out of the car to see my fake future mother-in-law striding over to me. With her 5'9" frame, she cut an imposing figure, and I found myself shrinking back. After quickly sizing me up, a smile spread across her attractive face. "Hello, Addison. I'm Jane Callahan. It's so very nice to meet you."

Instead of being formal and shaking my hand like I expected, she leaned in and kissed my left cheek and then my right. "It's very nice to meet you, too," I replied breathlessly.

When she pulled away, her gaze dropped to my ensemble. "I see Everett took good care of you, just as I instructed."

I smiled. "Yes, he did. Thank you for sending him to me."

Her hand trailed down my shoulder to my sleeve. "Carolina Herrera or Diane von Furstenberg?"

"Carolina Herrera for both the coat and suit."

"It's just to die for. You're going to turn heads today." She smiled as she cupped my chin. "Of course, with your gorgeous face, you'd turn heads even if you were wearing a burlap sack."

"Thank you for your kind words and compliments." I motioned to her tailored blue suit. "I like yours as well."

"I owe everything to Everett. I suppose he told you he's been styling us for years."

"He did."

Her red lips turned down in a pout. "I don't know what I will do without him when he retires. I guess I'll just have to stay home and style my bathrobe."

I smiled. Less than five minutes with Jane, and I already liked her a lot. Since she came from a pedigreed background, I had been afraid I would find her snobbish. At the very least, I imagined her swapping sugar with me in public and then giving me the cold shoulder in private.

"I understand you spent the weekend with Barrett."

"Yes ma'am, I did. We had a pretty intensive get-to-know-you session."

Jane waved her hand dismissively. "Oh honey, you don't need to call me ma'am. Just Jane is fine."

"Okay then, Jane."

A wicked look flashed in her ice-blue eyes. "Since Barrett's still breathing, I imagine you fought the natural urge to strangle him?"

I blinked several times as I tried to decide if she was serious. When I realized she actually was, I still couldn't help wondering if it wasn't some kind of test. At her girlish giggle, I finally laughed. "Yes, we both somehow managed to survive unscathed."

Jane waved one of her gloved hands. "He's my son and I love him dearly, but he is just horrible when it comes to women." Sadness washed away the amusement in her face. "Sometimes I worry it's my fault. Before he had his surgery and outgrew his heart condition, I was so terribly afraid of losing him. I ended up indulging him more than I should have. I certainly hope you won't do that."

Hmm, interesting. Now I had a little more insight into Barrett's character. Of course, I wasn't exactly sure how being spoiled as a kid made him into a womanizer, but I couldn't help wondering if it hadn't had something to do with it.

"Rest assured, I won't be indulging him. More than anything, I'll be putting him in his place."

"Good for you."

"Are you two done talking shit about me?" Barrett questioned.

Laughing, Jane turned around and gave Barrett a hug rather than kissing him on the cheeks. "Aren't you the narcissist thinking if two beautiful women are talking, it must be about you?"

Barrett crossed his arms over his chest. "You're deflecting, Mom."

She winked at him. "I'm a politician's wife—I always deflect away from the truth. Besides, we weren't 'talking shit', as you say. We were merely swapping secrets."

Wearing his usual dapper smile, James came up to me. "How are you feeling about today, Addison?"

"Great," I lied.

"You know, it's okay to be nervous," he said.

"I'm glad to hear you say that, sir, because if I were to be honest, I'd say I'm very nervous."

He gave my shoulder an encouraging pat. "You'll do great."

"Thank you, sir. I certainly hope so."

After I made my way up the narrow jet stairs, I stepped inside the cabin. I couldn't help standing stock-still and just staring at everything. Of course, that caused Barrett to bump into me. "Oof," I muttered as I toppled over one of the leather seats and landed in a heap on the carpeted floor.

"Wow, you sure as hell aren't graceful, are you?" Barrett asked as he pulled me to my feet.

"I would've been fine if you hadn't mowed me down," I protested as I swatted his hands away.

Once we realized our bickering had an audience, we ducked our heads and took a seat on the couch. Jane sat on the other side of Barrett while James and Bernie sat in two of the captain's chairs. Some of the other advisors filled up the back of the cabin, along with Saundra and Everett. The jet had barely started moving down the runway when Bernie took out a piece of paper and placed it on the table in front of us.

"Here's the game plan for today: we're going to be mimicking the whistle-stop train tour both Reagan and Truman took of Ohio, going from Dayton down through Perrysberg with five stops along the way."

James grunted. "Which means five speeches for me."

Jane smiled at him. "I've got your cough drops in my purse, and I've alerted Mary Anne to ensure there's lemon honey tea at every stop."

"Thanks sweetheart."

"A train tour? That's an interesting strategy," Barrett remarked.

"You don't like the idea?" James asked.

Barrett shrugged. "It just seems like a waste of valuable time. I mean, we could cover more ground by plane."

Eyeing me curiously, Senator Callahan asked, "What about you, Addison—what do you think?"

I furrowed my brows. "Me? You want my opinion?"

"Yes I do."

Nothing like being put on the spot. "Um, well, I kinda like it."

"Why is that?"

With everyone's eyes on me, I exhaled a nervous breath. "To me, a train provides an air of nostalgia in our modern era. Because you need to appeal to the farmers and blue collar workers of this area, a train is much more relatable than using your private jet."

James smiled. "Yes, those are the exact reasons."

While I basked in his praise, Barrett stiffened beside me. "Give Addison a cookie, she got the right answer."

Jane reached over to pat Barrett's leg. "Don't be petty and jealous, son. It's unbecoming." When I caught her eye, she winked at me.

Ignoring her comment, Barrett asked, "What would you like Saint Addison and me to do?"

I bit down on my lip to keep from telling him to quit being a petty bastard. Instead, I focused on Bernie.

"When we first exit the train, there will be roped off crowds. You're to greet them by shaking hands and smiling. We have seats for you in the front rows during all the speeches," Bernie replied.

"Got it," Barrett replied.

Once we were in the air, everything became very business-like. Some of the advisors talked on cell phones and worked on their laptops. Bernie appeared extremely old school as he read print copies of several newspapers.

It was James's actions that took me totally off guard. Taking a remote off one of the tables, he rose out of his chair, and music soon filled the jet's cabin. It didn't take me too long to recognize the oldies, and more specifically, it sounded like Motown. Maybe the Temptations or the Four Tops.

Barrett, who had his head buried in his iPad, turned to me and rolled his eyes. "This is the music Dad insists on using to get pumped up before a rally."

"Really?"

"Dad's Rocky-climbing-up-the-stairs-to-fist-bump isn't to 'Gonna Fly Now', but to the Four Tops."

"Don't knock it. This is what I grew up on," James argued. He extended his hand to Jane, and she smiled and rose off of the couch. She eagerly went to her husband and let him wrap his arms around her, their bodies moving in sync with the beat of the song.

Warmth flooded my heart at the sight, as well as the green-eyed monster of jealousy. As a hopeless romantic, I wanted what James and Jane had. The adoration and mutual respect was endearing, and something you rarely saw in political marriages.

An idea blossomed in my mind. "You guys should film this," I said over the music.

"Don't encourage them," Barrett replied.

"I'm serious. This would be a positive way to promote yourself. I mean, you'd be hard-pressed to find someone who doesn't appreciate music, and it shows that you're approachable and not pretentious."

James appeared thoughtful. "You know, that isn't a bad idea. We could put it with a compilation of speeches and appearances along the tour."

Jane laughed. "I'm all for it, just as long as I get to be in the editing room to make sure my best moves get put forward."

"Of course," James assured her. "What do you think Bernie?"

After glancing up from his computer, Bernie nodded. "I'll have someone look into it right away. We could use some backstage footage for the website."

"Addison, you're already becoming indispensable," Jane remarked.

"Yes, she is," James said. He whirled Jane back to her seat. "Thanks for obliging me, sweetheart."

She winked at him. "Any time."

I thought he was finished dancing, but James came over to me next. "Care to take a spin?"

"Here? Now?"

"With your theater background, I assume you're a wonderful dancer," James stated.

"Well, I'm not exactly wonderful, but I'm not too bad either."

He held out his hand. "Come on, get rid of some of that nervous energy."

As I rose off the couch, the song changed, and the Beatles' "I Want to Hold Your Hand" started playing. "This is one of my dad's favorite songs."

"Is it?"

I nodded. "He had it on vinyl, and he used to take this beat-up record player with us on our trips. Even though my siblings and I argued with him that CDs were way less cumbersome, not to mention better quality, he argued vinyl was the best because it was more authentic."

"I like his style," Barrett mused from his seat on the couch.

I craned my neck over James's shoulder to look at him. "You're a record kind of guy?"

"I have a whole collection."

At the desk, Bernie grunted in frustration. "I knew there was something I left off your questionnaire—things you collect."

Barrett laughed. "I think that's a pretty random question for a reporter to ask."

"Better safe than sorry," Bernie replied.

James eyed me curiously. "Speaking of your father, what did your parents say about your engagement?"

"Thankfully, I called them when I went back home to my apartment the first day, so they didn't have to see it on the news." They had been very surprised, and I even heard a hint of disappointment in their voices that I had been partaking in a secret relationship. One day I hoped to be able to tell them the truth.

"That's good. I can imagine that would have been quite a shock."

"Yes, it would."

Our dance came to an end to the last strains of the song. "Thank you for the dance, Addison."

"You're welcome."

"Feeling any better?"

I tilted my head in thought. "Actually, I do feel a little better."

"It's the power of dancing."

With a laugh, I replied, "I'll have to remember that."

The captain came over the speaker to inform us we were about to begin our descent, and I couldn't help marveling at how much speedier a jet traveled than a plane. Saundra came around to fluff Jane's and my hair and touch up our makeup.

Once we landed, the car took us the short drive to the train station. Even though it wasn't an official stop on the tour, there were people waiting to see us, but our tight schedule didn't permit us doing any kind of walk-through there. Instead, we boarded the train and headed for our first stop just down the tracks.

We arrived to the fanfare of waving flags and *Callahan for President* signs as John Mellencamp's "Little Pink Houses" blared over a loudspeaker. After the train came to a stop, James and Jane stood on the platform for a few moments, posing for photographs. Once they had made their way down the stairs, it was time for Barrett and me to come out.

As we stepped onto the platform, Barrett took my hand in his. A cheer went up at the sight of us, and we smiled and posed for the press who stood below us. Thankfully, just as my face felt completely frozen in place, Bernie motioned for us to come down the stairs.

When I started to take my hand away, Barrett squeezed it tighter. Speaking through his smile, he said, "Let me help you down the stairs."

"I can make it on my own just fine," I replied back through gritted teeth. With my free hand, I kept waving to the crowd.

"It'll look better for the photographers." He turned to me. "Besides, after what happened earlier, I don't want you face-planting."

"That wasn't my fault," I protested.

"Just let me help you."

"Not happening," I muttered. Honestly, I didn't know why I was being so stubborn. I mean, did it really matter if Barrett helped me down the stairs? No, but something within my feminist self was repulsed by the thought.

A low growl came from deep within Barrett's throat, which reminded me of the Beast in *Beauty and the Beast*. "Why do you have to be such a shrew?"

"Why do you have to be such a misogynistic douchebag?"

To those below us, we looked like a happy couple taking in all the supporters and perhaps commenting on the crowd. Our faces stayed frozen in enthusiastic expressions as if we had just had Botox. Of course, if anyone in the crowd was a lip reader, we were screwed.

When I moved toward the first step, Barrett still hadn't released my hand. "Let go," I hissed.

"Fine."

What happened next was simply a matter of physics. The energy I was putting into tugging against Barrett sent me propelling forward once he removed his hand, and that forward momentum sent me rolling down the platform's three stairs and into a tangled heap at the bottom.

A gasp of horror rang throughout the gaggle of reporters in front of me. I wasn't sure if their reaction was because I'd just face-planted in front of them, or if it was more about the fact that my skirt—the one with the fun and flirty hemline—had flown up around my waist. I was having a distinct feeling of déjà vu—or I guess in this case, it would be déjà moon.

Even though I'd lost a great portion of the skin on my knees and searing pain radiated from them, I fumbled to jerk my skirt down before scrambling to stand. Every molecule in my body hummed with the same mortification as the classic naked-in-public dream.

Barrett's hands came around my waist and he lifted me upright. "Just out of curiosity, where the hell is your underwear?" he hissed in my ear.

"Everett told me not to wear any so it wouldn't show panty lines through the suit," I snapped. Turning my back to the crowd, I pretended to be examining the damage to my bummed-up knees. "It's not like I don't have on pantyhose."

"It sure as hell didn't look like it."

"The color is called nude. You should google it."

"Yeah, well, that might true, but you still pretty much mooned the reporters."

Jerking my head up, I scowled at him. "Yes, I'm aware of that. What about the crowd?"

"No. Thankfully, they were blocked by the press corps."

"Thank God for small mercies," I grumbled.

"You forget those reporters have cameras."

Great. Kill me now. At that moment, I had two choices: I could sprint into the building and collapse into hysterics over my giant faux pas, or I could put on my big girl panties—in today's case, panties *period*—and do the job I'd been sent to do. From that day on, I would have WWJD moments—What Would Jackie Do. While I'm pretty sure Jackie Kennedy never mooned the press corps, she did put on a happy face and soldier on for the sake of JFK's campaign and later presidency.

Drawing my shoulders back, I plastered a smile on my face. Without another word to Barrett, I headed over to work the rope line of people. "Hello. Thank you so much for coming out," I said through a toothy grin.

When I reached out my hand, an elderly lady took it. "Are you okay, honey? That was quite a tumble you took."

"I'm fine. Thank you so much for asking. Nothing too bruised but my pride," I responded good-naturedly.

I moved on to shake several other people's hands. "What happened?" another woman asked.

What I did next was not something I'm very proud of, but in the moment, it seemed necessary. "I was too nervous about my first campaign event to eat, and I tend to get lightheaded. It was a little bit of hypoglycemia that cause me to tumble."

The woman's expression melted into pity. "Bless your heart. I hope you're feeling better."

"I am. Thank you." As I continued greeting people, the pain of both my physical and emotional injuries dissipated, and I began to enjoy myself. The exuberance of the crowd bolstered my mood and I could have kept on talking to people for hours, but soon I felt Ty's hand at the small of my back. "It's time to take your seats for the speech," he whispered into my ear.

I nodded as I waved goodbye to those I hadn't been able to reach yet. Ty ushered us down a long aisle of chairs to our seats and after a small band struck up a merry tune, James and Jane climbed the stairs of the platform. The music came to an end when James took a place at the flag-draped podium. "My fellow Americans and Ohioans, what an honor and privilege it is to be speaking before you today!"

The crowd immediately erupted into wild applause and cheering. James grinned at the response then began speaking about the problems the country currently faced and how he would remedy them if he was elected president. The speech itself probably lasted around ten minutes. When he finished, he turned to Jane, who rose from her seat to join him at the podium so they could smile and wave before leaving the platform. After they started down the aisle, Barrett and I followed behind them. We smiled, waved, and shook a few hands on our way back to the train.

The moment I picked my leg up to board the steps, agonizing pain shot through my knee and I yelped. Before I could lift my other leg, Barrett's strong arm came around my waist. "I'm helping you." His eyes bored into mine. "It's not up for negotiating, got it?"

I hurt too bad to argue so I just leaned on him, and a chorus of awwws rumbled through the onlookers at the sight of heroic Barrett helping his battered fiancée. I fought the urge to roll my eyes; if they only knew he was just doing it for the cameras, they would think differently of him.

While James took some questions from the press, Barrett and I were ushered into the private family car where Everett and Saundra awaited us. Their eyes widened at the sight of my bloodied knees. "Sorry about the pantyhose," I sheepishly said to Everett.

He waved a hand at me. "Oh honey, forget the pantyhose. I have five pairs on reserve. I'm more concerned with you being hurt."

Barrett snorted. "Maybe you should be more concerned with the fact that your no-panties rule led to Addison mooning the press corps."

Everett rolled his eyes. "Honestly, Barrett, she was wearing pantyhose—do you not hear the word *panty* in that? It's not like I had her in a garter belt."

Barrett's eyes flared, and I realized he must be a lingerie man. After shaking his head, Barrett said, "Regardless, if she'd had on panties, it would have lessened the damage of the photographs."

In that moment, I saw red before my eyes. "Is that all you care about? How my ass is going to look bad for your father's campaign?"

"That's not what I meant."

"Yeah, well, that's sure as hell what it sounded like."

"For your information, I was alluding to the fact that if Everett hadn't told you not to wear panties, your ass would have been covered."

"Only if I wore granny panties and not my usual thongs," I countered without thinking.

Barrett opened his mouth to argue, but then closed it. A curious look came over his face. "You wear thongs?"

"Yes, although that is none of your business."

"Good to know," he teasingly replied. At my death glare, he added, "Look, I really wasn't blaming you for what happened." He jerked his thumb at Everett. "It's all his fault."

"Don't blame me, blame fashion," Everett replied.

"Whatever. Let's just get ready for the next stop."

Although I assured her I could do it myself, Saundra insisted on cleaning and bandaging my knees. Thankfully, they didn't show through my pantyhose when I was standing, though things got a little more dicey when I was seated.

We spent the rest of the day keeping up a manic pace, which kept my mind off my ass. On our third stop, we had a sit-down lunch before James gave his speech. I didn't know how he managed to keep his voice throughout the day—I guess the cough drops Jane carried helped, along with his request of tea with honey and lemon.

I was thoroughly and completely exhausted by the time we trudged up the train stairs for the last time. When I entered the first car, all the advisors and minions were crowded around a couple laptops. At the sight of me, panic broke out as they scrambled to close the screens.

They weren't quick enough, though, and I got an eyeful of one of the headlines.

Assgate: How the future first daughter-in-law bared all to reporters at campaign stop.

I screeched in horror, which caused Pete, one of the aides assigned to Barrett and me, to come over. "Don't worry, Addison. Most legitimate newspapers are not being so crass about what happened."

"Wait, does that mean they're still covering it?"

Pete swallowed hard, sending his Adam's apple bobbing up and down. "Unfortunately, there have been a few mentions, a few photographs, and…some video."

"Oh. My. God." If there was ever a time in my entire life when I wanted the floor to open up and swallow me whole, it was this very moment. Even more than that, I wished for time travel so I could go back to earlier in the day and let Barrett help me down the stairs instead of fighting him.

Deep down, I didn't know why I was surprised. We lived in a world where a photo could go viral within seconds. Did I honestly think the reporters weren't going to publish the pictures of my ass? Could I not fathom being YouTube infamous in a compilation video of people falling on their ass?

"What's the matter?" Barrett asked from behind me.

"It appears the press has taken a comical approach to what happened earlier," Pete replied.

"Thankfully, they're not ridiculing Addison's character," another staffer, Martin, chimed in.

"They're just making fun of me and my ass," I argued as I fought the urge to throw up.

Jane's arms came around me. "Oh honey, I'm so sorry. It's one thing for you to fall and hurt yourself on your first day, but now the media has to take a shot at you emotionally."

"Thank you," I muttered weakly.

"Listen, why don't you have a seat, and I'll go get you a drink from the bar car?"

"You don't have to do that."

Jane cupped my chin. "I'm sure you could use something stiff."

"I guess so."

"Trust me, I know."

After she steered me to a seat, she headed out of the car. The others scattered back to their laptops, discussing the other headlines that didn't involve my ass. Overwhelmed by my emotions, I knew I needed to be alone. Without a word to anyone, I rose out of my seat and made my way down the aisle. Air whooshed around me as I stepped outside the train car.

Once the door had shut safely behind me, I finally allowed the hot tears of embarrassment to flow freely. Although I could have been selfish and only mourned for me, I also mourned for the shame I'd brought to James's campaign. This was the last thing he needed. He'd killed himself today giving speech after speech, yet all the media was focusing on was my ass.

Through my sobs, I heard the door open. Whirling around, I swiped my tear-stained cheeks. I had expected Jane or perhaps Saundra to check on me, but instead, Barrett stood before me, concern etched across his handsome face.

After staring him down for a moment, I asked, "Did your dad or Bernie send you out here?"

"No, they're in a strategy session at the moment, and before you can worry even more, it doesn't involve your ass."

"Thank God for small mercies." Groaning, I buried my head in my hands. "This has to be the worst day of my life."

"You don't mean that."

"Fine, but it does rate up there with the day I caught Walt banging his intern."

"Come on, it's not as bad as that." When I didn't respond, Barrett said, "Look on the bright side: at least there isn't an article that says something insulting like 'Full Moon Rising'."

I rolled my eyes. "That *so* doesn't make me feel any better."

"What about this?" He fiddled with something on his phone before shoving it in my face. "Buzzfeed is rating your ass with an overall nine out of ten stars."

Staring at the screen, I shook my head in disbelief. "I don't even have a response for that."

"The one thing that could be worse than mooning the world would be for everyone to be repulsed by your ass. That's not the case. You're getting mad ass love."

I couldn't help laughing at the absurdity of it all, and Barrett grinned. "Man, I'm glad to hear you do that. For a minute there, I thought I was going to have to hold you back from jumping off the train."

"It's still a temping thought."

"Trust me, tomorrow there will be a bigger story than your ass."

"No offense, but that isn't exactly comforting coming from the guy who is still known for his nude pics from multiple years ago."

"Hey, something that impressive is unforgettable."

I laughed once again. "You would think about it that way."

"In the end, we make quite the couple, don't we? The ass and the dick."

"Yes. We do," I replied with a smile.

"Come on, let's go back inside." He flashed me a wicked grin. "I want to see if any of the advisors are secretly checking out your ass on their laptop."

I didn't feel ready to face anyone, especially with tears still fresh on my cheeks, but Barrett was right. There was nothing I could do, so might as well keep moving forward—both me and my ass.

I smacked him playfully on the arm before letting him lead me back inside.

CHAPTER NINE

BARRETT

JUST AS I had foretold, Assgate dropped from the top of the news stories after a few days. Thankfully, it didn't even cause a blip in Dad's polling numbers. Instead, momentum grew. When voters went to the booths on Super Tuesday, they were all about James Callahan. Dad swept each and every primary.

Bolstered by the overwhelming victories, we stayed busy on the campaign trail. With just a week until primaries in Kansas, Louisiana, and Nebraska, the Niña, Pinta, and Santa María kept the roads hot while crisscrossing around the states. I didn't know how Dad still had a voice left after delivering so many speeches, but he managed to bring the same conviction and power to each and every one of them—regardless of the size of the venue or the crowd.

Whenever Addison and I made an appearance, the press came out in droves to cover it. I didn't think anyone in the campaign could have anticipated just how popular our engagement would actually be. To reiterate Caroline's assessment, people "shipped us"—whatever the hell that meant.

At the end of the day, it was really more Addison they were enthralled with. After all, she was the working girl who had won the heart of an eligible billionaire bachelor. She embodied the fairytale of beauty taming the beast, and damn if the girl didn't know how to turn on the charm. She effortlessly transitioned from talking with farmers in the heartland to chatting up seasoned politicians. Some of the aides had jokingly started calling Addison "Kate", referring to Prince William's wife, Catherine Middleton. Others remarked that Addison had the same effect as Princess Diana when she had breathed life into the stuffy House of Windsor, except in this case, she was breathing life into the sometimes boring world of political campaigning.

Of course, anything would be an improvement over Dad's closest rival, Cliff Waterston. The man could have easily played Winston Churchill in a movie, and his two sons had the same bulldog features. Since America was obsessed with superficial youth and beauty, they were falling for us hook, line, and sinker.

The more time I spent with Addison, the more I found myself not having to pretend so much. She was incredibly easy to be around. Yeah, we argued—a lot—but I didn't feel that she despised me anymore. Initially, I hadn't cared if she liked me or not, but now…now I felt determined to make her see me in a different light.

Addison was becoming more to me. I loved her humor, her charm, and her warmth. People loved her, and I was beginning to wonder if I hadn't also fallen under her spell a little. *Get a grip, Callahan.*

Ty snapped me from my thoughts by waving a beer in front of my face. "Want one?"

"Hell yes," I replied before taking the longneck from him. After popping the top, I took two long pulls before setting the beer down then ground my fists into my eyes to clear my blurring vision. I'd spent the last few hours on the bus trying to get some work done, and I needed a break.

When Addison emerged from the bathroom, I did a double take at her appearance. It wasn't the fact that she'd shed her dress for a pair of leggings and an oversized T-shirt; it was that she looked sick as a dog. She hadn't complained, but she'd been nursing a cold for the last week. Tonight, her eyes had dark bags underneath them, which contrasted sharply with her ghost-white face. I hadn't gotten a good look at her since she'd collapsed on the couch, bundled herself in several blankets, and buried her head in her laptop. I couldn't believe how quickly her condition had worsened.

Since I had never been good with expressing myself tactfully, I blurted out, "Man, you look like hell."

Ty smacked me in the back of the head. "Idiot," he mumbled.

Addison scowled at me. "For your information, I couldn't care less how I look at the moment." She swiped a tissue under her runny nose. "I can assure you I feel much worse than I look."

Rubbing the back of my neck, I sheepishly said, "I'm sorry. That didn't come out right at all."

"I promise Saundra will make me camera-ready for tomorrow's rally, and I won't shame you." *Shame me? She's worried about shaming me?*

When she suddenly swayed on her feet, I bolted out of my chair and placed my arms on her shoulders to steady her. Her glassy-eyed gaze met mine. "Thanks."

"Look, I don't give two shits about the rally. I'm worried about you." When her brows shot up into her hairline, I replied, "Yeah, I am. You've been sick for a week now, and you're not getting any better."

"It's just a cold."

I shook my head. "I don't think so. Maybe we should stop and take you to an urgent care or something."

"No, no. We don't have time for that."

"We can make time."

"I'm fine. I'll grab some cold medicine at the next stop."

"That's a start, but why don't you go lie down for a little while?"

Addison glanced over her shoulder at her laptop. "But I need to go over the notes my replacement sent."

"Theo will manage just fine without you. You need to get in bed." Before she could protest any more, I wrapped one of my arms around her waist and started leading her down the aisle to the bedroom. After opening the door, I shooed her inside and ushered her over to the bed. "Do you want anything to eat or drink?"

Addison paused in taking off her shoes, peering at me curiously. "Are you being real?"

"Huh?"

"I mean, is this all part of the"—she made air quotes with her fingers—"fake fiancé act, or are you actually offering to take care of me?"

Damn if her words didn't sting a bit, like I was such a heartless bastard I couldn't possibly care about the wellbeing of another individual. "Since everyone on the bus is in on the engagement ruse, I really don't have a reason to pretend, do I?"

"What about Sutton?" she countered.

Oh for fuck's sake. I hadn't stopped to consider the one outsider we had picked up in Georgia. Every family has a rogue member, and Sutton Callahan was mine. Although he had a genius IQ, he lacked basic common sense. If he hadn't been one of the best political strategists in the business, I didn't think Dad would have admitted he knew him, least of all that he was his cousin. Although he had an Ivy League education, he was rough around the edges from never abandoning the backwoods where he had grown up after his father, my grandfather's brother, had married "beneath him", as Grandmother Callahan called it, which basically meant he married a girl who was far outside the society realm.

"Okay, fine, there's one person not in on the jig, but trust me when I say, that has nothing to do with how I'm treating you."

Addison stared me down with such intensity that it felt like at any moment, she was going to shine a light bulb in my face and interrogate me to get to the truth. Finally, a look of acceptance came over her face, and she went back to taking off her shoes. I walked past her to turn down the sheets and duvet. When I finished with that, I fluffed the two pillows, wanting to make sure it was as comfortable as possible. Once I finished, I stepped back to make way for Addison, and when I looked at her, I found her staring wide-eyed at me. "What?"

She blinked a few times. "You're so…domestic."

I laughed. "You should know by now that I'm a man of many talents."

Addison snorted. "Always the egomaniac."

"I am consistent."

"Consistently bigheaded."

I glanced down at my crotch before meeting her gaze again. "That too."

Instead of yelling at me to stick my innuendo up my ass, she laughed. "As my granddaddy would say, you're a mess, Barrett."

"That I am. Now come get in bed."

As her knees dipped down onto the mattress, she glanced back at me over her shoulder. "You're not going to try to make something out of getting me into bed?"

Now it was my turn to laugh. "Nope. You beat me to it."

"How disappointing."

I busied myself with tucking her in. Just when I thought I couldn't shock her more, the expression on Addison's face told me otherwise. "Now, I'll ask you once again: do you want anything to eat or drink?"

She shook her head. "No thanks. I just want to sleep."

"Good." I handed her the TV remote. "I think it's best you stay in bed until we get to the hotel." Wagging a finger at her, I added, "Don't put your feet on the floor except to go to the bathroom. If you wake up and decide you need something, just text me, okay?"

Addison smiled. "Okay."

Satisfied that I had done all I could do for her, I decided it was best to go. When I started toward the door, Addison called, "Barrett?"

"Yeah?" I replied, glancing over my shoulder.

She smiled. "Thanks for taking care of me…for caring."

"No problem."

After closing the door, I started back to my seat. When I reached for my beer, I felt Ty's curious gaze searing into my back. Turning around, I questioned, "What?"

"You put Addison to bed."

"Yes, Captain Obvious, I did."

Ty shook his head slowly back and forth. "I don't think I've ever seen you do something so giving for a woman without expecting something in return, especially one that was sick and out of sexual commission." *What the fuck? Even Ty?*

"You know, I'm really starting to get tired of the 'Barrett the Bastard' theme that seems to be running rampant tonight. First, Addison questioned my motives about caring for her, and now you're floored that I showed an ounce of compassion outside of sex."

With an apologetic look, Ty said, "I'm sorry man, I didn't mean it to come out like that. More than anything, I don't want to give you shit for it. I want you to know I'm proud of you."

"Get real."

"I am," he argued. When I turned to stare incredulously at him, Ty smiled. "Whether or not you want to admit it, you have always been a fucker when it comes to women."

I scowled at him. "I'm mature enough to admit I've been an asshole to the opposite sex."

"You know, the first step to recovery is admitting you have a problem."

"Thanks, Dr. Phil. I didn't realize you were staging an intervention."

"I'm not. Addison is."

"Excuse me?"

"She's changing you."

I snorted. "Whatever."

"It's not a bad thing, Barrett."

"I didn't say it was."

"You didn't have to say anything. Your body language says it all."

"Give me a break," I huffed. Since I didn't want to hear any more bullshit theories from Ty, I pulled my computer back into my lap. Thankfully, he got the message and took out his iPad. Within a few minutes, I tuned out the world around me and became engrossed in the world of The Callahan Corporation. I didn't know how much time passed, but it was probably close to an hour or two.

All of a sudden, the bedroom door flung open, banging against the back table. A few seconds passed before Addison came staggering out. "Oh my God! Why is it so hot on this bus?" she screeched as she weaved up the aisle. Hiking one of her legs up on one of the seats, she began stripping off her leggings. She balled them up and through them in a guy named Ed's face. "There you go, sweetie."

Ed's cheeks turned several shades of red as he scrambled to push the leggings off his lap and into the empty seat next to him. Thank God she was wearing a tunic top that covered her ass—not that they hadn't seen it before on television. Even so, I knew Addison would be even more mortified when she came to if she had flashed most of the aides on the bus.

Ty and I exchanged a look. "Is she drunk?" Ty questioned.

"Considering she just took her pants off, I'd say completely wasted. A better question would be where the hell she got the booze."

"It's not booze. I gave her a little medicine about an hour ago," Sutton piped up.

I sighed and glared at him. "What medicine?"

"Just some of my cough syrup."

I widened my eyes in horror. "You're fucking with me, right?"

"She's sick as a dog and needed to kill off whatever heinous bug she has," Sutton argued.

"What's wrong with some cough syrup?" Ty asked.

"Maybe the fact that it's made with moonshine?"

"You're shitting me."

"Sadly, no."

"It is a tried-and-true mountain recipe," Sutton countered.

"She's totally plastered!"

"Hey man, that's not my fault. I told her just to do a tablespoon or two."

"How much did she have?"

"Half the jar."

"Oh fuck," I muttered as I jerked my hand through my hair.

"Do you think she needs her stomach pumped?" Ty asked.

"Hey, I always buy from a reputable source with a clean still," Sutton said.

"How comforting," I bit back sarcastically. As I was contemplating what we needed to do, Addison lumbered up to my seat. She flashed me a wicked grin while wriggling her fingers in greeting.

"Hey Bare, how's the Bear?" Her voice had taken on a husky tone, which I wanted to believe was from the all the coughing she'd been doing and not from coming on to me.

"Addison, I think you need to sit down."

With a wink, she replied, "If you insist."

Instead of taking a seat across from me, she straddled my lap. The heat emanating from her bare thighs scorched the skin beneath my pants, and the more I thought about it, the more I realized the temperature was too intense; it wasn't normal. I brought a hand to her forehead. "Jesus, Addison, you're burning up."

A sexy grin spread across her face. "It's cause I'm so hot for you."

"No, you have a fever—a high one." Turning to Ty, I asked, "We don't have a thermometer in the first aid kit, do we?"

"I don't think so."

"Pete, start mapping to the closest urgent care or hospital."

"I'm on it," he replied.

Addison slid her arms around my neck, drawing me closer to her. At the same time, her hips began to rise and fall, rubbing her pussy against my crotch. "Wanna initiate me into the mile-high club? I hear you're a frequent flyer." *Oh hell.*

"We're on a bus."

"Oops!" she cried before collapsing onto my chest into a fit of giggles. When she raised her head, she tilted it at me. "How about the *if the bus is a-rockin', don't come a-knockin'* club?" When Ty laughed, I glared at him.

"No. No clubs."

"Fine then." One of her hands dropped from my neck and gripped my swelling cock. At the touch, I shrieked like a prepubescent boy whose balls hadn't dropped yet. "Does the Bear want to come out to play?" she purred.

Oh yeah. He was more than ready to come out of hibernation. Just as he started poking his head out of the cave, I shoved Addison's hand away. "Don't do that."

"Why not?"

Because if you do, I'm going to rip your panties off and pound you until you scream my name right in front of everyone. "For starters, you're sick."

Her mouth curved into a wicked grin. "I'm not too sick to fuck your brains out."

I pinched my eyes shut and tried thinking non-sexual thoughts. It didn't help that the Bear was practically roaring behind my zipper. Regular

Addison with the sassy mouth was hot, but inebriated Addison with the dirty mouth was fucking combustible.

"No. It's wrong on so many levels."

Her lips turned down in a pout. "Don't you find me desirable?"

How the hell could I not? She was five-foot-seven of pure, sinfully sexy woman. Yes, the Bear was very, very interested. I swallowed hard. "Of course I do, but that's not the point."

She flashed her diamond in front of my face. "As my future husband, you have a duty to satisfy me."

Lowering my voice to make sure Sutton couldn't hear, I replied, "Addison, you need to stop. We're not really engaged, remember?"

"Come on, do your duty, Barrett—do me." She ground her hot core against my crotch and I groaned in agony. It had been too long, and she was too tempting.

Addison's hands came to my cup face. "It's okay, Barrett. Don't cry."

"I'm not crying."

Nuzzling her head to my chest, Addison said, "I don't ever want you to cry for me." Suddenly, her head whipped up. "Don't cry for me Argentina. The truth is I never left you."

"She's good," Pete mused beside me.

"Oh shut up."

After executing the one line, Addison scrambled off my lap and made her way to the front of the bus. Considering how plastered she was, she lunged and dipped more than she actually walked. Once she stood by the stairs, she turned around to face the door. "Oh Jesus," I muttered as Addison raised her arms and began to recreate the balcony scene from *Evita*, which my mother had forced me to see on Broadway many years ago.

"It won't be easy. You'll think it strange," she began singing.

With a grunt, I rose out of my seat to go get Addison. She needed to be lying down instead of belting show tunes. Suddenly, she stopped singing. She shook her head as if disoriented, then swayed again. Her glazed eyes sought me. *Shit.*

Before I could reach her, she collapsed to the floor. "Addison!" I cried as I dove down beside her. I pulled her into my arms. "Addison?" As I gently patted her cheek, her eyes rolled back in her head, and my heart jolted to a stop in fear. "Call an ambulance!" I barked at Pete.

"There's a hospital off an exit two miles up the road. We can get to it before an ambulance can get to us."

"Floor it, Carl," I ordered.

At my command, the bus lurched forward with rising speed. Ty bent down beside me and placed two fingers on Addison's wrist. At that moment, I was thankful that part of his many skills was having taken a medic course. After a few moments went by, he said, "Her pulse is little slow."

"Jesus," I muttered.

"Normally, I might entertain the thought of it merely being alcohol poisoning, but I don't like it combined with her high fever," Ty said.

"Are we getting closer?" I demanded.

Carl nodded. "We're just about to take the exit."

"GPS says the hospital is just a half a mile to the right," Pete added.

We wheeled into the hospital parking lot before screeching to a halt outside of the ER. Once we came to a stop, I strengthened my hold on Addison before rising to my feet. Ty had the presence of mind to throw a blanket over Addison's lower half, covering her bare legs and thong-clad ass.

I carried her down the bus stairs. As soon as I felt the pavement beneath me, I began to run. Damn, she felt so light. Addison moaned at being jostled around. "I'm sorry. I'm getting you help, I promise."

Ty caught up with me as I barreled through the ER doors. "Help! I need help!" I cried as I skidded to a stop at the registration desk.

The receptionist rose out of her chair. "Sir, I need you to calm down and answer a few questions."

"She's unconscious with a high fever. She needs help. Now!"

I was fully aware I was making a scene, but I didn't give a shit. I was going to do everything within my power to get Addison taken care of, even if I got thrown out in the process. Thankfully, for my sake, more level heads prevailed. Ty flashed his badge, and Pete informed the receptionist who we were. Recognition filled her face. "Yes sir, we'll take you right on back."

The mechanized doors leading into the heart of the ER opened, and I rushed through them. We were met in the hallway by a nurse and she escorted us into an empty room. "You can put her down now, sir," the nurse said as she motioned to the stretcher.

I hated the moment I eased Addison down onto the crackling paper sheet. I knew it was necessary for me to step away for the nurse to be able to work on her, but it went against every instinct I had, which were all telling me not to. She looked so small lying there, so fragile. She'd felt so right in my arms, so protected. Pain like I'd never known crisscrossed through my chest. I'd spent more time with Addison than I had with any other woman, had given more of my emotional self to her than anyone outside my close circle. Inexplicably, I didn't see her as the bane of my existence anymore, my ball and chain. I also didn't see her as an off-limits piece of ass, either. She'd become more than I'd ever imagined she could, and if I was completely honest with myself, she'd become more to me. Much more.

I didn't have a clue how sick she really was, but I knew I couldn't bear losing Addison. Not now. Not now that I'd actually found someone I wanted to be with.

If I was really honest with myself, I didn't think I would be ready come November either.

CHAPTER TEN

ADDISON

"BP IS 120 over 70. Pulse rate 60," a voice called from above me.

As I drifted in that shadowy state between sleep and consciousness, the medical jargon being spouted made me think I was in a *Grey's Anatomy* episode. *Did I forget to turn the TV off before I went to sleep?* The more I thought about it, I realized I couldn't remember even turning it on. If I really thought about it, none of the voices sounded like the cast.

When my eyes fluttered open, I stared up at a blinding fluorescent light. My body felt weightless, as if it were floating along on the surface of water. It took a few moments to process that I wasn't outside or in a pool. Instead, I was riding along on a gurney through the halls of a hospital.

Whoa. How did I get here? The last thing I remembered was being on the bus. After succumbing to a coughing fit, a knock had come at the bedroom door, and Barrett's weird cousin offered me some medicine. He swore it would stop my coughing and help me sleep, and against my better judgment, I took some. After taking the dose he recommended, I still kept coughing. I desperately wanted sleep, so I ended up chugging a bit more of it. And then some more. Then I went to sleep…or maybe I passed out. I wasn't sure.

"Is she going to be okay?" a voice vibrating with emotion asked. When I eased my head to the side, I saw Barrett. He wore an ashen expression, and the fear in his eyes was palpable. Instantly, my heart beat a little faster. Did he care that much for me?

"We just need to get her temperature down and some fluids in her. She'll be fine."

I wanted to tell Barrett not to be so scared, that I was okay, maybe a little hungover, but my tongue seemed to be glued to the roof of my mouth. The light bearing down on me became too intense, so I closed my eyes. Within a few seconds, I floated away into the darkness.

THE NEXT TIME I woke, it was to my bladder screaming in agony. When I reached down to toss off the covers, I caught a glimpse of the IV tubing attached to my hand. "What the…" Oh right, I was in the hospital.

A gentle snore drew my attention to the left side of the bed. "Oh my," I murmured at the sight of Barrett sleeping in an uncomfortable-looking chair. With his head lolled over like that, he was going to wake up with an awful crick in his neck. I marveled not only at the fact that he had stayed with me, but that Mr. VIP wasn't stretched out in a cot. Although I couldn't see him, I imagined that Ty was somewhere outside the door.

At the sound of my name, my gaze snapped from Barrett to the television on the wall across from me. "Holy shit," I muttered at the sight of my face plastered across the screen.

"Yes, Harry, we're live outside McKinley Hospital in Farmington where Addison Monroe has been admitted. Earlier this morning, Pete Chandler came out to speak to us. He assured us that Miss Monroe's condition was not critical, and said she was kept overnight merely for observation after being diagnosed with pneumonia. She is expected to be released later today with strict R&R orders. Back to you."

I gasped at the scene that played on the television. It seriously looked like something out of a romance movie. Barrett appeared every bit a larger-than-life superhero as he swept through the hospital doors with me cradled in his arms. His frantic gaze spun around the ER as he desperately pleaded for someone to help me, the fear in his eyes achingly authentic. The panic in his voice wasn't exaggerated. He wasn't trying to keep up the façade for the people in the waiting room. Then I remembered waking up in the ER and how he'd looked then. He wasn't acting then either.

He cared about me.

A lot.

I would have to say it was quite surreal hearing your medical diagnosis on the news rather than from a doctor or nurse, but it was even more earthshattering that your fake fiancé exhibited such feeling for you—especially when you weren't sure you felt the same. As I watched him sleep, I couldn't help noticing how sweet and innocent he looked. Sure, he was still hot as hell, but there was something endearing about him when he was at rest. The cockiness and arrogance he normally wore were washed from his expression.

After a loud snore erupted from Barrett's lips, he jolted awake, and his brows furrowed as he took in the unfamiliar surroundings of the room. Once he realized where he was, he whipped his gaze over to me. Relief instantly replaced the tension in his face.

"Hey," I said with a smile.

"Hey," he croaked. As he ground his fists into his eyes, he asked, "How long have you been awake?"

"Not long."

"You've been unconscious since last night."

"Really?"

He nodded as his mouth gaped open in a yawn. "Of course, I shouldn't be surprised considering the amount of alcohol a lightweight like you had."

"Whoa, wait a minute—I wasn't drinking last night."

"Oh yeah you were. That cough syrup Sutton gave you has a moonshine base."

I widened my eyes. "You're joking."

"Sadly not."

After sweeping a hand over my mouth, I muttered, "Oh God."

"I'm sorry I wasn't paying better attention. If I'd seen Sutton offering you any of that garbage, I would have tossed it out the window, and maybe him along with it."

I laughed. "It's okay. I should have known better than to take unmarked 'medicine' from someone I don't know."

"When I talked to Dad last night, I insisted he find somewhere else for Sutton."

"Was that really necessary? I mean, it wasn't like he was plying me with alcohol to try to take advantage of me or something."

Barrett gave an angry shake of his head. "He should've been more cautious. With your fever, your body could have gone into shock with the alcohol. It could've been a lot worse."

While I didn't think my condition would have been that serious, I decided it was best not to argue with Barrett considering how adamant he was. After shifting in bed to see him better, my bladder demanded immediate relief, causing me to wince in pain. Barrett's brows creased. "What's wrong?"

"Um, I, uh…" God, this was mortifying. Sure, I'd shared close quarters with Barrett in hotel rooms and on the bus, but I'd always been able to be discreet about Mother Nature calling.

At my hesitation, Barrett rose out of his chair. "Are you in pain? Do you need the nurse?"

Refusing to look at him, I replied, "Actually, I need to pee."

The concern in his face evaporated and amusement danced in his eyes. "You got that worked up over having to take a piss?"

I wrinkled my nose. "Ugh, do you have to say it like that?"

"Would you prefer me to say *urinate*?"

"While I prefer not hearing any of the names for it, at this moment I'm much more concerned with the act itself."

"You have two choices: you can ring for the nurse to come help you and probably piss yourself before one makes it here, or you can let me help you."

I sighed. Barrett had a point about it taking forever for a nurse come. "Okay. You can help me."

After easing the bed up, I swung my feet over the edge. When I started to stand, my rubbery-feeling legs caused me to wobble. Before I could fall back in the bed, one of Barrett's arms slid around my waist. "Easy there, Miss Independent. I'm here to help you, remember?"

"I thought you meant just guiding the IV pole."

"I can do both."

Since I was too weak to argue, I leaned against Barrett and let him steer me and the IV pole across the room. Silently, I lamented the draft I felt behind me where my hospital gown gaped open. When we got to the bathroom door, it was a tight squeeze for us to make it through. As I hovered beside the toilet seat, Barrett remained glued to my side.

"Um, a little privacy please."

He shook his head. "With you so weak, I'm not taking a chance of you falling."

Oh God. The situation grew more and more mortifying by the second. "Could you at least turn around once I'm sitting down?"

Even though I could tell he didn't like the idea, he nodded. Once his back was facing me, I tugged at the hem of my gown and eased down on the toilet seat, groaning in ecstasy as a steady stream began to flow. When Barrett snickered at my response, I groaned again, but this time out of embarrassment.

"I can't believe you have to see me like this."

"Trust me, this is a cakewalk after what happened on the bus."

"What are you talking about?"

Barrett's shoulders tensed. "Nothing."

"No, tell me what you meant."

"Let's just say the cough syrup coupled with your fever made you act out of your head."

A reel of images from the previous night on the bus charged through my mind, causing me to shudder. "I sang, didn't I?"

"Yep." *Oh—oh shit. I gave Barrett a lap dance.* When I shrieked in horror, he whirled around at my reaction. "What? What's wrong?"

I buried my head in my hands. "I just remembered coming on to you."

Barrett sucked in a breath. "I was hoping you would have blacked all that out."

"Why? Why do I have to remember? There are entire nights of partying I can't recall from back when I was in college, but no, I have to have to the image of straddling your lap burned into my memory."

He chuckled. "You were pretty disappointed I wouldn't initiate you into the mile-high club."

Peeking at him through my fingers, I said, "But we were on a bus."

"Yes, I did explain that to you."

"I didn't try to come on to anyone else, did I?" The thought of me grinding against Pete or Ed was even more horrifying than Barrett.

"Thankfully, it was just me." He winked at me. "Even in your inebriated state, you were true to me."

A relieved breath whooshed out of me. "I'm a woman of my word. I might be high as a kite on moonshine cough syrup, but I still keep my promises." I shuddered. "Ugh, *moonshine.*"

"It'll knock you on your ass for sure."

"You've had some before?"

"Unfortunately, yes. Once was more than enough."

I laughed. "I second that."

After flushing the toilet, I rose to my feet. Once I adjusted my gown, I said, "Okay."

Barrett turned around. "Now was that so bad?"

"Yes. It took me almost a year to be comfortable enough to pee in front of my ex-fiancé."

"It's never been an issue with me."

"Have you ever spent enough time with a woman for them to actually have to pee?"

With a chuckle, Barrett said, "Yes, smartass, I have."

"Hey, it was just an honest assumption."

"You know the adage about making assumptions right?"

"Yeah, yeah, I'm an ass, whatever," I replied as I started shuffling out of the bathroom.

Barrett had just escorted me back to bed when a knock sounded at the door. "Come in," Barrett called.

A dozen or so helium balloons bobbed into the room followed by Ty. "Good morning," he called.

"Good morning."

After he placed the balloons on one of the bedside tables, he placed a bag on my tray.

"I'm not sure if they've brought breakfast around yet, but here's your favorite French toast."

"Oh Ty, that's so sweet of you."

He jerked his chin at Barrett. "I'm not the one who thought of it, I'm just the one who picked it up."

When I met Barrett's eyes, he shrugged. "I used to hate hospital breakfasts when I was a kid."

"Then it was awful sweet of you. Thank you."

"You're welcome."

With my stomach rumbling, I reached for the bag. Like a mother hen, Barrett hovered over me, helping me get my plate in order. This was the man few in the public knew him to be. If only they knew how compassionate and caring he was deep down, it would change their perception of him. It certainly had for me.

"Did you get everything taken care of?" Barrett asked Ty.

He nodded. "I've spoken with your parents, and everything is in order for when Addison is discharged."

"Wait, what's in order?" I questioned through a mouthful of French toast.

"Your R&R."

I swallowed. "My what?"

"The doctor has insisted you take it easy and recuperate for at least the next week to ten days."

Widening my eyes in horror, I shrieked, "A week? I can't be gone from the campaign that long, not now."

"Yes, you can be gone that long, and yes, you will. Besides the pneumonia, you also were dehydrated and a little anemic, not to mention the ridiculous amount of alcohol in your system," Barrett replied.

I wasn't too surprised about the dehydration thing; I hadn't been drinking water like I should—finding a bathroom in the middle of a campaign stop was not the easiest thing in the world. "I'm being sent home?"

Barrett shook his head. "I'm sending you to our house on Martha's Vineyard." When I started to protest, he held up a hand to silence me. "You don't need to go back to your apartment all alone. You need to be somewhere you can be looked after."

"Evan can do that back in Arlington."

"Not full-time."

"You're hiring someone to stay with me?"

"Nope. Ty and I will be staying with you."

My mouth gaped open. "You're joking."

"No, we're not." He grinned at Ty. "Are we?"

Ty laughed. "Nope."

I shook my head. "It's one thing for me to be off the trail for a week, but your dad can't afford to lose you, too, not when we're so close to getting enough votes for the nomination."

"Look at it this way: I'll appear far more sympathetic to the media if I stay with you while you recuperate." *Well that's true.* So he was doing it for sympathy and image, not because he really wanted to be with me.

Having seen true concern in his eyes, I couldn't help wondering if that was his only motivation behind staying with me. In the end, I really didn't have a good reason to argue against staying at a house on the beach with two hot men looking after me. "Okay, fine."

With a chuckle, Barrett said, "I'm glad you could finally see things my way."

"I'm only agreeing to it because I can't pass up the opportunity to have you cooking and cleaning for me."

Barrett snorted. "Like I would actually do either of those things. I'll be hiring someone to come in and do all that."

"Bummer. I really wanted to see you wearing an apron."

"I'll be happy to put one on if it fulfills a fantasy of yours," Barrett replied teasingly.

"That won't be necessary."

Barrett motioned to my plate. "Hurry up and finish your breakfast so we can bust you out of here."

"I thought we had to wait for a doctor to discharge me?"

He winked. "Addie, you should know by now, I'm not one to follow the rules."

CHAPTER ELEVEN

BARRETT

AFTER A WEEK of sunshine and relaxation at Martha's Vineyard, a doctor cleared Addison to return to the campaign trail. Although it felt great being back on the Niña, I kind of missed having time with just Addison. Although the weather had been chilly, we'd had several days of bright sunshine. We took a few short walks on the beach every day with Ty giving us plenty of distance, but mainly we just holed up in the house, watching movies or Addison reading while I worked. All too soon, it was time to get back to reality.

Dad still had a few votes to gain before clinching the nomination. He was unstoppable in the following weeks, crushing primary after primary. Finally, he amassed enough votes to secure the nomination, and it was one of the best nights of my life—well, at least the best night outside of a sexual escapade.

We celebrated by taking over a Mexican restaurant. The margaritas flowed like water, and it wasn't long before we were all shit-faced, Dad and Mom included. Somehow we all kept it together as we boarded the bus in front of the press. Thankfully, the bodyguards along with the newly allocated Secret Service kept them from getting too close to us, or they would have been able to smell all the liquor.

Now that Dad had the nomination, we had a brief moment to breathe. It meant the campaign would be heading back to DC for a weekend to strategize for the upcoming months, and Dad and Mom would also be getting time to go back home to Alexandria.

Addison and I were also off the hook, at least when it came to working on the campaign. We obviously would still need to spend some time together to keep up the front of our engagement, but we could go our separate ways. Although we probably could have used some time apart, I secretly hoped Addison wouldn't insist on it.

The truth was, I liked spending time with her. I especially enjoyed just hanging out and watching movies on the bus or in the hotel. That's when Addison and I got to just be ourselves without having to worry if a camera lens was pointed at us or if someone was analyzing our conversation. We talked about anything and everything. One moment we might be engaged in a very intellectual conversation, and the next we would be laughing over a funny meme we saw on Instagram.

Although I was still too stubborn to admit it to Ty, he had been right when he said Addison was changing me. Since I'd become fake engaged to her, I no longer cared about jet-setting or staying out all night partying. I also began to appreciate the hidden allure of being with just one woman—and more specifically, being with just Addison, and that was even without sex involved.

A wiser man in the ways of the heart might've realized where this was headed. Alas, I was fucking clueless to the subterfuge I was being swept up in, and I remained that way until it was far too late.

We landed at Dulles at a little after five. Addison and I exited the jet and hopped into the back seat of the waiting car while Ty slid into the front seat. As we began the drive back into the city, I turned to Addison. "Wanna grab something to eat before we go home?"

She quickly shook her head. "Actually, I need the driver to let me out at my apartment."

"Okay. Ty and I can grab some dinner and then swing back by and pick you up."

"No!" Addison exclaimed. Her cheeks flushed at her outburst. "I mean, thank you, but that won't be necessary. I have a million things I need to get done before the movers come in two weeks. I'll probably crash there after I get everything done." She yawned exaggeratedly. "I'm pretty tired already."

"You don't need to worry about any of that. I told you before we can have some people come pack you up."

"No, no, I'd rather do most of it myself."

"If you're sure. I mean, you're going to need your stamina for next week."

"I am."

A feeling of unease washed over me. I didn't have any reason in the world to doubt Addison's story, but something just seemed off with her. "Okay. We can just meet up in the morning."

"That sounds good."

We didn't speak for the rest of the drive, instead burying our heads in our phones. When Charlie alerted us we had arrived, Addison tossed her phone in her purse before fumbling for the door handle. It was like she couldn't get out of the car fast enough—or maybe she couldn't get away from *me* fast enough.

Just before the door slammed shut, she called, "Bye!"

"Bye," I replied, but the door had already closed behind her.

Ty turned around his seat. "What was that about?"

"I have no fucking clue."

"Did you say something shitty to her, Captain Insensitive?"

I threw Ty a death glare. "No, asshole, I didn't. Besides, you were on the plane with us. You know exactly what was said."

With a thoughtful look, Ty replied, "That's true." He shrugged. "Must be hormones."

I chuckled. "I sure as hell wouldn't mention that to her tomorrow."

Ty grinned. "Affirmative on that. So where do you want to eat?"

"I don't care what we eat as long as we eat now. I'm starving."

"Two blocks ahead there's a great Indian restaurant."

"Works for me."

Charlie let us out at the door of my favorite Indian place. The moment we brushed through the front door, the delicious smell of spices entered my nose, sending my stomach roaring. After the hostess seated us, the James Bond-looking watch Ty always wore dinged. When he glanced down at it, he frowned. "What's wrong?"

"I thought Addison said she was going to stay in tonight and pack."

"That's what she said."

He shook his head. "Then why did she just leave her apartment?"

"Wait, how do you know she left?"

"I have a tracking device in her phone."

I widened my eyes at him. "What the hell, dude? Don't tell me you've rigged my apartment with cameras, too?"

Ty rolled his eyes. "No, I haven't. Until your father officially accepts the nomination and the Secret Service assigns someone to you, I can't possibly trail your ass and hers at the same time."

"In the meantime, you decided to put a lojack on Addison's phone?"

"It was a necessary evil."

"You know she would flip her shit if she found out."

"At first, but then I think she would see reason once I explained about all the potential nut-jobs who could be stalking her."

I rolled my eyes. "Nice one, scare her into submission."

Instead of a comeback, Ty studied his watch, his brows lined in concentration. "Maybe she decided to go grab something to eat?" I suggested.

"That's what I originally thought, but she's en route somewhere."

"What the hell does that mean?"

"She's in a cab or on a bus." Ty squinted. "Okay, she just got off on 8th Street."

"Well, 8th Street is full of restaurants, so that makes sense if she's getting something to eat."

"But why would she travel that far to eat alone?"

I sucked in a breath as a feeling of being sucker-punched washed over me. "She's going out."

"Yeah, ace, that's pretty obvious."

"No, I mean, she's going out-out, like she's meeting up with someone." Swallowing hard, I added, "A man."

"You don't know that. She could be meeting up with some friends."

"Then why didn't she tell me? Why did she lie about staying in and resting?"

A worried look flashed in Ty's eyes. "I don't know. I just know Addison isn't the type to break a deal. She knows what is at stake. She couldn't possibly be seen in DC with another man without causing a complete scandal."

"The more I think about it, the more I realize she's been a little secretive lately, like taking hushed phone calls in the middle of the night—not to mention, the last two times we've been back home, she's left to go visit her brother in Arlington." I shook my head.

"I'm starting to think visiting her brother is code for getting the D."

Ty snorted. "Once again, Addison doesn't impress me as the type to screw around. If anyone was going to do it, it would be you."

"Well, I'm not the one sneaking off to 8th Street, am I?"

Ty didn't respond. Instead, he looked at his watch again. "She's stopped somewhere."

"Where?"

"I don't know, it's not that advanced. It only tells me an address, not the name of the place."

I slammed my palms down on the table, causing the water glasses to shake and overflow. "Okay, enough speculation. Let's go bust her cheating ass!"

Pursing his lips at me, Ty countered, "Don't you think the more rational thing to do would be to call her? Or maybe just ask her about it in the morning?"

"When in my life have I ever made a rational decision?"

Ty snorted. "Never."

"Exactly." Since he still didn't appear completely convinced, I said, "Okay, Mr. Protector, what if someone recognizes her and slips a roofie in her drink to take compromising pictures to sell to the press?"

My suggestion sent the wheels in Ty's head spinning in overdrive so fast I could almost see smoke curling from his ears. "They could take advantage of her," he growled.

"Yes, they could," I goaded.

Just as the waitress appeared to take our drink order, Ty bolted out of his chair, almost toppling the middle-aged woman to the floor. Always the gentleman, he reached out to steady her. "I'm very sorry ma'am, but we have to go."

Without even checking to see if I was behind him, he started for the door. After joining him in two long strides, I pulled out my phone to let Charlie know we were ready to be picked up. When Charlie let me know he was just across the street, Ty and I darted into traffic and began weaving our way to meet him. Charlie had just scrambled out of the car to get the door when we met up with him.

"Would you like a different restaurant choice, sir?"

"No. I need you to take us to—" I glanced back at Ty.

"143 8th Street," he answered.

Charlie gave a quick nod as Ty and I got into the car. Once he shut the door behind us, he hustled back around to get inside. Since it was a Friday night, traffic was slammed, and my impatience grew as we inched along at a freakin' snail's pace.

As I drummed my fingers against my thigh, I kept a constant look at Ty's phone. At any minute, I expected him to say that she was on the move again, but he never did. Wherever Addison was, she appeared to be staying there.

"There it is!" Ty suddenly exclaimed. Of course, it would be on his side of the car. I practically dove across him to peer out the window. "Looks like a club," Ty remarked.

Although I hated to admit it, he was right—the flashing marquee and line out the door screamed club. "Figures she would be out looking for a quick hookup."

Ty laughed as he shoved me off him. "Do you realize how ironic it is that you're saying that?"

"Whatever." I patted Charlie on the back. "We'll get out here."

"Yes sir. I'll wait for your call."

"Oof," Ty muttered as I elbowed him in the gut in my efforts to scramble out of his side of car. "Barrett, you don't have to be in such a rush. She hasn't left."

"I want to catch her in the act before she has the chance to leave."

After making our way between the traffic-stalled cars, we stepped onto the sidewalk where a giggling bachelorette party outfitted in boas and tiaras stood in line in front of us. A couple months ago, I might've tried hitting on some of the inebriated bridesmaids-to-be, but at the moment, all I cared about was getting to Addison. I was just about to ask Ty to pull his badge to get us inside quicker when another bachelorette party arrived and we got sandwiched between the crazy groups. My ears rang from the ear-splitting squeals and screeches of conversation.

Then the line burst forward like a rushing river, and Ty and I were carried along on the wave of bridesmaids. The current finally poured us out into a blackened room with multicolored neon lights, and steady bass thumped from behind a velvet curtain.

It was at that moment that my mind starting putting two and two together. A club plus lots of drunken bridesmaids equaled the probability that

Magic Mike-type shit was about to go down. Was it actually possible that Addison had abandoned me to get dry humped by some oiled-up dude in a banana hammock?

Leaning over closer to Ty, I asked, "Are you thinking what I'm thinking?"

"That they should replace waterboarding with a constant loop of drunken women chattering?" Ty replied as he stuck a finger in one of his ears.

I scowled at him. "No."

"Fine. What?"

"This is a strip club." Since I could see Ty's mind was going to poles, platform heels, and a sea of tits, I added, "A *male* strip club."

A mask of horror came over Ty's face. "Are you shitting me?"

"I wish."

Ty started to protest, but then the wave of bridesmaids overcame us again as we all started moving toward the curtain. When we got to the pay stand, a shrill voice behind me said, "They're with us."

Before I could argue that we were most definitely *not* with them, a hand smacked me on the ass. I whirled around to see a stacked brunette wearing a blinking *Bride-To-Be* tiara. "Sit next to me, sweetcheeks," she slurred as she ran her finger provocatively down my chest. When she got to my belt buckle, I spun away from her, shoving Ty between us.

My action caused Ty to break out into a hysterical laugh, one fueled by both amusement and fear. It was certainly not one you would expect from an ex-military man. If I hadn't been so freaked out myself, I would have given him serious shit about it.

Thankfully, Miss Happy Hands was distracted by one of her friends passing her a sparkly flask. When we dipped through the curtain, I braced myself for what I was about to experience. In my mind, I expected half-naked men to be thrusting on women's laps or twerking in their faces while dollar bills got stuffed into g-string clad bulges.

What I actually saw shocked the hell out of me, mainly because it was nothing like I expected. Sure, there were the usual strobe lights and disco balls hanging from the ceiling as well as a lighted stage in the center of the room. The long tables set up throughout the room were draped in white linen, and they were set with real plates and glass goblets. For a minute, it felt like being at a political fundraising dinner. Never having been in a male strip club before, I had nothing to compare to, and I figured it just boiled down to the fact that women were a hell of a lot classier than men.

While my gaze swept around the packed room for any sight of Addison, Ty steered us over to an empty table for two. Thankfully, we weren't going to have to sit with any horny bachelorettes. The overhead lights flickered on and off, signaling the show was about to start.

An attractive waitress appeared before us in a Day-Glo pink wig and glittering dress. "What can I get you gentlemen to drink?"

Normally, I would have just gone for a beer, but tonight called for something a little stronger. "A shot of your best scotch and a Heineken."

Ty bobbed his head. "I'll have the same."

Just as the waitress moved on to the next table, the lights went completely out, plunging the room into pitch blackness. Immediately, the crowd erupted into cheers and whistles.

"How the hell are we going to find Addison in all of this?" Ty questioned.

"I say when the lights come back on and the men come out, we start going table to table."

Ty chuckled. "Have you really thought out that plan?"

"What's wrong with it?"

"Oh, I don't know, maybe the part where we go from table to table of drunk, horny women in a male strip club."

I cringed. "I see what you mean."

"Although it's been a while for me on the sex front, I'm still not in the mood to have my junk randomly groped," he added.

"It might do you some good," I countered.

"I haven't come in my pants since I was sixteen years old."

"Fine, here's a better plan: you go hang out with the bachelorettes while I look for Addison. I'm pretty sure any one of them, Miss Happy Hands Bride included, would be happy to take you to the bathroom and screw your brains out."

"I am not abandoning you to the wolves, not even for some ass."

Just as I was about to thank him, music blared out of the speakers. Recognizing it as Aerosmith's "Dude Looks Like a Lady", I thought it was an odd choice, but once again, what did I know.

The stage lights blazed on, momentarily blinding me. When my eyes adjusted, I peered at the stage. It wasn't a bunch of Magic Mikes who came strutting onto the stage. Don't get me wrong, they were men, but they were dressed in glittering sequins and intricate beading. Wearing wigs in every color of the rainbow, their lips glistened with shiny gloss.

Ty and I slowly swiveled our heads to stare at each other. We both wore the same *What the fuck?* looks.

Yes, ladies and gentleman, we had just officially chased Addison down to a drag show.

Our waitress then returned with our drinks. Peering up at her, I realized what I had missed before: she was also a he in drag.

As she served Ty, I couldn't wait any longer. I needed alcohol stat, so I grabbed my scotch off her tray and downed it in one gulp. "I think I'm going to need another," I said, placing the glass back down.

"Yes sir."

When the waitress left, I shook my head. "We've somehow stumbled into the fucking Twilight Zone. I mean, what the hell could Addison possibly be doing here?"

After Ty threw back his scotch, his expression became extremely grave. "You haven't seen Addison naked, have you?"

"No, of course not. Why?"

"I'm just wondering if she might really be a dude."

Now it was my turn to do the hysterical laugh. "Bullshit. There's no way Addison is a dude." *Not with all those luscious curves of hers.* At Ty's continued skeptical look, I added, "Dad had the FBI run a background check when she started at the campaign, along with another one before he asked her to be my fiancée. If there was a dick on her, don't you think the feds would have sniffed it out?"

He stroked the stubble on his chin thoughtfully. "True, but why does the lead guy remind me of Addison?"

When I followed Ty's gaze, my stomach jumped into my throat. The guy—or girl—did look like Addison in the face. Same bone structure, same eye color. *Holy fucking shit.* Was it possible that Addison was a man?

At the end of the song, applause and cheering rang out around us. While the other ladies exited to the left and right, the Addison lookalike came to the center of the stage. "Good evening. Welcome to Divas. I'm so glad you could join us tonight. I am Estrella, your hostess this evening." When more applause and catcalls followed, Estrella bowed. "Thank you, thank you. I appreciate your enthusiasm. My cleavage also appreciates your green enthusiasm, if you know what I mean." Bending over, she flashed her chest to the crowd, showing it was stuffed with money.

"We have a really phenomenal show for you this evening, and I am proud to welcome a very special guest tonight. It isn't very often that her talent gets to grace the stage here at Divas, so hold on to your tits and your dicks, and put your hands together for the lovely and talented Adriana!"

The curtain went down, and the lights once again dimmed as an upbeat, 80s-sounding tempo filled the air. The multicolored stage lights began to flicker before the curtain flung open. The giant swig of beer I'd just taken spewed out onto the table at the sight of Addison—the real Addison—striding down the stage. She might've had on a long black wig, platform heels, and an inch of stage makeup, but it was definitely her. Part of me exhaled a relieved breath that it was Addison and that there wasn't a chance she was Estrella and hiding a dick.

"Holy hell, she's Cher," Ty muttered.

Oh yeah, she was Cher all right. She was Cher circa 1987 in the "If I Could Turn Back Time" video—and before you revoke my man card, I would argue that my mother was a huge Cher fan. In fact, I met her when she performed at my mother's fiftieth birthday party.

In case you've never seen the video, Cher basically sports fishnet stockings and black electrical tape worn like a skimpy body suit to moderately cover her tits and ass along with a black leather jacket. Even after Assgate and sharing a hotel room for the last few months, I'd never seen so much of Addison on display. It was incredibly unnerving and so incredibly sexy watching her perform.

After Addison danced past our table, Ty elbowed me. "You know, she's really good."

"You said the same thing when she was belting *Evita* on the bus."

"Yeah, I meant it then, and I mean it now, too. She's one hell of an actress to be able to sound like Cher."

"Let's not forget the fact that she can act like she's in love with me."

Ty chuckled. "That's true."

When the music ended, Addison brought her fingers to her lips and then blew a kiss to the audience. After taking a deep bow, she waved and then started off the stage.

Estrella came back out, and this time she was Cher, but Cher circa 1965 with the long, straight hair. Her blue bell-bottoms sparkled along with her silver halter top. "Good evening again, friends. It's no secret that we're big fans of Cher around here." She tossed some of her dark hair over her shoulder while licking her tongue over her top lip, mimicking Cher's signature early moves. "Whenever Adrianna comes to Divas, we can't help but put on a few extra Cher songs."

The opening strains of "I've Got You Babe" began, and Addison reappeared from behind the curtain. This time she wore a short black wig and a white button-down shirt with a fuzzy vest and pants. Her transformation into Sonny circa the late 60s was completed by a black mustache. It was like a Victor/Victoria moment where she was a girl pretending to be a man, leaving me to feel like I was on some sort of acid trip.

After clasping Addison's hand with her own, Estrella began, *"They say we're young, and we don't know. We won't find out until we grow."*

With a slightly lower voice than from before, Addison chimed in with, *"Well, I don't know if all that's true…"*

Once again, I was mesmerized by Addison. She possessed a hell of a lot of talent to be able to belt out Evita sick as a dog and also do a great Sonny Bono impression—not to mention the fact that she could start singing in Spanish if the mood hit her. She was unlike any other woman I'd ever known.

In that moment, with her in drag, I began to fall a little more for Addison Monroe.

When Addison and Estrella finished the song, the room broke out in roaring applause and cheering. I myself whistled and catcalled a few times, which earned me a look from Ty. After taking a bow, Addison headed off stage while Estrella began announcing the next act. I craned my neck to watch as Addison slipped behind the curtain once again. Once a Gloria Estefan lookalike came out to do "Conga", I smacked Ty's arm before rising out of my chair. "Come on."

We worked our way through the maze of tables. After making it across the room, I saw a doorway leading to a long hallway. Before we could enter, a tall, buff drag queen who looked a lot like RuPaul stepped in front of Ty and me, blocking us from going any farther. She wagged her finger at us. "I'm sorry, sugah, but no one but the divas are authorized in the hallway."

"Yeah, well, I really need to see Addison—I mean, Adrianna."

"You'll see her one last time in the finale."

"I need to see her privately, and I need to see her *now*."

Ru narrowed her eyes at us. "This isn't a strip club, sweetie. No one gets a private dance with any of the divas."

"Uh, yeah, that is *so* not what I was insinuating."

Pursing her red lips, Ru said, "Mmmhmm. It's always pretty boys like you playing at being straight who want to get freaky."

With a grunt of frustration, I glanced back at Ty. He nodded and dug his badge out of his suit pocket. He flashed it at Ru. "I'm going to need you to step aside."

"Oh hell no, not until I thoroughly examine this." She snatched the badge out of Ty's hand. "You wouldn't believe the shit some psychos pull," she said as she read over the details of Ty's bodyguard badge. Once she was satisfied, she handed it back to him. "Fine, but I'll be watching you."

"Thank you," I muttered as we brushed past. At the end of the narrow hallway was an exit sign, and there were three doors on both the right and left sides. "Fuck. How do we know which one?" I asked.

"We don't," Ty replied. He tried the first door on the right then rushed inside with me following close on his heels. Instead of Addison, I got an eyeful of a dude bent over taping his dick back.

"Yeah?" he asked, his head between his legs.

"Sorry. Wrong room," I replied as I stumbled back out into the hallway. After Ty slammed the door, I said, "Hey ace, maybe we should knock first?"

Ty's Adam's apple bobbed as he swallowed hard. "That sounds like a good idea."

At the next door, I rapped my knuckle against the wood. "I'll be ready in five," a falsetto voice replied.

"Not her."

"Nope."

"Who are you looking for?" the voice called.

"Um, Adrianna."

"Last door on the left."

"Thank you."

We bypassed the other rooms and headed to the end of the hallway. After knocking on the door, I was stoked to hear Addison's voice call, "Come in."

I threw open the door and stalked inside with Ty close on my heels. Addison stood in the middle of the room. She had managed to shed not only her wig, but her pants as well. She stood in a thong with her blouse unbuttoned, and instead of a bra, a spandex-looking fabric wrapped around her chest, binding her breasts. She would have looked sexy as hell if she still hadn't been sporting the handlebar mustache.

At the sight of me, her eyes widened. "B-Barrett, wh-what are y-you d-doing here?"

"I believe I could ask you the same the question."

Once she had a moment to recover from the shock of seeing me before her, she grabbed the lapels of her shirt and pulled them tightly closed. "Did you follow me here after you let me out at my apartment?"

"Actually, Ty tracked you with the GPS in your phone."

A gasp of horror escaped Addison's lips. "He did what?"

"Thanks for throwing me under the bus, buddy," Ty growled behind me.

Addison stomped over to him. She jabbed a finger into his chest. "How dare you violate my privacy by tracking me like some dog!"

"Told you she'd be pissed," I muttered.

"I'm sorry, but your security is my utmost concern at all times. The tracking is a necessary evil to ensure your safety during the times I cannot be physically in your presence."

The anger in Addison's eyes dissipated a little as she appeared to be processing Ty's words. After exhaling a long breath, she replied, "Okay. I get it." She shook her head. "I don't like it, but I do get it."

I crossed my arms over my chest. "Now here's something I would like to get: just what in the hell is my fiancée doing performing at a drag club?"

"You know, a simple call to question my whereabouts would have sufficed. You didn't have to come snooping around."

"Considering you'd already lied about staying in for the night, what possible reason would I have for believing you?"

As I stared into Addison's mustached face, the absurdity of the moment hit me. Reaching over, I grabbed the right side of the mustache and ripped it off. Unfortunately, I didn't realize how well it was glued on.

Addison shrieked in pain as her hands flew to her face. "What did you do that for?"

"I couldn't have a serious conversation with you with that thing flapping at me."

She glared at me through her watering eyes. "Could you not have simply asked me to take it off?"

Remorse filled me at the sight of her reddening skin. "I'm sorry. I'm just a little wigged out right now." At the sight of the mustache still in my hand, I quickly tried to toss it to the floor, but it wasn't going anywhere. I spent the next few seconds flapping and flailing my hand to try to get it off.

"What the hell is going on in here?" a voice boomed behind us.

I spun around just as Estrella marched into the room. She'd exchanged her Cher costume for a Dolly Parton one, and for a moment, I was completely transfixed by her enormous tits in the revealing dress. She shoved Ty and me out of the way with the strength of a linebacker. Placing her hands on Addison's shoulders, she questioned, "Are you okay, Addie?"

"I'm fine, E."

Estrella threw a suspicious glance at us over her shoulder. "And just who are they?"

"That would Barrett, who I've been telling you about, and his bodyguard, Ty."

Recognition flickered on Estrella's face before she whirled around and came over to me. "Oh my God! I can't believe I didn't recognize you."

"I guess you've been following us on the campaign trail, huh?"

"Of course, but it's also more about the fact that Ginger—the redhead in the opening act—has a poster-size picture of you and your junk on the wall in one of the dressing rooms."

While I laughed, Addison shrieked with mortification. "Did you have to tell him that, E?"

"I was just stating a fact." Estrella thrust out her hand. "I'm Estrella here at the club, and I'm Evan in real life." She—he jerked his chin back at Addison. "I'm her older brother."

I glanced between the two of them. "Ah, now it makes sense."

"What makes sense?" Estrella questioned.

"Why Ty thought Addison might be a man."

Addison's eyes widened at Ty. "Excuse me?"

I laughed as a flush filled Ty's face. "It's just we didn't know why you would have snuck off to somewhere like this. Then you and Estrella looked a lot alike…" Ty smacked my arm. "He thought it, too," he tattled.

"Seriously, Barrett? After all these months together, you still thought I could be a man?"

"Come on, you two do look alike."

Estrella laughed. "While I'm honored you thought I could really pass for a woman, Addison should be insulted because you thought she was a man in drag."

I held my hands up. "For the record, it was a paranoia-induced thought on both of our parts."

"You're both idiots," Addison huffed.

"Trust me, after your Cher performance, I know without a shadow of a doubt, you're a woman."

As her cheeks reddened, Addison ducked her head. "Whatever."

"You looked good out there." When Addison looked up at me, I winked. "*Real* good."

"Thank you."

A guy with a headset on appeared in the doorway. "Estrella, you're on in three minutes."

"Coming, Monte." Evan reached out and cupped Addison's chin. "I just needed to check on my baby sister for a minute after I heard two strange men were after her."

"I'm fine. You can put your terminator side away for now, big brother."

"I'm glad to hear it." He jerked his chin at the door. "Go on and get out of here."

"You don't need me to help close up?"

Estrella snorted. "Honey, the last thing you two need is to get caught in this club."

Addison gasped as she turned to me. "He's right. We've got to get you out of here before the crowd leaves."

"Why just me?"

"I came to the club disguised, so I can easily sneak out. You, on the other hand, are an entirely different story."

"We can always disguise him, too," Evan suggested with a wicked grin.

I shook my head quickly back and forth. "Oh hell no! Don't you even think of sending me out in drag like they did to Gene Hackman in *The Birdcage*!"

"I think you would look good in a dress," Estrella remarked as she eyed me up and down.

Addison nodded. "He already has his chest waxed, so a plunging neckline won't be a problem."

"For your information, I had laser hair removal on my chest," I protested.

Addison and Estrella laughed heartily while Ty said, "Seriously dude?"

"Shut up," I grumbled. Thanks to my comment, Ty would be giving me shit for days about being such a metrosexual. "Look, as long as I'm seen here with Addison, what does it matter if I'm in a drag club? If any pictures surface, we can simply say we were enjoying a night out by supporting the arts."

"Nice spin," Addison replied with a smile.

"I learned from the best."

After giving Addison a knowing look, Evan said, "While that would certainly work, I don't want any extra scrutiny on the club."

"I agree."

"Are you sure about that? Think about all the publicity," I argued.

"We're doing just fine without a media circus."

"If you say so."

Monte poked his head in the door. "You're supposed to be on stage now!"

"Calm your tits. I'm coming." He turned to Addison. "Go out the back, and then go two doors down to La Trattoria. Knock on the back door and tell them Evan sent you. You can leave through there just in case anyone was following Barrett."

Addison grinned. "You always come up with the best plans on the shortest notice."

Evan winked before hurrying out the door. "Love ya," he called.

"Love you, too," Addison replied.

Ty cleared his throat. "Barrett, why don't you and I wait outside so Addison can get dressed."

"I'd like to talk to her for a minute first."

"Okay. I'll be just outside."

"Thanks man," I replied.

After the door closed behind Ty, Addison gave me a sheepish look. "I'm pretty sure I know what you want to talk to me about."

"The campaign's foreign policy stance?"

She laughed. "No. About Evan."

"Bingo."

With a sigh, she said, "I was afraid this was going to happen."

Crossing my arms over my chest, I asked, "That I might find you singing in a drag club?"

The corners of Addison's lips twitched. "No, that you would find out the truth about Evan."

"He was in your FBI file, but there sure as hell wasn't anything about him that drew a red flag."

"That's because when Evan was twenty-five, he had his name legally changed."

"Why?"

"Even though my parents completely accept him being gay, Evan felt it would be a lot easier on my dad if he kept this aspect of his lifestyle hidden. People at his church accept that he has a gay son, but I'm pretty sure they wouldn't be so forgiving about having a gay son who owned and performed in a drag show."

"Yeah, probably not."

"In the end, Evan didn't want Dad to lose his job because of him."

"That was noble of him."

"That's Evan for you." Pure love radiated in Addison's eyes. "He has the biggest heart in the whole world," she said with reverence.

"Not only that, but he has one hell of a singing voice." With a wink, I added, "Just like his sister."

Redness once again tinged Addison's cheeks. "Thank you."

There was something seriously endearing about her humility; it made her even more attractive. Of course, the fact that she was practically naked under her shirt was also very appealing. I cleared my throat to clear my mind of the highway to hell it was barreling down. "With Evan changing his name, he didn't show up in any of the files."

"If anyone dug deep, they would find that Evan Nelson owned the club, rather than Evan Monroe." Addison rolled her eyes but then smiled in spite of herself. "He chose his last name after Prince."

I laughed. "Good choice."

Addison's expression grew serious. "Barrett, the reason I didn't tell you about Evan is not because I am ashamed of him."

I held up a hand to silence her fears. "I know that just as much as I know the real reason why you didn't tell me."

"You do?"

"You were afraid of what it might mean for Dad's campaign."

Her eyes widened. "You don't think I lied because of the money?"

"While I'm sure you didn't want to do anything to screw up your chances, I know in your heart you worried what the news might do to Dad's chances."

She nodded. "That day I met with your father, he and Bernie were so sure that there weren't any skeletons in my past, I couldn't bring myself to tell them about Evan."

"Although I'm pretty sure my dad wouldn't give a shit, I'm sure some of his advisors would've been less than pleased by the news."

After nibbling on her bottom lip, Addison asked, "Should we tell him now?"

"I think he has the right to know, especially if something comes out in the media after us being here. It would be better if he wasn't blindsided."

A worried expression overtook her face. "You think he's going to be mad at me for lying?"

I smiled that she cared so much about what Dad thought, and that she was obviously so oblivious as to how much he absolutely adored her. "Don't worry. He'll understand."

"I hope so."

"He will."

Addison smiled. "Thanks for being so understanding about all this, Barrett."

"You're welcome."

"But I'm still pissed you thought I could be a man."

I laughed. "Like I said, it was a delusion brought on by extreme paranoia." When she gave an exasperated roll of her eyes, I countered, "Put yourself into my shoes for a minute. After you say you're going to be home all night, we track you down to this club. What other conclusion could I possibly come to?"

"Maybe I was here to watch the show." Tilting her head, she continued, "Or any other scenario that doesn't have me as a man?"

I threw up my hands. "Look, I'm sorry. If it makes you feel any better, I first thought this was a *male* strip club."

Addison cocked her brows. "Please tell me you're joking."

"No, I'm not."

"How could you possibly think that?"

"All I could deduce when Ty and I got here was that it was some kind of club, and we were surrounded by a bunch of drunken bachelorettes. It just made sense that it would be a strip club."

"With your less than stellar deduction skills, it's amazing you managed to get an MBA," she teased.

"Why is it so unfathomable that I thought you'd snuck out because you wanted to see some naked men?"

"Well, for one, I signed a contract to be your fiancée, and in my experience, most engaged women do not frequent strip clubs unless it's their bachelorette party. Second, you should know me well enough by now to know I'm not really the strip club type."

"I know that. I just wanted it to be a strip club because that meant you weren't out looking for another man—well, one that wasn't oiled up in g-string."

Addison's eyes widened. "You thought I might be meeting up with another man?"

"Although I'm not proud to admit it, yes, I did."

"Oh. My. God."

"What?"

"Barrett Callahan, you were jealous!"

"I just said I didn't want you meeting up with another man, not that I was jealous of one."

Addison gave me a toothy grin. "You were totally jealous, and you know it."

"Okay, you know what? I'm done talking about this. Go get dressed so we can get out of here."

"Fine, fine. You can play it off all you want to, but we both know the truth."

I rolled my eyes before I started to the door. "Keep dreaming, sweetheart." When I got out in the hallway, Ty leaned up against the wall, wearing a shit-eating grin on his face. I knew then he'd heard every word of our conversation. "Don't you start with me."

He held up his hands. "I didn't say a word."

"You didn't have to—it's written all over your face."

A shriek of pain followed by a grunt of frustration came from inside Addison's dressing room. Turning back to the door, I called, "Are you all right?"

"The pin on my binding is stuck. I can't seem to get it undone."

"Do you need some help?"

"Unfortunately, yes."

Without another word to Ty, I reentered the dressing room. The sight of Addison with one arm wrapped around her back like a contortionist made me laugh. "You could have asked me to do this before I left. You don't always have to be so stubborn and independent."

"At the moment, this stupid pin is the one being stubborn. It's no wonder considering how fast they had to get me into this costume."

"Would you just stop and let me get it?"

"Fine," Addison replied as she dropped her arm and stood straight.

When my fingers brushed against her skin below the binding, she shivered. I tried to focus my attention on the pin instead of her reaction, and after working with it for a few seconds, it finally popped open. "There," I said as I pulled it out of the fabric.

Addison took the pin from me and promptly tossed it into the trash. She smiled at me. "Thanks. I was beginning to think you might have to cut me out of it."

Eyeing the scrunched material, I asked, "How do you get out of that stuff?"

She laughed. "It's kinda like an ace bandage. You just unwrap it."

Without thinking, I stood watching as she began unraveling the binding. Just before she got to the very end, she glanced up at me, and our eyes locked for a moment. *God, she is so beautiful, even with all that makeup.*

Shit.

More than anything in the world, I wanted to rip away the binding and jerk her into my arms. I wanted to crush her lips against mine, tasting her mouth and tongue, but this time it wouldn't be because we were practicing or selling our relationship to the cameras.

No, it would be because I was dying to taste her. I wanted her. I wanted to fuck her, own her, *keep* her.

Fuck.

I could not go there with Addison. I was already confused as hell about what I felt for her. If I threw in the physical, it would mess everything up.

I took two steps away from her. Clearing my throat, I said, "I'll be outside."

"Okay."

I was so incredibly screwed.

CHAPTER TWELVE

ADDISON

TWO WEEKS AFTER Barrett unmasked me—or maybe I should say unwigged me—singing at Divas, I found myself preparing for quite a different performance on a far bigger scale. As I stood backstage, the thundering roar of the crowd was so deafening it seemed to cause the floor beneath my Jimmy Choos to shudder. Peeking from behind the curtain, I anxiously eyed the multitude of people packed shoulder to shoulder in the George R. Brown convention center in downtown Houston.

In just a few short minutes, I was going to be in front of a crowd of thousands, not to mention the millions watching on television and their computers, to introduce Jane as the potential future First Lady. As I clung to one of the velvet curtains to steady me, I wished I had never agreed to do this. When the idea had first been broached, I had immediately voiced my opposition and suggested Caroline do it instead. She would be in attendance at the convention, and after all, she was a blood relative. I was just the woman masquerading as Jane's son's fiancée.

Even so, both Jane and James assured me I would be the best for the job. While their confidence was encouraging, it did nothing to soothe my nerves or calm my fears. After all, the convention was a big deal. I would be in front of all the delegates giving their support, not to mention a huge television audience. Sure, I hadn't had a slipup since Assgate—unless you counted when I got high off the moonshine cough syrup—but my luck could always run out.

A tap on my shoulder caused me to shriek as I jumped out of my skin. Whirling around, I stared into Barrett's concern-filled face. Fifteen minutes ago, I'd left him in the family box, the seats where the candidate's family sat in the front row of the balcony, to come backstage to await my turn to speak. "What are you doing here?" I demanded.

"I came to check on you."

Instantly, my heart did a funny little flip-flop at his chivalrous gesture. "Thanks. I appreciate it."

"So how are you holding up?"

"Just peachy," I replied, my voice rising an octave. When Barrett cocked his brows at me, I sighed. "I feel like I'm going to puke."

He smiled encouragingly at me. "It's just nerves. You're going to do great."

"I just have this fear that I'm going to walk out there and forget everything I'm supposed to say."

"That's why the teleprompters are there," Barrett reassured.

"What if I fall again?"

"That won't happen." His brows creased slightly. "You are wearing underwear this time, right?"

I widened my eyes. "Oh my God, you really think I could fall?"

Barrett laughed. "No, I don't. I was just teasing you."

"Well I'm not in the mood."

He placed both his hands firmly on my shoulders. "I want you to listen me," he commanded.

"Okay."

"You are going to go out there and knock them dead, not only because you're a gifted speaker, but because you wrote a kickass speech that comes straight from that enormous heart of yours."

I blinked at him a few times. "You really think that?"

He nodded. "Yes, I do. The entire campaign feels that way. Dad would have never suggested you do it if he didn't believe in you and your abilities."

"Thank you, Barrett. That means a lot."

"Come here."

Barrett drew me into his strong embrace. We'd come a long way since the day we'd had to practice holding hands. With everything that had transpired over the last few months, we'd built a strong friendship. We also shared an intimacy I hadn't found with any other man. A pang of sadness entered my chest as I thought about how much I was going to miss it after November, not to mention the fear of never finding it with another man.

At the sound of my name echoing over the loud speakers, Barrett pressed his lips to my cheek. "More than anything, I believe in you."

His comment, coupled with his close proximity, made my already weak knees even less stable.

"Th-That means a l-lot," I stammered. *Good lord.* What was happening to me? One hug and a nice word from Barrett had me acting like a lovesick school girl whose crush had actually waved at her. I hated when he was able to do that to me, and it seemed to be happening more and more lately. I couldn't let my heart become any more invested in him. It was too dangerous. He had to stay in the friend zone.

"Now get out there and knock 'em dead." He then proceeded to smack me on the ass, hard. My outrage at his gesture overruled my nerves, and I practically stalked out from behind the curtain. Then, when I started out onto the stage, I momentarily had a deer-in-the-headlights moment with the spotlight. Thankfully, I only faltered for a moment before striding confidently on. Once my fingers gripped the sides of the podium, I couldn't help doing a small fist bump in my mind that I hadn't fallen. My gaze stretched past the crowds to the teleprompter in the back, and at the sight of my speech scrawling across the screen, I took a deep breath before looking away. I knew I didn't need it.

"Good afternoon. It is my honor to stand before you today to introduce a woman whom I greatly admire. A woman who has fought tirelessly for the underprivileged and the disenfranchised even before her husband became a senator. A woman who worked to slash illiteracy rates by implementing a reading initiative for low-income areas not just in her home state of Virginia, but throughout the southeast. Through all of this, she has also been a wife and a mother of three. She has been the anchor for her husband through the rough political waters of a thirty-year senatorial career. She has been the rock for her children to lean on and the soft place to fall. Please help me in welcoming my future mother-in-law and the future First Lady of the United States, Jane Callahan."

My ears rang at the deafening noise that erupted around me and I turned to watch as Jane made her way down the stage. She appeared poised and dignified in her white suit, and when she reached the podium, she hugged me. "You did fantastic," she shouted into my ear.

"Thank you," I replied.

After pulling out of Jane's embrace, I waved once more to the crowd before I hurried off the stage. This was Jane's triumphant moment, and I didn't want to take one second away from it. When I rushed behind the curtain, Barrett was waiting for me.

Overwhelmed with emotion, I dove into his waiting arms. It felt so good to be able to share this moment with him. Our connection as a couple felt so true and genuine.

"You were fantastic!" Barrett exclaimed.

I pulled away to stare into his face. "Really?"

He grinned. "Quit fishing for compliments. You know you rocked the house."

I laughed. "I sorta did, didn't I?"

"You sure as hell did."

Gazing into his eyes, I realized I'd gained more than a friend during the last few months. I'd learned that leaning on someone wasn't such a bad thing, that leaning on *Barrett* wasn't such a bad thing. I liked being a recipient of his caring side. "I couldn't have done it without you."

"Oh please, you could've given that speech blindfolded."

"No, I mean it. You coming back here and saying you believe in me gave me the confidence I needed." Acting on impulse, I reached up and pecked him on the lips.

Barrett stared wide-eyed at me. "What did you do that for?"

I shrugged. "I don't know. As a way to say thank you." That was the honest-to-God truth; I hadn't had any ulterior motives. I certainly hadn't thought about how Barrett might take it for something else, but his expression told me he did.

"I'm sorry if you don't want me kissing you."

With a scowl, he replied, "That's not it." *Right, why else would you suddenly be acting all weird?*

"Considering how pissed you look, that must be it."

"You just took me off guard, that's all." He took my hand. "Come on, we better get back to the family box."

Any elation I'd felt over my speech was suddenly dampened by Barrett's obvious loathing of my lip-lock. I hadn't even considered that the idea of kissing me could be repulsive to him. *Tuck away your heart, Ads. You know the sort of woman Barrett truly likes, and even after all this time, it isn't going to be you.*

CHAPTER THIRTEEN

AS EVERETT FUSSED around me trying to get the tie on my tux just right, I felt like I was being choked, but it wasn't the tie that was leaving me suffocating—it was my growing feelings for Addison. When she kissed me out of the blue, it had knocked me emotionally on my ass. Sure, we'd kissed a ton of times before, but they had all been orchestrated for the media's benefit. This one was different. It had been off the cuff and driven by her emotion. Sure, it hadn't been a passionate *I wanna rip your clothes off* kinda kiss.

It was an even more dangerous one.

The night after Dad had stood on stage and officially accepted the party's nomination, we were ditching the business attire for evening wear to attend the Cattleman's Ball. It was the first time Addison and I had attended anything black tie for the campaign, and tonight we would be hobnobbing with campaign donors. That fact coupled with a large media presence meant Addison and I would be on constant display as the happy couple. I hadn't dreaded having to pretend in a long a time, and I thought maybe I was doing so now because the lines between pretending and what I truly felt were blurring.

"There, got it!" Everett exclaimed, drawing me out of my thoughts.

"Thanks man."

Everett handed me my cufflinks, the heirloom ones that traveled in the safe with the other family jewels. As I started putting them on, Everett said, "Oh hell, I forgot to get Addison's necklace to her."

"I'll take it to her."

"Are you sure?"

"I'm heading that way now to pick her up to head downstairs to the car."

Everett nodded before handing me a small velvet box. Addison had been corralled into my parents' suite about an hour ago so Saundra could work on her and Mom simultaneously. After bypassing the Secret Service outside the door, I entered the main room. "Addison, we need to go."

"Coming!" she called.

I walked in a smile. At the sight of Addison bedecked in a red strapless gown with her long hair swept back in a loose knot, my smile slowly faded. I blinked several times at the breathtaking image before me. *Fuck. Me.* It'd been several long months since I'd had sex, and seeing her in *that* dress was not helping my very *blue*-balled situation. "Wow," I murmured.

"Does that warrant a 'thank you' or a 'what's wrong with me?' response from me?" she teasingly asked.

"You look beautiful."

A pleased expression came over her face. "Thanks. What's in the box?"

"Huh?"

"The box in your hands."

"Oh yeah." I walked over to stand before her. "Everett forgot to give this to you."

When Addison opened it, she gasped at the sight of the necklace. After she stood there just silently staring for a few moments, I jumped at the sound of her sudden laughter. Furrowing my brows at her, I asked, "What's so funny?"

"These feels like a scene out of a movie—*Pretty Woman* to be more exact, like you're going to snap the box on my fingers like Richard Gere did to Julia Roberts."

"I've never seen it."

"Please tell me you're joking."

"Is it a chick flick?"

"I suppose you could call it that."

"Then trust me, I've never seen it."

"We're just going to have to remedy that ASAP."

"On one condition."

"What's that?"

"You watch a macho movie."

Wrinkling her nose, Addison asked, "Like one with The Rock or Vin Diesel?"

I flashed her a wicked grin. "Oh yes."

She sighed resignedly as she put the ruby earrings on. "Fine, it's a deal."

After taking the necklace out of the box, I guided it over her head before bringing it to rest against her neck. As I closed the clasp, my eyes dropped down to take in an eyeful of her cleavage. My hand itched to dip into the dress to cup one of the perfect round globes, to feel her nipple harden beneath my fingers.

"Eyes up here, Mr. Callahan," Addison teased.

"I was just checking to make sure the necklace was hanging right."

"Sure you were."

With a wink, I replied, "Fine, I was totally checking out your tits in that dress. Are you satisfied?"

Addison wrinkled her nose. "Ugh, I hate that word."

"Tits?" I repeated, solely to aggravate her.

"Yes."

"Would you rather me say breasts? Or maybe boobies?" I scratched my chin thoughtfully. "Knockers."

She smacked my arm. "How about you say none of them?"

"I can't make any promises."

With a sigh, she took my arm. Thankfully, I had managed to bring some levity to the moment. The last thing I needed was to be fantasizing about doing anything to Addison. The stakes were just too high, and there was too much to lose.

THE BALL WAS being held at an exclusive country club just outside of Houston. When we got out of the car, flashbulbs went off all around us, and we stood and posed for the photographers on the makeshift red carpet before heading inside. Instead of the usual classical or big band music, a full country band belted out tunes.

We made the rounds, smiling and shaking hands before we were herded over to our table for dinner. Once dinner was over, it was time to put on a show with the photographers by taking a turn around the floor. As the band struck up "Carry Me Back to Virginia", Dad threw back his head and laughed as he led Mom onto the dance floor. A pleased shock reverberated through the crowd as he high-stepped Mom around the floor, much like one of the Virginia reel dances of the past. "Do you know how to do that?" Addison asked as she clapped in time with the others.

"Would you revoke my man card if I said yes?"

She laughed. "No, I wouldn't."

"Then yes, I know how to do that."

Addison's eyes suddenly widened. "You guys don't expect me to do that, do you?"

"I have a feeling if we win, it'll make its way into one of the inaugural balls."

"Count me out on that one."

"It's not that hard," I reassured her, although Addison didn't seem convinced.

Once the song ended, Dad and Mom received raucous applause. As they went back to their seats, it was time for Addison and me to take our turn. Thankfully, more couples walked out onto the dance floor so we wouldn't totally be on display. The last thing we needed was to have a giant spotlight following our every move.

As the band began playing a cover of Chris Stapleton's "Fire Away", I drew Addison closer against me. She pressed her cheek against my face, tucking her chin to my shoulder. Closing my eyes, I inhaled the sweet fragrance of her shampoo; it smelled like a mixture of vanilla and coconut, and I immediately thought of our week at Martha's Vineyard. I couldn't wait until the election was over and we had time to go back there again.

And then it hit me: we wouldn't be going back there together. When the election was over, *we* were over.

My heart clenched at the thought of Addison not being around. She had become such an integral part of my life. No longer did I think in just me terms, but it was always about us, or more importantly, about her. What did she want for lunch? How could I make her feel better when some fashion hack criticized one of her campaign dresses? What could we do to unwind after a long day of events?

Maybe we would somehow remain friends after all this. It might work better for the press if we remained on good terms. I sure as hell didn't like the thought of not ever hearing her laugh or seeing her roll her eyes at something I said. Pain continued to work its way through my chest, and I had to fight to breathe.

More than anything, I didn't like the thought of her meeting someone else. Having some other man's lips pressed against hers. Having their hands on the perfect curves of her body. Just the thought caused my body to tense in anger.

"Are you okay?" Addison asked.

"Yeah. Fine. Sorry."

Dipping my head, I buried my face into her neck. Before I could stop myself, I began placing tender kisses along the soft skin of her shoulder. After shivering slightly, Addison sighed, her breath warming the top of my ear. My thumb rubbed a trail on the exposed skin between her shoulder blades as I kissed a trail up her neck and onto her cheek.

With my mouth inches from hers, I stared into her eyes. Just like her impulsive kiss at the convention the day before, I brought my lips to hers, but I didn't give a quick peck like she had. Instead, my mouth stayed fused to hers like it was a lifeline in a turbulent sea.

At the sound of applause, I jerked away from her. *I want more. More of her. More of her lips. More.* Confusion had replaced the longing in her eyes. Forcing a smile to my face, I waved to the crowd before leading her off the dance floor. Although I wanted nothing more than to escape to somewhere I could be alone, Caroline bounded in front of me. "My turn, big brother."

Gritting my teeth, I let Caroline push me back out in the spotlight. Once again, I fought to breathe as my tie felt like it was strangling the life out of me.

Deep down, I knew the truth. I didn't want us to end. I didn't want us to be *just friends*. I didn't want to think in terms of just me. I wanted to keep wondering what she wanted for lunch. I wanted to continue unwinding together after a long day.

In that moment, it was crystal fucking clear that I wanted Addison. The real question was if I was I actually going to do anything about it.

CHAPTER FOURTEEN

ADDISON

AFTER THAT NIGHT in Houston, I no longer knew how to act around Barrett. The lines had been blurred, although neither one of us would admit it. Some days I tried to distance myself as much as possible, while other days I acted just plain weird around him. When I say weird, I mean I found myself doing all the weird crap women do when they really like someone and want to catch his attention. Basically, I was acting like an inexperienced teenage girl with her first crush.

Barrett, on the other hand, acted as if nothing had happened, like the moment we left Houston, he had entered a time warp where things were exactly the same as in the beginning. He still aggravated the hell out of me with a barrage of sexual innuendo on a daily, if not hourly basis. His ability to transcend made me wonder if the whole thing had been some figment of my imagination.

Now a week after Houston, we were back on the Santa María and deep into the heart of Ohio. After our third rally of the day ended at eight, I had been so thrilled to climb the bus stairs that I fought the urge to kiss the top one. I made a beeline for the couch before anyone else could stake a claim. Since we weren't campaigning with Senator Callahan, we had a skeleton crew. Besides Ty, we just had Pete and two of his minions helping run our schedule and appearances.

I had just pulled my Louboutins off my swollen feet when Barrett appeared. "Scoot over."

"But there are plenty of chairs."

"Yes, I'm aware of that, but I want the couch."

"And I *need* it so I can prop my feet up. When you've worn heels for thirteen hours, we'll talk."

"What if I offered to give you a foot rub?"

Cocking my head at Barrett, I asked, "Don't tease me."

"I'm not. Hell, for part of the couch, I'd be willing to suck your toes."

I wrinkled my nose. "Ew. I'll pass on that one."

Barrett laughed as I scooted down the couch. The moment he sat down, I plopped my stocking-clad feet in his lap. "You're really holding me to it, aren't you?"

"Damn straight."

After cracking his knuckles, Barrett said, "All right, I'm going in."

When his fingers started kneading my foot, my head lolled back against the back of the couch and a low groan of pleasure emanated from deep in my chest. "Man, you're really good at that. You might have a future as a masseuse."

"Comes from practice massaging other areas."

Tilting my head, I peeked one eye at him. "Like the Bear?"

Barrett laughed. "I meant areas on a female's body."

"Of course you did."

"Although he does get plenty of attention."

"You mean he hasn't gone into hibernation with the sex drought that's been imposed on you?"

"He never hibernates. He's always ready and willing should the opportunity arise."

Cocking my brow at him, I asked, "Have there been any opportunities lately?"

He wiggled his fingers at me. "You mean besides with my hand?"

I laughed. "Yes."

"I told you before, I've never cheated on a woman."

"But we're not really a couple."

"Doesn't matter."

I nibbled on my bottom lip as I processed the enormity of what he was saying. "During all this time, you haven't snuck in a hookup?"

Barrett paused in massaging my foot to scowl at me. "No, I haven't. Considering we're practically joined at the hip, I'd love to know when you think it would have been possible for me to bang some random bimbo."

He had a point. There was so little of our time that was spent apart, let alone any time completely alone. Since the beginning of our relationship, our schedules had been so regimented. Not only did I feel bad for doubting him, I was seriously impressed that he had been celibate this long.

I placed my hand on his shoulder. "I'm sorry. It was wrong of me to doubt you, especially since I don't have any reason to suspect you."

Barrett grinned. "Apology accepted."

He then rubbed a spot that had been aching all day, and as it had been so long since I'd been touched like this, I hitched a breath in. *Oh*. With those magic hands of his on my feet and knowledge of the Bear via the internet, an ache began to spread between my thighs. When I shifted my hips, Barrett's nostrils flared. "Is there a problem?"

To save face, I bent over to massage the top of my calf. "I had a cramp."

"I must be loosening up some of the tension," Barrett replied. His eyes dropped to watch his fingers working my calf muscle through my hose-clad skin. When his tongue darted out over his bottom lip, I sucked in another breath. If I was reading him correctly, his expression told me he'd like to run his hand up my foot, past my calf, and between my legs, and damn me to hell if I didn't want the exact same thing.

I was just about to teasingly move my foot over his crotch when Pete stuck one of the secure phones in Barrett's face. "It's your dad."

I immediately jerked my foot back as a feeling of unease washed over me. Secure phones were untraceable, and they also couldn't be cloned. I knew for Senator Callahan to call Barrett on one meant something serious had happened, something he didn't want anyone else to know about.

Barrett cupped the phone to his ear. "Hey Dad." Whatever Senator Callahan said sent Barrett shooting up off the couch. "What?" he demanded. His free hand went to jerk its way through his hair.

Icy apprehension trickled down my spine. Leaning over, I peered around Barrett to give Pete a questioning look. He shook his head, which told me he didn't know what the conversation was about.

The rigid tension in Barrett's body loosened, sending his shoulders drooping. He hadn't said another word. Instead, he had been listening intently to what James was saying. After what felt like an eternity, he said, "Okay. Call me the minute you know more. Give Mom my love." He nodded. "Yeah, I love you too."

When Barrett ended the call and turned around, his face was white as a sheet. I jumped off the couch to stand in front of him. "What happened?"

"The convoy Thorn was leading was hit by a roadside bomb. Three of his men were killed. He got hit in the leg with some shrapnel, but other than that, he's fine."

I exhaled the breath I'd been holding. "Thank God."

Barrett nodded. "They're about to release the story to the media, and Dad didn't want me to hear it over the news since they won't release the soldiers' names yet."

I couldn't imagine how scary it had been for Barrett during those few seconds when he thought Thorn had been killed. When a shudder ran through Barrett's body, I didn't hesitate to pull him into me for a hug. He welcomed my embrace by wrapping his arms around me, and then he shocked the hell out of me when he said, "I need to light a candle for Thorn's men."

"Of course."

"And I need some whiskey."

I smiled into his shoulder. "After that call, I'm sure you do." Easing back, I looked at Pete. "Can you google the closest Catholic church to us while I get Barrett a drink?"

Pete nodded and pulled his cell phone out of his pocket. "I'm on it."

"Thank you."

Ty appeared from the bedroom where he'd been catching up on some missed sleep.

"My phone just went off with a secure call alert. What's going on?"

After squeezing Barrett tight, I turned us around and then pushed him down on the couch. "You fill in Ty, and I'll get that whiskey."

"Okay."

Ty hurried down the aisle to sit by Barrett. After digging around in the liquor cabinet, I glanced over my shoulder at them. "Um, I don't see any."

"It's the Glenmorangie Pride—the oval bottle."

"Oh, okay." I pulled it out. "I was looking for Jack Daniels with the black label."

Ty snorted next to me. "Barrett's palate is far too discriminating for cheap whiskey."

Eyeing the bottle, I said, "Is this kind more expensive than Jack?"

"Try four thousand a bottle."

"F-Four th-thousand?" I was so shocked that I fumbled the bottle and almost dropped it. Breathing a sigh of relief, I quickly sat it down on the counter. "You've got to be kidding me."

"Nope."

Opening the top, I inhaled the amber-colored contents. "Hmm, I would've thought for that price you would get high just from inhaling it."

Barrett chuckled. "Not quite."

After a grabbing a glass out of the cabinet, I poured it half full. When I handed it to him, Barrett said, "Thanks."

"You're welcome."

He brought the glass to his lips and took a long gulp then quirked his brows at me. "Aren't you going to have any?"

"I'm not much of a whiskey girl."

Barrett held out the glass to me. "Try it. You might change your mind."

"I might change my mind about Jack Daniels, but there's no way in hell I'd ever be so extravagant as to buy this stuff," I replied as I took the whiskey. With Barrett's eyes on me, I took a bigger gulp than he had. Instantly, I regretted the urge to one-up him. Although the liquor had a smooth feel, something about the taste was just wretched. If it had been cheap, I would've spit it out, but instead, I swallowed it down.

"Nope. Still not a whiskey girl."

Barrett just laughed as I handed him back his glass.

A moment later, Pete came over with his phone. "St. Francis is ten minutes from where we are now, and it's open until midnight."

With a nod, Barrett said, "I can pay my respects, and then we can grab a bite to eat."

"Good, I'm starving."

Barrett had downed his whiskey by the time the bus turned into the church parking lot. Ty immediately got off the couch when we parked and headed to the door; I knew he was going to do a quick sweep of the parking lot on the off chance there was somebody out there who wanted to hurt Barrett.

When I remained seated, Barrett glanced over his shoulder at me. "Aren't you coming in with me?"

"Oh, um, I didn't know if you wanted to be alone."

"I'd like the company if you don't mind."

My heart beat a little faster at his declaration. I felt the urge to argue that with Ty trailing behind him, he wouldn't be alone, but I didn't. "Of course I don't mind."

I quickly rose off the couch and headed over to him, and he motioned for me to go first down the stairs. When we got off the bus, we started down the walkway and into the church. Over the years, I'd toured many Catholic churches, always admiring the architecture and the beautiful art and stained glass windows. St. Francis was a lot smaller than the churches I'd been in before, and while it didn't have the impressive architecture, it di have a warm, inviting feeling.

Instead of hanging back, I stuck to Barrett's side. A small fount with holy water sat just inside the vestibule, and Barrett dipped his fingers in then crossed himself. When he caught my eye, he grinned. "Were you afraid it was going to burn me?"

I laughed. "No, it's just interesting seeing this side of you."

"Although it might be surprising, I am a man of faith."

"If you tell me you were an altar boy back in the day, I might faint."

"No, I was never an altar boy, but that doesn't mean I was any less holy." He gave me a pointed look. "At least as a kid."

As we started up the aisle, Barrett knelt down on one knee and crossed himself again. At the top of the altar, the amber flames of numerous candles flickered on a tiered table. My head turned left and right as I took everything in. It was after nine, but there were still two other people kneeling on the risers with rosaries in their hands.

When we reached the table, Barrett took a fresh candle out of the box. He reached out to light it, but then he froze. "What's wrong?"

"I just realized I don't know their names."

"I think God will know who you mean."

Barrett considered my words for a moment before nodding. He then lit his candle on one of the others before bowing his head. I felt it only right to do the same, and I said a few words in prayer for the families of the men who had been killed.

When I lifted my head, I turned to see Barrett had his eyes on me. His expression was unreadable, but standing there with him in the candles' illumination, I once again felt electricity swirling in the air, just as I had that night in Houston. The growing spark between us once again grew a little stronger.

Just as soon as it came, it vanished once again, like snuffing out the flame of a candle. Barrett took a step back, breaking the spell. "I, uh, I'm going to pop in the confessional," he stated.

"Okay, take your time. I'll wait for you."

He nodded before heading over to the built-in boxes that housed the confessional. After he dipped out of sight behind the dark curtains, I turned and walked back down the aisle then sat down on one of the last benches. As I gazed around the church, I tried not to overthink what was going on between us. I had to once again ask myself if I even wanted it to be anything. A fake relationship was complicated enough during the campaign, and I couldn't imagine trying to maintain a real one, especially with someone like Barrett who didn't do relationships. In the end, wouldn't I just be setting myself up for heartache?

Barrett emerged from the confessional and came over to meet me. His mood seemed lighter, and I was thankful he was feeling better. "It went well?" I asked.

He grinned. "Yeah. It did."

"Good."

As we started out of the church, I said, "I think people would have paid good money to see what I just did."

"What do you mean?"

"Bare Callahan voluntarily going to confession." I turned to him with a smile. "Now *that* is a headline."

Barrett chuckled. "I guess me in a confessional would turn people's perception on their ass."

"You know, John F. Kennedy faithfully attended mass."

"Thanks for the tidbit."

"What I meant was just because you have a womanizing reputation, that doesn't mean you don't have faith."

"Most would argue that I should probably sin a little less."

"That's not for them to judge. Your sin is yours alone."

With a grin, Barrett said, "I like your way of thinking, Addison."

"I'm glad," I replied.

Walking to the bus, Barrett jerked a frustrated hand through his hair. "Jesus, I can't even begin to imagine what Thorn is going through right now, not to mention having to do it thousands of miles away from his family."

"Can your parents visit him in the hospital?"

"Dad mentioned something about it, depending on how long he had to stay."

"Maybe you could go with them?"

From the expression on his face, I could tell Barrett hadn't even thought of it. "That's not a bad idea." He gave me an earnest look. "But not for some photo op bullshit."

"Of course not. Because he's your big brother and you love him."

"Exactly." When we reached the bus, he patted his stomach. "Now how about some food?"

I laughed. "Sounds good to me."

AFTER GETTING GREASY burgers and fries at a truck stop down the highway, we got back on the road. Barrett and I once again took the couch, although this time he didn't offer any foot rubs. Instead, we propped our feet on the table in front of us and started watching some of the campaign coverage on the television. The combination of a full stomach and the swaying of the bus lulled me to sleep.

I didn't know how long I'd been out when I awoke to the voice of our bus driver, Shane. When I popped open one of my eyes, he was staring down at us. "Sir?"

"Dammit, Shane, stop calling me sir," Barrett grunted.

"I'm sorry, but the bus's engine has been having issues for a few miles. I think it's best we stop for the night."

"Sure. Whatever."

At the feel of his chest rumbling beneath my ear, I realized I had somehow fallen asleep on Barrett. Quickly, I popped straight up. My mortification intensified at the sight of a wet stain on Barrett's shirt where my face had been. *Oh God.* I had actually drooled on him.

Barrett glanced down at the puddle before looking back at me. I gave him an apologetic look.

"I'm so sorry about that."

He grinned. "Don't worry about it. I'm used to chicks drooling when they're around me."

I laughed. "God, you're such an egomaniac."

"I like to consider it stating the facts."

After a quick look at my phone, I saw it was after midnight. Inwardly, I groaned. I knew we'd back on the road by seven, so that didn't give us much time to sleep. I pulled myself up off the couch, slung my purse over my shoulder, and headed for the door.

After stepping off the bus and getting a look at where we were staying, I had serious thoughts about turning around and getting right back on the bus. Ohio was famous in the campaign circuit for its eclectic roadside hotels and motels. Most were charming little mom-and-pop places, and although most of the décor was outdated, they were still nice. While I'm certainly not a five-star hotel person, I would have to say our digs for the night probably didn't even qualify for one star.

The one-story motel was painted Pepto Bismol pink with teal accents. A giant teddy bear-shaped sign that looked like it had been designed in the 60s sat in front of a swimming pool not much bigger than most kiddie pools.

Barrett got off behind me. "The Teddy Bear Motel? Charming."

Shane grimaced. "I'm sorry, sir—uh, I mean, Barrett, but there's not another hotel for a hundred miles. I don't want to push the engine too much."

"It's okay, Shane. This will do for the night."

While Ty and Shane unloaded the luggage, Pete worked on getting our rooms, standing outside a booth since the motel didn't even possess a lobby. With our roller bags trailing behind us, we crossed the parking lot to meet up with him.

Pete's forehead was lined with concern. "We're on opposite ends of this hellhole, which is going to be a security nightmare for Ty."

Barrett snorted. "Since this looks like the last place on earth I would be at, I think we're fine."

Ty crossed his arms over his massive chest. "I'll still be putting you into your room, and I don't want you leaving without calling me. Then I'll come get you in the morning."

"Fine, Mom, whatever you say."

Pete flashed a teddy bear-shaped key in front of Barrett's face. "They only had one room with a double bed. The rest were twins."

Barrett and I cut our eyes over to each other. If anyone needed the twin beds, it was us. We might've shared hotel rooms over the last few months, but we sure as hell hadn't shared a bed. Maybe there would be a couch one of us could sleep on, perhaps even a pull-out.

Reaching his hand out, Barrett took the key from Pete. "Thanks. Six AM wake-up call?"

Pete nodded. "Unfortunately, yes. We need to be on the road by seven."

Shane cleared his throat. "Yeah, about that. There's no way I can get the bus seen by seven. I'm going to have to call around for a mechanic. It'll be at least eight, if not nine."

"Son of a bitch," Pete groaned.

"Take it easy, man. Worst case scenario, we rent a car, and then Shane can meet us at the convention center."

Pete tilted his head, weighing Barrett's suggestion. "That could work. Okay, I'll find a rental car for backup as soon as I get inside."

"Good deal. The best thing we can do right now is get some rest," Barrett said.

"I'll call you in the morning with the revised itinerary."

"Thanks. Night."

"Night guys," I said.

True to his word, Ty walked over to our room with us. Sliding the teddy bear key into the lock, Barrett opened door. After fumbling on the wall for a switch, light flooded the room. We both stared at the double bed.

Shiiiiit.

I mean, it would have been slightly easier if it had been a king or even a queen-sized bed, but no, it had to be a double.

There was nothing else in the room but two uncomfortable-looking chairs that no one could sleep in. After dropping his suitcase, Barrett walked over to the bed and grabbed a pillow before turning back to me. "I'll sleep on the floor."

I shook my head. "That's awfully chivalrous of you, but you don't need to do that."

Barrett's brows wrinkled in confusion. "Wait, you want it?"

"Of course not. I meant neither of us is going to sleep on the floor. We can sleep together."

"Are you sure you really want to do that?"

"After all these months together, I think we've reached a level of intimacy where we can deal with sharing a bed. You've helped me pee for goodness sake."

With a laugh, Barrett replied, "I didn't actually help you pee. I just stood there in case you passed out."

"Same difference."

It was then I realized Ty was still standing in the doorway, and the expression on his face told me he thought Barrett and I were entering dangerous territory by sharing a bed. I imagined he was thinking the minute we went horizontal, we would attack each other out of pent-up sexual need.

"If you guys are good, I'm going to ask you to lock yourselves in," Ty said.

"We're fine, bud. Go get some rest," Barrett replied.

Ty gave him a pointed look. "You guys make sure to do the same."

From the look on his face, Barrett wasn't picking up on the double meaning of Ty's statement. He merely smiled and shut the door in Ty's face. After bolting the locks, Barrett said, "We're good."

"Goodnight," came Ty's muffled reply.

"Night," Barrett called back.

With the door shut, the room seemed even smaller, and I inhaled a deep breath as the walls seemed to close in around me. Even though it was the *last* thing I needed, "Touch-a-Touch-a-Touch-Me" from *Rocky Horror Picture Show* began playing in my mind.

"Did you say something?"

"Oh, uh, no. I was just humming."

"Go ahead and grab the bathroom," Barrett said.

"Okay. Thanks."

I grabbed my suitcase and wheeled it across the threadbare carpet into the bathroom. Once inside, I locked the door, though I wasn't sure why. It wasn't like we hadn't experienced this setup up tons of times before when we ended up in smaller hotel rooms. The glaring difference this time was the fact that I'd be coming out to only one bed, not two, and that one bed was a very tiny double.

There was also the fact that things had changed between us since the last time we'd been in close quarters in a hotel. Maybe they hadn't changed for Barrett, but they sure as hell had for me. In my somewhat old-school version of romance, the act of sleeping with a man could sometimes be more intimate than actually having sex. Usually, the sharing the same bed part came after a night of sex, but it was still pretty intimate, so I wasn't thrilled with the prospect of getting so very intimate with Barrett when my feelings for him were currently so very volatile.

Trying to calm my nerves, I went about my nightly routine of taking off my makeup and brushing my teeth before slipping into my pajamas. Once I was finished, I tossed everything back into my suitcase. Since I was sure Barrett needed the bathroom, I couldn't continue hiding out, so I unlocked the door and stepped into the bedroom.

Apparently I'd taken longer than I'd thought to get ready for bed because Barrett was already fast asleep. He must've been pretty exhausted after the events of the day because his shirt and pants lay crumpled on the floor next to his side of the bed. When I pulled back the spread, I gasped. In his exhaustion, Barrett hadn't bothered to put on his pajama pants. He remained in his black briefs, exposing his upper thighs—his hard, very muscled upper thighs.

Get a grip, Addison—and no, that grip can't be on the Bear!

The mattress dipped down as I slid into the bed. Barrett was a major bed hog, so I scooted over until my leg was on the very edge of the mattress. As if his sexual Spidey senses were alerted of a female presence, Barrett rolled over, slinging his arm over my breasts while he covered my thigh with his. His warm breath fanned against my neck.

Oh God. This was so, so bad. His close proximity caused my male-neglected vagina to sit up and take notice. I pressed my thighs together, trying to lessen the growing ache between them.

Pinching my eyes shut, I willed myself to go to sleep. Instead of counting sheep, I tried counting all the lead roles I'd had in musical theater, but I could barely get through middle school before I was biting my lip from the overwhelming need for sexual healing I felt.

Okay, this was never going to work with him sleeping so close to me. I had to get him to move. "Barrett?" I whispered. When he didn't respond, I repeated, "Barrett?"

Dammit, the man slept like the dead. Taking his arm, I moved it off my breasts. Of course, the friction caused my nipples to harden, which just increased the ache between my legs. I tucked Barrett's arm at his side before shoving his thigh off of mine.

Even though I was free, I wasn't going to be able to ignore how horny I was. I would never fall sleep without relief. When Mary Anne had mentioned necessities on the trip, I hadn't actually thought about how necessary my vibrator would be. On a whim, I'd tossed it into my bag, and over the last few months, I'd used it a time or two in the shower so the water would drown out the noise. Those times had just been maintenance getting-off sessions; they hadn't been brought on by any male interaction, especially not with Barrett.

I slipped out of bed and padded over to my suitcase. After unzipping it, I dug into the secret section where I kept tampons and panty liners. Once I had it in my hand, I threw a glance at Barrett over my shoulder. The last thing I needed was for him to catch me with a vibrator in my hand. He would never let me live it down.

Thankfully, he let out a snore, and I knew I was safe. After hustling into the bathroom, I dropped my pajama shorts and panties. Tonight there would be no fantasizing about Henry Cavill or Charlie Hunnam.

Gazing at the vibrator, I closed my eyes and wished it were the Bear.

CHAPTER FIFTEEN

BARRETT

A TRAIN'S WHISTLE jolted me out of a deep sleep. Disoriented, I rubbed my eyes and tried remembering where the hell I was. Oh yeah—Bumblefuck, Ohio, at the Teddy Bear Motel. Reality was scarier than any nightmare that might've plagued me.

When I rolled over, I found Addison's side empty. Rising up in the bed, I peered around the darkened room, but I didn't see her anywhere. At the sound of a long moan from the bathroom, I threw back the covers and got out of bed. I hoped Addison hadn't got food poisoning from the drive-in-from-hell we'd eaten at.

"Addison?" I questioned at the door.

My chest tightened apprehensively when I didn't get a response. Throwing up my fist, I started to knock on the door, but then a picture of an unconscious Addison flashed before my mind. Okay, forget decorum—I was just going in. Thankfully, when I turned the knob, I found it unlocked, but nothing could have prepared me for what I saw.

Instead of Addison's head hanging over the toilet throwing up or her crumpled in a heap on the floor, she had one foot hiked up on the tiny sink. Her pajama shorts and underwear lay wadded beside her left foot, and one of her palms was splayed out behind her on the tile wall for balance. Her other hand was between her legs, moving a pink vibrator in and out of her pussy.

Addison hadn't heard me because she was too intent on getting off, and from the looks of it, she was close. Her eyes were pinched shut, and concentration lined her brows. Her chest rose and fell with heaving breaths in between moans of pleasure.

Holy. Fucking. Shit. My mouth dropped open, sending drool dribbling down my chin and onto my chest. The sight of Addison touching herself sent the Bear roaring to life. He clawed against the confines of my underwear to be freed, sending me shifting on my feet.

Wait, what were the odds that this was really happening? Surely I was still asleep, and this was all some sort of erotic dream. When I reached to pinch myself, my elbow banged into the door. "Dammit," I muttered.

The sound of my voice caused Addison's eyes to pop open. At the sight of me, she let out a screech of mortification rather than pleasure as her foot fell from the counter and she scrambled to shield her vag from my intense stare. In her melee, the vibrator fell from her hand and rolled to a stop at my feet.

Refusing to look me in the eye, she stammered, "J-Jesus, h-haven't you ever heard of kn-knocking?"

"I called your name, but you didn't answer. I was afraid you were sick again."

"Well, I wasn't." She snatched her pajama shorts off the floor and covered her crotch with them.

This scenario could go one of two ways: I could leave the bathroom and let Addison recover her dignity, or I could offer my services to help her achieve the orgasm she'd just lost. I just needed to know where we stood.

"Look at me," I commanded.

Although she resisted at first, she finally swept her gaze off the floor. Where I expected embarrassment, I got fire. Jerking her chin up, Addison said, "Go ahead, make fun of me for being so desperately horny I'd get out of bed in the middle of the night to get off in a skanky bathroom. And while you're at it, go ahead and gloat about how just lying next to you got me hot because it's the truth."

I'd never been someone to be rendered speechless. I usually had some biting remark or smartass comeback just waiting to be released, but with the smell of Addison's arousal fresh in my nose and her declaration of being turned on by me ringing in my ears, I was utterly and completely speechless. Seconds ticked by as we stood there having a stare-off.

"When you were touching yourself just now, did you wish it was my fingers stroking your wet pussy?" I questioned hoarsely.

Electricity crackled and popped in the air around us. "Yes," she whispered.

That acknowledgement was all I needed to hear. I closed the gap between us, grabbed Addison by the shoulders, and jerked her into my arms. Dropping my head, I slammed my mouth against hers. Her lips were so much different this time than when we had practiced kissing. Desperate desire and aching need poured out from their softness.

As I swept my tongue into her mouth, Addison moaned. Damn, if it wasn't the sexiest sound in the world. Our tongues intertwined and danced around each other as I raked one of my hands through the long strands of her hair and brought the other to cup her breast. When I ran my thumb over the hardened nub, Addison rewarded me with another moan, which caused the Bear to once again claw against my underwear for release. He was just going to have to be patient; this moment was about giving Addison pleasure.

I jerked back to stare her in the face. "Do you want to come?"

"Mmm, yes."

"Do you want me to make you come?"

"Yes. Please, Barrett."

"Mm, I do like hearing that sassy mouth of yours beg me."

Addison grunted. "Do you have to ruin this by talking?"

"Does that mean you want my mouth somewhere else?"

When she bit down on her lip, I knew exactly where she wanted it. Grabbing her by the hips, I hoisted her up and placed her ass on the edge of the sink; thankfully, even though it was old as the hills, it was way more solid than I expected. After pushing her legs wide apart, I licked my lips at the sight of her glistening pussy. Then I dipped my head to lick her there. Addison sucked in a breath and arched her hips against my face. After a few teasing licks, I placed my mouth fully on her clit before sucking it into my mouth.

"Oh God! Yes!" Addison cried. While one of her hands clutched the edge of the sink, the other came to my head. With each pull of my mouth, she yanked the strands of my hair.

One of my hands once again sought out her pajama-clad breast while the other went between her legs. While my mouth worked on her clit, I slid two fingers inside her wet walls. Addison shrieked in pleasure as she began to move her hips furiously against me. "Barrett, Barrett, Barrett," she murmured as her head lolled back. I seriously loved hearing my name coming off her lips.

When her walls started clenching around my fingers, I glanced up to watch as she came completely apart. Her eyes pinched shut as she sucked her bottom lip between her teeth. *Fuck me.* It was so sexy. *She* was so sexy.

Once she finished convulsing, I took my fingers out of her, and she glanced at me with glazed eyes while her face relaxed into a post-orgasm haze. "I'm sure your overinflated ego doesn't need the compliment, but that was amazing."

I grinned. "Thank you. I'm glad to be of service."

As she eased down from the sink, Addison slid down my body as she got to her feet. When her pussy met the Bear, I groaned and bucked my hips against her. She reached between us to cup my bulge. "Does the Bear want to be in my mouth or my pussy?"

My mouth dropped open in surprise. First of all, I couldn't believe she had actually said the word *pussy*—it was so not her style. I really dug the sound of it coming off her lips, not to mention the fact that she had indulged me by acknowledging my dick as the Bear. Secondly, I couldn't believe she was giving me a choice. Most chicks wanted to bypass giving the Bear a lick-down. If this meant she was a fan of giving head, I thought I might come right there in my boxers.

"I want in your pussy. Now."

Tilting her head at me, she said, "Then take me."

Like the caveman I felt like, I grabbed her by the waist and hoisted her up to wrap her legs around me. Addison circled her arms around my neck and drew my head down to hers. Our lips met in a frenzied kiss as I stumbled out of the bathroom, and as we crossed the short distance to the bed, Addison rubbed herself against me.

After we collapsed onto the bed in a tangled heap of arms and legs, Addison tore her mouth away from mine. "Condom?" she questioned breathlessly.

I ripped open her pajama top before dipping my head to nuzzle her tits. God, they were even more gorgeous than I'd expected, full globes of firm perfection. "Aren't you on the pill?" I questioned against one of her breasts.

She shook her head. "Stopped getting shots when my ex and I broke up. No insurance for a while," she panted out.

"Damn," I grumbled as I reluctantly unhanded her breast. I rocked back onto my knees before hopping off the bed. "Way to kill the mood."

Addison rolled over on her stomach and propped her head up on her arm. "Newsflash, ace: even if I was on the pill, I wouldn't dare let you ride bareback without being tested considering the number of women you've been with."

I smirked at her. "While I should find that insulting, I'll take it as a compliment."

"I would expect nothing less," she replied with a grin.

I snatched my wallet off the nightstand and eyed the remaining two condoms, not having imagined they would be coming out of retirement so soon. I ripped open the wrapper before tossing it to the floor. With one hand, I jerked my briefs down, sending the Bear officially out of hibernation.

At Addison's gasp, I met her somewhat bewildered gaze. After blinking a few times, she swallowed hard. When her eyes trailed from the Bear up to mine, she gave me a shy smile. "The camera doesn't do it justice."

I threw my head back with a laugh at both her comment and the fact that she had googled my dick pics. "I'm glad you think so." After sweeping the condom on, I placed my palms and knees back on the bed and crawled over to her.

"Are you ready for the Bear to ravage your cave?"

Addison rolled her eyes. "If you say anything remotely like that again, my alleged cave will be permanently closed to you."

Smirking at her, I slid one of my hands over her buttocks and between her legs. She gasped at the contact. "Your cave might have other ideas."

With a grunt of both irritation and frustration, she flipped over onto her back. "For the love of all that's holy, just shut up and fuck me."

"Your wish is my command," I replied as I climbed on top of her. Addison widened her legs obligingly, and I settled between them. Taking the Bear in my hand, I guided him toward her. I began rubbing the length against her slit, circling her clit with the head.

Addison's hands came to grip my shoulders. "Now, Barrett. Please."

Slowly, I eased inside her slick walls. When I was halfway, I glanced down to gauge her reaction. At what must've been my overly concerned expression, she giggled. "Keep going. You're not about to tear me in half."

I laughed. "I'm glad to hear that."

When I was buried fully inside her, we both moaned. Damn, it felt so fucking good being inside a woman again. It had been too long—multiple months too long—but being inside Addison felt different, and I wasn't talking about the fact that she was ultra-tight after going without for a while.

My hips remained motionless as I stared into Addison's eyes. What I saw in them momentarily scared the shit out of me. It was something I'd never seen in any other woman's eyes: connection. A truly *emotional* connection. One that transcended the physicality of the moment. But the look wasn't just in Addison's eyes; it was being reflected back at me from my own. Although I hated to admit it, I really liked the feeling. I liked it almost as much as being buried balls deep inside Addison.

"Are you okay?" I croaked out.

Addison slid one of her hands down my back to cup my ass cheek while the other came up to touch my face. "I'm more than okay."

I eased slowly out of Addison before plunging back inside. Thankfully, she shrieked with pleasure, not pain. I then took up a punishing rhythm. With every thrust, I went deeper than before. God, it felt good, maybe better than it ever had before.

I flipped us over so that Addison was riding me. My hands came to grip her buttocks to rock her harder on and off of me, and the friction felt out of this fucking world. One hand snaked up her abdomen to pinch and tease one of her hardened nipples while the other went between her legs to massage her clit. "Holy shit!" she shrieked, which had me increasing my pace.

"That's it, babe. Take it," I growled. Digging my heels into the mattress, I began raising my hips to meet hers, pounding in and out of her. We both began to breathe heavier. Two of my favorite sex sounds filled the room: the slapping of skin and pants of pleasure. It was even better because it was Addison's skin and Addison's pants. It was better because of her, and I wanted nothing more than to give her my everything.

CHAPTER SIXTEEN

ADDISON

"OH GOD, OH God, OH GOD!" I screamed as my walls convulsed around Barrett. I came so hard it felt like a locomotive was charging through my abdomen. The muscles in my thighs trembled, and my arms felt rubbery. After I collapsed onto Barrett's chest, he continued pumping his hips furiously until he gave a loud groan of pleasure and came as well.

Rolling off of him, I flopped onto my back on the mattress. While I worked to regulate my breathing, I swept the sweat-soaked strands of hair out of my face. Meanwhile, my vagina was still recovering from the massive orgasmic quake with tiny aftershocks. I'm pretty sure if it could have lit up a cigarette, it would have. It felt that good.

When I cut my gaze over to Barrett, his dazed expression took me somewhat off guard. After all, he was a known sex god. I would have assumed what I had just experienced was probably everyday stuff to him, but apparently not.

I cleared my throat. "So..."

His head slowly turned on the pillow to stare at me. "That was..."

I giggled. "Yeah, it was."

A sexy grin spread across Barrett's face. "I didn't know you had it in you."

"Had what?"

"The ability to fuck me senseless."

With a laugh, I replied, "I guess all those sexless months of pent-up desire count for something."

"If I'd known sex after abstinence would be so amazing, I would have gone without more often."

"Ha! I doubt that very seriously."

Barrett winked at me. "You're probably right. Even after all that time, the sex between us could have turned out to be a dud instead of being explosive."

His over-the-top descriptions of our sex kept my ego on cloud nine, but even as I languished in post-coital bliss, I couldn't ignore the questions swirling in my mind. "Barrett, what happens now?"

"Another round?"

I laughed. "Although tempting, that's not what I meant."

"Well, I'm serious. Give the Bear a few minutes of hibernation, and he'll be raring to go."

After smacking Barrett's bicep, I turned over on my side to face him. "I meant, what happens now that we've had sex?"

"Like with our engagement?"

"Yeah. I mean, do we go back to the way we were until Election Day, or do we keep having sex?"

He snorted. "You've lost your mind if you think I'm going back to celibacy after that mind-blowing fucking."

"You thought it was mind-blowing?"

"Hell yes."

My ego, which had been bruised and battered by Walt's cheating, did a little victory dance. "It was pretty amazing."

"Then what's the problem?"

"I'm just worried, that's all."

"Worried I'll end up breaking your vagina?"

I laughed. "No, that's not what I meant."

"Hmm, you're worried you'll be too tired from our sexathons to keep up your campaign duties?"

"Would you please be serious?"

Barrett sighed. "You're alluding to how sex complicates stuff."

I nodded. "We have such a great thing going, and I don't want to mess it up."

"Why don't we just take each day one at a time?"

"Or each fuck one at a time?" I countered.

He chuckled. "That's one way to look at it."

Every rational thought in my mind told me that continuing to have sex with Barrett wasn't a good idea, but in the end, I understood what it was like for a man to think with his penis because I totally let my vagina make the final decision.

"Okay. We'll take it one day at a time."

"Can we enforce that ideology tomorrow? The Bear is ready to go again."

I glanced down to see Barrett's erection already at half-mast and grinned. Yeah, there was no way on earth I would be denying myself more of that. I might've just had two amazing orgasms, but my lady parts were feeling greedy and craved even more. They were ready to binge on the Bear. "I guess it wouldn't hurt."

"Thank God."

"I suppose we better get the Bear fully operational," I mused as I took his cock in my hand and pumped up and down his shaft. When I licked my lips, Barrett's eyes flared. "Lie back. I'll take care of this."

"Yes ma'am."

Barrett's head fell back against the pillow. As I started kissing my way down his chest, my lips slid across a small raised mark over his left pec. I couldn't help pausing to look at it. "Is this from one of your surgeries?"

"Actually, I got that one in a gang fight."

"Ha, very funny."

He grinned. "Yes, it's from my last heart surgery."

"How old were you?"

"Two."

"You haven't had to have any more surgeries?"

"Nope. They managed to fix the ol' ticker then, or at least the damaged valve."

"Damaged," I murmured. I couldn't help fixating on that word, both the physical and emotional meaning.

"What about it?"

"I was just thinking it was a little ironic you had a damaged heart."

"And why is that, Miss Alanis Morrisette?"

"I guess I was just thinking it's a little ironic you've never been able to love a woman before and you have a damaged heart."

"Come on, you don't actually believe there's a correlation, do you?"

"I just said I found it ironic. Obviously, it's more symbolic since anatomically, the actual heart does not control our ability to love."

Barrett groaned and threw an arm over his head. "Would you please hold off on the psychoanalyzing me and suck my cock?"

I laughed. "Fine, fine." I quickly kissed and licked the rest of the way down his chest and abdomen. When I slid the tip of the Bear in my mouth, Barrett's hips bucked forward. I took my time sucking and licking the head then began to lick my way down his shaft. Barrett's hands gripped the sheets. "Please, babe."

"I do so love to hear you beg," I said, throwing back his line from earlier.

He sucked in a breath. "I'll say or do anything you want as long as you suck my cock."

I winked at him. "Your wish is my command." I then sucked him into my mouth, taking in half of the Bear. A satisfied grunt came from his lips as my head began bobbing up and down, alternating between suctioning light and hard. While my mouth dominated his cock, my hands cupped and caressed his balls.

"Oh yeah, just like that," he panted. His moans and pants of pleasure fueled me on, taking him deeper and deeper. His hips began pumping up and down on the bed. "Fuck. I'm getting close," he rasped.

Although I was fine with him coming, Barrett pushed me away. "I want to save it for inside you," he explained.

"Works for me," I replied with a grin.

As he fumbled on the nightstand for another condom, I asked, "How do you want me?"

"Let's get that fabulous ass of yours up in the air."

I rose up on my knees before leaning forward to place my palms on the mattress. As I swayed my hips provocatively, I threw a glance at him over my shoulder. "How's this?"

"Good. Very, very good."

The mattress dipped as Barrett got back in bed. His hands came to the back of my thighs, pushing my legs apart, and instead of sliding the Bear inside me, I felt the warmth of his wet tongue against my clit. "Oh God!" I cried as my head dipped down. His hands caressed my buttocks as his mouth pressed against me.

Just when I was about to come, Barrett replaced his tongue with the Bear. We both moaned with pleasure at the joining of our bodies, and Barrett's hands then came to my hips. With each thrust, he pulled me harder against him, going deeper and deeper. I seriously began to wonder if I would be able to walk in the morning. Considering how good it felt, I stopped caring about walking ever again.

When I kept getting closer and closer but still hadn't come, Barrett slid one of his hands off my hips and between my legs. He began stroking me, alternating between pinching and rubbing my clit. The added friction was enough to send me over the edge. "Yes, yes, oh yes!" I cried, my eyes squeezing shut with pleasure.

Barrett continued pounding into me for a few minutes until he tensed and came with a shout. He lay with his chest against my back, panting to catch his breath. "Fuck me," he muttered.

"You sure did," I teased.

He chuckled. "I didn't think it could be as good this time…"

"But it was."

"Hell yeah it was." Barrett eased out of me before removing the condom and tossing it in the trash. I flopped over onto my back, bringing my hand up to push the hair out of my face.

When Barrett returned to the bed, he covered us up. "We better get some sleep."

"Not to mention, if we don't stop now, I'm not going to be able to walk in the morning."

Barrett grinned. "The Bear and I appreciate the compliments."

I fluffed my pillow before rolling on my side. "You both are egomaniacs."

"Yes, yes we are."

"Goodnight, egomaniacs," I said as I closed my eyes.

With a chuckle, Barrett replied, "Goodnight."

My eyes popped wide open when Barrett spooned up next to me. At what must've been my body tensing in surprise, he asked, "Is this not okay?"

"No, no, it's fine." I threw a glance at him over my shoulder. "I just didn't take you for someone who spooned."

"There you go making assumptions again."

"I stand corrected."

"You want to know what one of the best things is about our time together these last few months?"

"What?"

"The fact that you've been able to see how very wrong you were about me."

Rolling my eyes, I replied, "Yes, I have, but don't start gloating or I'll change my mind."

He laughed. "Goodnight Addison."

"Goodnight Barrett."

CHAPTER SEVENTEEN

ADDISON MONROE WAS a sex goddess, an out-of-this-world, knock-your-socks-off, sex goddess—and I wasn't just saying that because I'd been stuck in the seventh ring of abstinence hell for the last several months with only my hand to sustain me. I was saying that because I'd been with enough women to know what I was talking about.

I'd been quick to initiate Addison into my appreciation of sex outside the box. We'd christened the bathrooms on the Niña, Pinta, and Santa María, and I'd taken her doggy style on the jet's couch then she'd ridden me reverse cowgirl in one of the captain's chairs. Although I was ready to sneak some quickies in during campaign events, Addison balked at the idea.

Our scorching summer sexathons melted into fall. As Dad's leads in the polls gained momentum, my feelings for Addison continued to grow. They transcended the physical into something much, much deeper. I was completely falling in love with her, even though I wasn't really sure I knew what that was, but I didn't know how to tell her. At the same time, I didn't know if I should. I didn't want to risk what we already had. For the life of me, I couldn't begin to read her, so I sure as hell couldn't afford to get it wrong. The one thing I was certain of was that I didn't want us to end. What we had was beyond what I'd ever known to be possible with a woman, and sometimes I even swore I'd seen her look at me the same as Mom looked at Dad—*adoringly*, with *love*.

With two weeks to go until Election Day, Addison and I found ourselves at rallies in southern California. After a full day of speeches and hand shaking, we'd headed out to Napa to stay the night at the estate of one of Dad's old buddies from Yale. Although Addison and I would have loved nothing more than to just crash, Lucas and his wife, Elaine, were throwing a huge dinner party for us. Cue having to break out the formal wear again.

While waiting to be called into the dining room for dinner, Addison and I mingled around the front hall, exchanging the same boring small talk with people. She looked gorgeous as usual in a glittering silver dress. Considering the low neckline of the dress, I owed Everett a thank you note. As I snuck peek after peek of Addison's peaks, the Bear began growing restless.

Unable to restrain myself, I led Addison over to a private corner. Leaning over, I whispered into her ear, "I really want to fuck you right now."

The champagne Addison had just sipped went spewing from her lips. While dabbing her mouth—which I would have loved to have wrapped around the Bear—she shot me a murderous look. "We're in public," she hissed.

"I know, that's what makes it so much hotter."

As she glanced around, I could tell the wheels were turning in her head. "You want us to go back upstairs before dinner?"

"No. I want to take you into one of the empty rooms and fuck you up against the wall, or maybe take you from behind while you're bent over a couch."

Addison's eyes bulged. "But someone could catch us," she protested.

I snorted. "I should have known you would be too much of a goody two-shoes to have sex in public."

"Is that something you're used to doing? Like with other women?"

"Sometimes."

Her brows scrunched as she gnawed on her bottom lip. Trying to put her out of her misery, I said, "Look, it's okay. You're not the brazen, sex-in-public type of woman."

"I can be brazen," she countered.

"Oh really?"

"Yes. I just don't think now is the right time, considering what could happen to your father's campaign if we were caught."

I grinned at her. "Blaming your lack of a sense of adventure on the campaign is low."

When Addison opened her mouth to argue, Lucas and Elaina began herding everyone into the dining room where they had one of those huge tables that seated thirty people. While I had expected to be separated from Addison like at most dinner parties, I was glad to see we were seated beside each other.

After we all sat down, wine was poured, and we began the first course of soup. I had just dipped my spoon into the fine china bowl when Addison's napkin dropped beside me. When I started to reach for it, she shook her head. "I've got it."

I'd just taken a bite when Addison's hand landed on my knee. She then slid her hand up my thigh to cup the Bear, causing me to shoot straight up in my chair. Turning to me with an innocent expression, Addison asked, "Is something wrong?" All the while, her hand continued caressing my growing erection.

Feeling the eyes of everyone on me, I forced a smile to my face. "Just a little cramp in my foot. I'm fine."

"You've been on your feet too much today. Make sure you put them up after dinner," Elaina said.

"I will," I croaked out.

As Addison continued to give me a hand job through my pants, she calmly ate her soup like nothing was amiss, like my eyes weren't about to roll back in my head. When she increased her tempo, my hands gripped the sides of my chair so hard my knuckles turned white. As I subtly pushed my hips back and forth, sweat began to break out along my forehead. Just when I thought I was going to come in my pants like a teenage boy, Addison removed her hand.

I stared at her in both sexual frustration and disbelief as she took her wine glass and took a dainty sip. She smiled at Elaina. "This is delicious. I simply must get a few bottles to take back with us."

What. The. Fuck? I was sitting there with a raging hard-on and blue balls while she calmly critiqued the wine. The truth was Addison had strung the Bear too far along for him to just deflate on his own. I had to have relief, and I had to have it then. After pushing my chair back, I remained hunched over to hide my tented pants. "I'm so sorry, but I'm going to have to excuse myself."

"Oh my, you don't look well, Barrett," Elaina commented.

"I'm afraid a sudden headache has taken hold." *No pun intended.*

When I stood up, I doubled at the waist to hide my erection while keeping one hand on my allegedly aching head. Just as I started to leave the table, Addison's chair scraped back on the floor. "Lucas, Elaina, my apologies, but I won't be able to eat a thing unless I see Barrett safely to bed."

"Yes, you most certainly should accompany him," Lucas replied.

Elaina nodded. "We'll have a tray sent up in a bit for the two of you."

"That's very kind," Addison replied. She then slid her arm around my waist. "Here, sweetheart, let me help you."

"Oh, I think you've done plenty," I hissed under my breath.

Addison had the nerve to giggle. Once we were out of the dining room, I stood upright before glaring at her. Instead of cowering back, she gave me a shit-eating grin. "I told you I could be brazen in public."

"There's being brazen, and then there's being a cock tease, and now you're going to have to pay." Taking her by the arm, I started dragging her down the hallway.

"Where are you going? The stairs are back there."

"We're not going to the bedroom."

"We're not?"

I shook my head. "I want somewhere more public."

Apprehension rippled in Addison's eyes, but she didn't argue with me. Earlier in the evening, Lucas had given us a tour of the house, so I knew the second door on the left was the library. I opened the door and pushed Addison inside.

When the door shut behind us, Addison glanced over my shoulder. "Aren't you going to lock it?"

"Then no one could walk in on us, and what would be the fun in that?"

Her eyes flared as she took two steps back from me, but before she could escape, I pounced on her, jerking her against me. Our mouths crashed against each other while our tongues battled.

I steered us over to the huge mahogany desk in the center of the room. Once Addison bumped into it, I knelt down before her. Grabbing the hem of her dress, I slowly began inching it up her legs and thighs, and my nostrils flared at the smell of her arousal. Dipping my head, I began kissing the exposed flesh, licking a warm trail up to her pussy.

Addison's hands came to my hair, her fingers jerking through the strands. I ripped her panties down to the floor before spreading her legs, and one lick between her thighs told me just how ready she was for me. When I stood up, her eyes, which had been pinched shut with pleasure, popped open. Normally, I would have gone down on her longer, but she had already made me wait far too long.

Taking her by the waist, I hoisted her up to sit on the desk, keeping her ass on the edge. While I retrieved a condom from my wallet, Addison's hands came to the button on my pants. After she unzipped me, she pushed my pants and briefs over my ass and down my thighs.

"Do you want me to fuck you, Addison?" I asked as I rolled the condom on.

She dug her fingers into the lapel of my tux and jerked me closer to her. "Yes. Please."

"Right here where anyone could walk in on us?"

Licking her lips, she replied, "Mmhmm."

"Will you try to be quiet? Or will you scream loud enough for the others to hear?"

"I'll scream."

"Damn straight you will." Reaching around her, I unzipped her dress and jerked the front down around her waist. I ducked my head to lick and nip at her breasts in the fancy lace bustier. Then I slammed into her, causing her to shriek with pleasure. She wrapped her legs around my ass as I pounded in and out of her slick walls.

When her walls began tightening around me, I froze mid-thrust before pulling out of her. Panting, Addison's expression changed from pleasure-filled to confused. "What are you doing?"

"Giving you a taste of your own medicine."

Her swollen lips turned down in a pout. "You're not just punishing me you know—the Bear is suffering too."

I laughed. "That is true."

Widening her legs, she gave me a seductive smile. "Then get back inside me. Right now."

"There's no way in hell I would argue with an invitation like that."

Grabbing her by the hips, I flipped her over to where she was practically lying across the top of the desk. After giving her ass a resounding smack, I thrust inside her, burying myself balls deep. Moaning with pleasure, Addison held on to the edge of the desk for dear life as I fucked the hell out of her. Just when I thought it couldn't be any better between us, it was.

Addison cried out my name as she came, and two thrusts later I finished, collapsing onto her back. We lay there for a moment, desperately catching our breath.

At the sound of footsteps in the hallway, Addison and I threw a panicked glance at each other before staring around the room for a place to hide. "Curtain," I muttered before helping her off the desk. With my pants around my ankles, I had to waddle behind the desk, which caused Addison to burst out in a fit of giggles.

"Would you be quiet," I hissed.

We had just dipped behind the heavy curtains when the door flung open. Peeking through the side, I saw it was the butler. "What are you doing?" someone asked in the hallway.

"I could have sworn I heard somebody moving furniture around in here," the butler replied.

I snorted at his summation of our actions. I was sure when it came down to it, we probably had been moving the desk around some. When the door shut back, I exhaled a relieved breath before sliding the condom off the Bear and tossing it in the trashcan. Then I pulled my briefs and pants back up.

"That was a close one," I mused.

"No, that is exactly what happens whenever I try to be bad!" Addison moaned as she slid the straps of her dress back into place.

"Admit it, it was fucking hot."

She paused in fidgeting with the front of her dress, and a sly smile curved across her lips. "Yeah, it was." Then the moment passed. "Would you zip me up?"

"Sure." After Addison turned around, my fingers reached for her zipper, but then froze in midair. As the setting sun trickled in from the curtains, it illuminated her from the top of her head down to her feet in an angelic glow.

And then it hit me. There was no more wondering or questioning my feelings. I loved her. I really and truly loved her. Without even hesitating, the words tumbled from my lips. "Addie, I'm in love with you."

Addison whirled around. "What did you say?"

"I said…I love you."

She blinked at me in disbelief. "That's what I thought you said."

"I really mean it, Addison."

"I know you do."

My brows shot up. "You do?"

Bobbing her head, she replied, "I can tell by the look in your eyes." After exhaling a deep breath, she smiled. "I love you, too."

At the sound of those words coming from her, I thought my heart might burst right out of my chest. *Holy shit, she actually loves me.* "Man, I'm fucking glad to hear you say that. It wouldn't have changed the way I feel, but I'm glad you didn't leave me hanging out to dry."

Addison's hand came up to cup my cheek. Love danced in her eyes, coupled with a bit of mischief. I'd seen that look before, but I had never realized what it meant until today.

"Well, when I imagined saying it, it wasn't after we'd just almost gotten caught having sex," she mused.

I laughed. "Think of it this way: it just makes it more special."

"I guess you're right."

"Now come on and zip me up."

"Yeah, we better get out of here before the butler comes back."

"Or they bring the food tray to an empty room."

My stomach rumbled at the mention of food. "I'm starving."

Addison gave me a coy grin. "I quite enjoyed working up an appetite."

"Hey, I know— how 'bout after we eat, we work up an even bigger one?"

She laughed. "Sounds good to me." Then she cocked her head. "Now, will you please tell me where the hell my panties are?"

CHAPTER EIGHTEEN

BARRETT CALLAHAN WAS in love with me. Notorious *playboy* and *womanizer* Barrett Callahan was in love with *me*—regular old, non-supermodel me. After speculating about his feelings for me the last few months, I now had verbal confirmation. He had said those three little words without provocation and not under duress. They had come tumbling out of his lips of his own volition. Call me a little petty, but I basked in the fact that he had said it first. For a man like Barrett, that was a real coup, and I couldn't help feeling a little victorious as I snuggled under the opulent Frette sheets next to a snoring Barrett.

Don't get me wrong, I loved him, too. Over our months together, I'd come to fall in love with the kindness, integrity, and compassion that lay beneath his oversexed, party-loving surface. Time and time again, he had proven my stereotype of him wrong. He possessed all the qualities you looked for when it came to the type of man you wanted to fall in love with. He treated his parents with respect and deep admiration, and he had a deep bond with Thorn and Caroline. He exhibited a strong work ethic in his devotion to his job, and aside from the barrage of sexual innuendos that were a quirk of his character, Barrett always put my needs and wants first. He was a real catch, and I had reeled him in hook, line, and sinker.

But the longer I lay there, basking in our mutual declarations of love, the more my feelings of euphoria began to fizzle. While I should have been inwardly belting out "Something Good" from *The Sound of Music* or "One Hand, One Heart" from *West Side Story*, I couldn't seem to chase away the overwhelming sense of dread that coiled in the pit of my stomach. It even hung heavy in the air around me, making it difficult to breathe.

Questions swirled in my head at a manic pace. Did Barrett really love me, or after all these months of pretending, had he just succumbed to the hype? Would he change his mind in the light of day? Would it all fade after the election? When the paparazzi were no longer dogging us and we were no longer playing our parts in the charade, would his love survive? Was it even possible for someone like him to romantically love a member of the opposite sex?

Smacking my hand to my forehead, I willed the voices in my head to stop. But, no matter how hard I tried to think about something else, my anxiety continued working in overtime. One thing was certain: I wasn't getting to sleep any time soon. More than anything, I knew I needed to get away from Barrett. Rising out of bed, I tiptoed across the hardwood floor to the closet. After grabbing a pair of yoga pants and a sweater from my suitcase, I crept into the bathroom to change. Then I slipped into my sneakers, grabbed my phone, and hurried out of the room.

The house was quiet as I made my downstairs. Earlier when he was giving us a tour, Lucas had told us the alarm code to use in case we wanted to go for an early morning swim in the heated pool or a run through the vineyards. After punching it in, I exited one of the side doors.

With the full moon lighting the way, my shoes crunched along the gravel path. I'd almost reached the vineyards when another fear came ricocheting through me so hard that I actually stumbled. Once I righted myself, my hand rubbed my tightening chest. A scenario played out before me in lurid detail, one that was hauntingly reminiscent of what happened with Walt.

Barrett might love me, but could he ever be faithful to me and only me? With his past history with women, there was no grey area, only cold hard facts—facts I was finding it too hard to ignore or not be devastated by.

He'd never been in a monogamous relationship longer than a couple months. Because of his past indiscretions, he had to be programmed to cheat. To look around for the better offer. The more attractive arm candy. The woman who didn't want forever.

Not me.

As I stood on the hillside overlooking the vineyard, I sank down onto the ground and desperate cries overtook me. I wanted to be with Barrett more than anything in the world, but not if my heart would be broken beyond repair for trusting the wrong man with it—*again*.

Fumbling for my phone, I knew there was only one person to call, one person who could help me navigate the hell I found myself in. After the third ring, he picked up.

"It's Addison. I need your help."

CHAPTER NINETEEN

BARRETT

THE NEXT MORNING when my alarm woke me, it felt like my head had just hit the pillow. Maybe I felt that way considering I didn't roll off of Addison until late into the night. After eating dinner in bed, we burned all the calories we'd consumed by having a major sexathon.

Fumbling for my phone on the nightstand, I turned the alarm off. Yawning, I rubbed my eyes, and when I turned over to kiss Addison good morning, I found the bed empty. Craning my ear, I didn't hear the shower on.

Sitting up, I scanned the room for her. I finally found her over by the closet—hunched over, furiously packing her suitcase. "Addison?"

"Yes," she replied as she continued stuffing things in her bag.

"What are doing packing already? We don't have to leave until after breakfast."

When she turned around, my gut clenched like it had been roundhouse kicked. Her bloodshot eyes were swollen from crying. Throwing back the covers, I leapt out of bed. "What's wrong? Did something happen to your parents or one of your siblings?"

"No, it's nothing like that."

"Then what is it?"

An anguished sigh escaped her lips. "I'm so sorry, Barrett."

Dread entered my chest. "About what?"

"I just can't do this anymore."

"But there's only two weeks left."

She shook her head at me. "I'm not talking about the campaign. I'm talking about us."

I furrowed my brows at her. "Us? What's wrong with us?"

Her eyes pinched shut as if she were in agony. "I can't be with you."

My lungs constricted at her words, and I fought to breathe. I sure as hell hadn't been expecting her to say that. When I recovered enough to find my voice, I countered. "But I love you, and you love me—you said so yourself last night."

"I know I did."

"Then what could possibly be the problem?"

"You."

"Me?" When she nodded, I said, "Okay, I can work with that. Tell me what I did, and I'll fix it, I swear."

"It's not that simple, Barrett."

"It can be, if you would just give me a chance." The realization struck me in that moment that I had never asked a woman to give me a chance. It was always the other way around.

She went over to the bed and sat down. "Last night I couldn't sleep, so I ended up going for a walk. I needed to think about what you said, what we both said. No matter how hard I tried, I couldn't ignore the feeling that this was all just an extension of the campaign, that somehow your feelings weren't genuine."

What the hell? Has she lost her mind? "Now you're telling me how I feel?"

"It's more about what you *think* you feel. We've been in tight quarters together for months. Over time, we've grown to care about each other a lot. I think somewhere during all of that, you thought what you were feeling was romantic and physical love, but in actuality, it was just love for another person."

"That is bullshit!" I stalked over to stand in front of her.

"Maybe it is, maybe it isn't. Maybe it's the same thing for me. I just think I love you because of all we've been through together."

"What we have isn't fake. It's real—I know because I've never felt it for another woman in my entire life."

Addison's mouth gaped open and she blinked at me a few times, but then she shook her head like she was shaking herself out of a spell. "You don't know how much I want to believe that."

"Then believe it. Stay with me, and I'll make you see."

"I can't."

"Why are you being so fucking stubborn?" I growled.

"It's not just whether or not what we have is real. In the end, I realized that regardless of how I felt, I couldn't ignore your past."

Oh that's just fucking great. Nothing like my past coming back to bite me in the ass—again. "Let me get this straight, not only can you not be with me because you think I'm delusional in my feelings for you, now you're blaming my past?"

"You are a playboy, Barrett."

"*Was*—I *was* a playboy, but not anymore. People can change."

"I wish I could believe that. I've had my heart broken once by a man cheating on me, and I can't go down that road again."

"Just like I told you before, I've never cheated on a woman."

"And like I said then, you've never been monogamous for a long period of time. What happens six months or a year down the road when you grow tired of me and a piece of ass turns your head?"

"Are you blind? In all the months we've been together on the road, have I even once looked at another woman? Flirted with another woman?"

"You couldn't because of the contract and what it would mean for your dad's campaign. What happens after Election Day when it no longer matters?" she countered.

"I didn't do it just because of the contract. I did it because you fucking consumed me. I only had eyes for you, and I always will."

"You can't make promises like that."

I jerked my hand through my hair. "Isn't my word worth anything?"

Addison rose off the bed. "I wish it was."

"What happens now? You just call it quits and leave?"

"If you're worrying about the campaign—"

"I couldn't give a fuck less about that. Right now I'm more concerned with you and me."

"Outside of the campaign, there is no you and me, not really."

"Oh hell yes there is."

Addison turned away from me to throw the last of her things in her suitcase. "Look, I've taken care of everything. I called Bernie last night."

"You did?"

"Yes. He helped come up with a plan." After zipping up her suitcase, she turned back to me. "We're going to say the pneumonia I had earlier in the campaign has come back, and a doctor has ordered me on strict bed rest. I'm going to post a message to the blog from my bed, looking like hell, where I'll relay how disappointed I am that I can't be on the trail for the last two weeks. No one will be the wiser. It'll just be one more bullshit story in this façade of a relationship."

Grabbing her by the arm, I forced her to look at me. "It's not a façade. I love you, dammit!"

"In time, you'll see I was right."

When I opened my mouth to argue with her, a knock came at the door. "Who the hell is it?" I growled.

"Ty."

I narrowed my eyes at Addison. "You even told Ty you were leaving before you told me?"

"He doesn't know anything except that I need a ride to the airport. I led him to believe something was wrong with Evan."

"With your ability to lie at the drop of a hat, perhaps you have a future in politics." Even though I knew it was a low blow, I wanted her to hear me, to stop judging me for who I once was.

Ignoring me, Addison went over and opened the door. When Ty stepped into the room, he suddenly recoiled back as if he could feel the heavy tension in the air. At his hesitation, Addison grabbed her purse and bag. "Would you mind getting my suitcase, Ty?"

"Uh, yeah." As he bypassed me, his eyes searched my face for the answer to the questions I knew were swirling in his mind.

When she got to the door, Addison turned around. "Goodbye, Barrett."

Although there were a thousand despicable words I wanted to hurl at her, I instead forced a smile to my face. "I'm only saying goodbye because this is what you think you want. Maybe when you get your head out of your ass and think straight, you'll realize it was a huge mistake, and I'll be here when you do."

An agonized expression came over Addison's face. Without another word, she scurried out the door. Ty threw one last *What the fuck?* look over his shoulder before he hurried to catch up to her.

THE NEXT TWO weeks passed in a blur. I stayed on the Niña, making campaign stop after campaign stop for Dad. I ate artery-clogging food from mom-and-pop diners while guzzling cheap beer. Sleep evaded me, so I existed on a Red Bull cocktail that gave me the energy I needed to keep me going at events all day and part of the night.

True to her word, Addison posted a video explaining her absence from the campaign. She actually managed to sound sick, and although she had been made to look ill, she still looked breathtakingly beautiful to me. At every stop, I fielded questions about her health along with well wishes for her recovery. Sometimes there would be a stuffed animal or a bouquet of flowers for her; I handed each of them off to Pete to send to the local children's hospital.

With a week until election time, we made a swing through Colorado. Mom and Dad sat me down outside Denver and urged me to take a few days off. They must've been truly concerned about me because they even suggested I go back to Martha's Vineyard for some R&R.

I refused. I was going to see this thing through, even if it killed me. Being back at the beach would only make me think of Addison, and I desperately needed something to get her off my mind. I thought about what Marshall had said the day we were signing contracts about a discreet hookup; the truth was I probably couldn't get it up even if I tried. For the first time in my life, the thought of touching another woman held absolutely no appeal. The thought of looking into another woman's eyes while hammering her made me feel sick. I had absolutely no desire to fuck anyone other than Addison.

How could I? She was everything I never knew I wanted or needed. *But will that change? Do I actually have what it takes to be a one-woman man for the rest of my life?* I had promised her I would never want anyone but her. She had been burnt so badly before, but I knew I wasn't capable of cheating. Ever. It just wasn't in my DNA. If I ever fell out of love with her, I would divorce her rather than cheat, and the mere thought of not loving her caused my stomach to revolt.

Addison was wrong. She was it for me, and would be forever.

That was true, but for the time being, I needed to focus on the campaign. I would be everything my parents needed during the days and would drown in my pain at night. Since we were just points ahead in the polls, Dad's advisors decided to go balls to the wall the day before the election. Instead of the usual two-city stop, Dad would hit six cities. I guess some jackwad staffer thought it made sense to do a city for each point we were ahead. Because Dad was in it to win it, he agreed, and because I was also a glutton for punishment, I decided to accompany him.

We started off that morning in Miami, and I couldn't help remembering the time we were there before when Addison charmed the crowds with her fluent Spanish. After Miami, we flew to Cleveland, then to Chicago, Dallas, and finally Los Angeles. It was after midnight when we ended up almost crawling onto The Callahan Corporation jet for our flight back to Virginia.

Dad's advisors stretched out in the chairs in the main cabin while Dad and I bunked together in the bedroom. It was more than just a little odd to be in bed with my father, but at the same time, I knew if things went according to plan, our time together was about to drastically change.

I'd just fluffed my pillow for probably the hundredth time when Dad's voice caused me to jump. "Do you want to talk about it?"

I glanced over my shoulder at him. "The campaign?"

He turned his head to scowl at me. "Don't be coy."

"I wasn't, I just figured that was what you meant."

"Okay then, I'll make it simple—let's talk about what happened with Addison."

I groaned. "Come on, Dad. After the last twenty hours, she's the last thing I want to talk about."

"I think we need to talk about her."

I shoved myself up into a sitting position. "Fine, let's talk about Addison."

After rolling over, Dad propped his head on his hand. "Bernie told me she had to stop campaigning because of her feelings for you."

"Yeah."

"Did you lead her on?"

"Why is it automatically my fault?"

"When has it not been?"

"Damn, Dad, don't sugarcoat it."

"I'm sorry, but it's the truth. It's been the truth since you came out of your awkward phase as a teenager and girls started throwing themselves at you." Dad peered curiously at me. "I would think it was something your mother and I did wrong with our parenting if Thorn acted the same way."

"Oh yes, perfect Thorn," I muttered.

Dad furrowed his brows. "Is that it? Do you have intimacy issues with women because you think we loved your brother more than you?"

I chuckled. "No, that's not it at all."

"I certainly hope not. More than anything, I would hope you know how much your mother and I love you. We love all of you children equally."

"I know you do, Dad. Trust me. There isn't anything you or Mom did or didn't do that made me the way I am about women. It's just who I am."

"It doesn't have to be, son. You can change."

"But that's just it, I did change." I swallowed hard. "I told her I loved her, Dad."

Dad's mouth gaped open, and it took him a few seconds to find his composure. "You did?"

"Yeah, I did."

"And you really meant it?"

I threw my hands up in frustration. "Jesus, why doesn't anyone believe me?"

"I'm sorry, it's just…you surprised me."

"Trust me, I surprised myself, but it's the truth. I love her."

Dad's face lit up. "That's wonderful, Barrett. I'm so proud for you."

"At least you can see I'm sincere."

"Didn't Addison believe you?"

Shaking my head furiously from side to side, I replied, "Even though I said what I felt in my heart, Addison couldn't believe me."

"Why?"

"She said after all these months together, she didn't know what was real and what was fake."

"Oh, son, I'm so sorry."

I exhaled a ragged breath. "I never imagined telling a woman I loved her, and I sure as hell never fathomed her not believing me."

Dad patted my leg. "You have to make her believe you."

"How the hell am I supposed to do that?"

"By fighting for her. Show her how you truly feel. Make her believe without a shadow of a doubt that you love her."

As I stared into Dad's determined face, I knew he was right. Although I didn't have the faintest clue how to do it, I had to fight like hell to make Addison see she was the only woman for me. I had to launch a campaign of my own—one to win Addison's heart.

CHAPTER TWENTY

ADDISON

I SWEPT THROUGH the employee entrance of Divas wearing a baseball cap placed over a platinum blonde wig while sporting huge Jackie O sunglasses. Since my breakup with Barrett, I'd been living at Evan's apartment in Arlington. It was the easiest way for me to avoid the press. If they got a whiff I was back in DC, they'd be staked out at both Barrett's and my apartments.

At first, I'd lied to Evan and said I was off campaigning until Election Day. I just wasn't emotionally strong enough to unburden myself of what had happened. But then, a few days later, he caught me making one of my fake "I'm sick and that's why I'm off the campaign trail" videos. After that, I came clean to him about everything in a blubbering mess of snot and tears. To his credit, Evan had consoled me, but he'd given me space. He didn't question my actions.

It wasn't just Evan who was giving me space. I hadn't heard anything from Barrett since leaving him that morning in Napa. I didn't know what to make of it. Was he respecting my wishes to leave me alone? Or had he realized he had just been caught up in all the make-believe and really didn't love me like he thought he did? In the end, I was too chicken-shit to call or text him to see.

Although I hated myself for it, sometimes I couldn't stop myself from watching some of the campaign footage, specifically the clips that featured Barrett. He had been keeping a manic pace on the road since we'd parted. His appearance seemed somewhat haggard—he bore dark circles under his eyes, and his usually jovial expression had become somber. The part of me that wanted to give in to my feelings argued that the change in Barrett was because he really was lovesick, but the other part countered by saying his sullenness came from being rejected.

After too many nights holed up on Evan's couch eating Chinese takeout and watching *The West Wing* on Netflix, I'd decided I had to get out. More importantly, I had to get my mind off of Barrett. So, I'd taken Evan up on his offer to work at Divas. Initially, I thought it would be good for me to be somewhere I was guaranteed not to see Barrett. Unfortunately, the moment I entered my dressing room, memories of the night he'd come to the club came flooding back. I could almost feel Barrett's fingers feathering across my skin as he undid my taping. After all, things had really started to change between us that night.

With pain zigzagging through my chest, I flopped down into the makeup chair. As I took off the baseball cap, Evan breezed through the door. Wrinkling his nose, he remarked, "That's a hideous wig."

I laughed as I slid it off my head. "It's just for a disguise. I wouldn't dare disgrace your stage with this second-rate hairpiece."

"You sure as hell better not."

When I took my sunglasses off, Evan let out a low whistle. "I'm going to owe Bryan a raise considering all the work he's going to have to put into your makeup tonight."

"My life is in the toilet. Am I not allowed a good cry or two?"

"Or a hundred," Evan countered.

"Bite me."

He hopped up on the counter in front of me. "Why are you doing this to yourself?"

"Because I'm depressed."

He shook his head. "I mean, why aren't you riding off into the sunset with Barrett? The man told you he loved you, Ads."

"It's not that simple."

"Considering how hard it is for most men—gay or straight—to say those three little words, I'd say it was pretty simple."

"But his past—"

"Screw his past. It isn't fair to fault him for things he did before you." Tilting his head toward me, he countered, "How can you possibly be a missionary's daughter and not believe in the power of redemption?"

"Trust me, I want to believe in it. I want to believe Barrett—that he's truly changed, that he will never cheat on me."

"Then believe it."

Swallowing hard, I shook my head. "I can't, no matter how hard I try, and after Walt, I can't be so naïve."

"Just like it's not fair to punish Barrett for his past, you can't punish him for yours either. He isn't Walt."

I glanced down at my hands, and the glittering engagement ring stared up at me. I hadn't been able to take it off. The rational part of me argued that I couldn't take it off until after the election because being seen without it might raise speculation; the lovesick part knew that once I took it off, I would be symbolically severing my ties to Barrett.

"Maybe he isn't, but I know I can't survive having my heart broken again. Whatever I felt for Walt was just a tiny flake in the avalanche of what I feel for Barrett."

"You're making a big mistake, Ads."

I swiped the tears from my eyes. "Maybe I am, but in the end, I have to do what makes me feel safe. I have to love me more."

"Even if that love and safety comes at the price of your happiness?"

"Yes," I murmured.

Evan huffed exasperatedly before he hopped down off the counter. "Then you're a damned fool."

Maybe I was being a fool, but I was just too stubborn to do anything about it.

CHAPTER TWENTY-ONE

BARRETT

NOVEMBER 12th WAS *the* day in more ways than one. It was the day Dad was going to be elected President of the United States, and it was also the day I was going to win Addison back. I could feel it deep down in my bones. The Callahan men were going to be victorious.

The day started impossibly early as I woke up in my apartment for the first time in months. My offer for Mom and Dad to stay at my apartment had been vetoed, and instead, they had opted for a suite at The Plaza, which truthfully was closer to where he would be giving one of his final speeches.

Once Dad finished, he would be flying back to Alexandria so he and Mom could vote at their registered polling station. While Dad was speaking, I would make a quick run across town to cast my vote. Although we could have done absentee ballots, it was a time-honored tradition for a candidate and their family to vote in person.

With Addison registered in DC, I wouldn't have the chance to see her until later in the day when we took over the Jefferson as we awaited election returns. Of course, the moment I stepped out of the car at the polling station, the media bombarded me with questions about where Addison was. I assured them they would be seeing her soon.

On the flight home, I caught the video of Addison going to vote. Although she was without the benefit of Saundra and Everett, her appearance in a navy dress and white coat was impeccable. I was sure Evan had had something to do with that since she was staying with him. Ty helped her maneuver through the reporters as she made her way inside the polling building. With our group overrun with Secret Service agents, I had dispatched Ty to be with Addison. There was no man I trusted more with her safety.

When we got back to the Jefferson, I immediately began scouring the crowd for any sight of Addison. "She isn't here," Pete said from behind me.

Whirling around, I questioned, "Why not?"

"She let Bernie know she would be staying at volunteer headquarters until the polls closed. Then Ty will escort her here."

I glanced down at my watch. It was two hours until the polls closed. I couldn't possibly wait that long. I had to see Addison now. "Can you call a car for me?"

Pete shook his head. "You can't go anywhere. In thirty minutes, the press is coming out in droves to cover Thorn's FaceTime with your Dad. You and Caroline will both be expected to be there for a photo op."

"Fuck," I muttered under my breath.

"It's just two hours. Then she'll be here and you can undertake whatever grand gesture it is you have in mind to win her over."

I cocked my brows at him. "Win her over instead of back? Like I didn't do anything wrong?"

Pete winked. "Anyone with a pair of eyes can see she's crazy about you."

My heart did that funny flip-flop thing that made me question whether I needed to get an EKG. "Really?"

"Oh yeah."

"I hope you're right, man."

"Of course I am. Why else would your father put so much faith in my abilities?"

I laughed. "Just keep ego tripping, man."

With a grin, Pete motioned for me to follow him. "Come on. Let's get you in the family suite for Thorn's call."

THE NEXT TWO two hours seemed to pass in a dreamlike state. Everyone went crazy at the sight of a fully recovered Thorn back in the field with his men standing in front of a giant American flag. Even I got a little teary at the truly patriotic moment, especially when he saluted Dad and called him Forty-Eight. Hopefully in a few short hours, Dad really would be the forty-eighth president.

At seven, I started pacing around the family suite, waiting for Addison to show up. A half hour went by, and then an hour. When early precincts began reporting on Dad's lead, everyone started cheering and clapping. I, on the other hand, retreated to one of the corners. After taking my phone out of my pocket, I called Ty. "Where the hell is she?" I demanded.

"We've been tied up in traffic."

"Is that the truth, or are you just fucking with me?"

"Of course it's the truth. Take a look outside if you don't believe me."

I gave a grunt of frustration. "I really need to see her."

Ty's voice lowered. "I know you do, and I swear, I'm doing my best to get her to you."

"Thanks man."

"We'll see you soon."

I'd barely hung up the phone when a reporter appeared before me. "Was that Addison you were talking to? Why isn't she here?"

Instead of punching him, I forced a smile to my face. "She's stuck in traffic after spending the afternoon with her old coworkers at campaign headquarters."

"How kind of her. You certainly are a lucky man."

My chest constricted at his words. "Yeah, I am," I croaked. I excused myself before I did something completely unmanly like bursting into tears. Another half hour went by without any sign of Addison, and the exhilaration and triumph in the air surrounding me did little to boost my mood.

Finally, my phone dinged with a text from Ty: *We're on the way up.*

Without a word to anyone, I hurried out the bedroom door. Since I'd gone inside the family suite hours earlier, the penthouse had become packed with people. I craned my neck, searching for Addison. As I made my way through the crowd, people patted my back and gave me congratulatory hugs, but I couldn't be bothered to acknowledge them. Addison was my only concern.

I finally saw her. God, she was so beautiful. Her nose and cheeks were flushed from the cold, and her long, dark hair was windblown. As she chewed on her bottom lip, her gaze darted around the room, taking in all the people. Then, as if she sensed my presence, she stared right at me.

At the sight of me coming toward her with the steely determination of a lion stalking a gazelle, Addison's eyes widened. Her panicked gaze bounced left and right to see if she could make a quick escape, but it was too packed for her to make a getaway.

"I need to talk to you, alone," I shouted over the celebratory roar.

"There's nothing more for you to say. Today is Election Day, and the gig is officially over." She stared pointedly at me. "*We're* over."

I shook my head furiously back and forth. "No, we're not. I know you love you me."

"You're so infuriating!" she shrieked before she started pushing and shoving her way through the crowd. After glancing over her shoulder to see me close on her heels, she whirled back around. She poked me in the chest with one of her fingers. "Look, I know you're not used to being dumped by women, but trust me when I say, we're done. Now leave me alone!"

I placed my hands her shoulders. Dipping my head close to her ear, I said, "But I can't do that. Trust me, I tried to respect your wishes and walk away, but the last two weeks were absolutely miserable without you."

Realizing we had an audience of curious onlookers, I nudged Addison out the nearest door. Unfortunately, it was out onto one of the balconies. Biting cold air rushed at the two of us, causing us to shiver. Once we were hidden away from prying eyes, I pulled Addison into my arms. "I love you."

Her eyes pinched shut in pain. "Please stop saying that, Barrett."

"I'm going to keep on saying it until you understand I mean it with all my heart, body, and soul. I'm going to fight day and night for you." I drew in a deep breath. "I love you, Addison Monroe. If I'm honest with myself, I've loved you since that first weekend at the Jefferson. I loved you when you mooned the press corps and when you drank half a quart of moonshine and became Eva Peron. I loved it when you flashed your tits and ass on stage as Cher at Divas."

"Those are the things that made you fall in love with me?" Addison huffed indignantly.

"Yes—I mean, no, not just those. It was a million other things, like the way you genuinely care for my parents, and how you never meet a stranger. I love how intelligent and driven you are. I love how you want to make the world a better place with your empathy and your caring heart. I'm not sure there is a single thing about you I don't love."

When I dropped down onto my knees, Addison gasped. "Barrett, what on earth are you doing?"

"An incredibly grand gesture since the concrete is fucking freezing and these pants cost a ridiculous amount of money."

"Excuse me?"

I sighed. "Look, I'm on my knees before you to beg you to forgive and forget my past, to realize I am not the same man I was before I met you. I can tell you with absolute certainty that as long as I live, there will never be another woman I could love as much as I love you. You're the one and only."

Addison's eyes bored into mine, desperately seeking the answers to the questions I knew were swirling in her mind. More than anything, I knew she wanted to know if this was for real. "I love you for real and forever, Addison."

"You really do?" When a few tears slid down her cheeks, I desperately wanted to brush them away—anything to touch her.

"Yes, I do."

Addison's face lit up, and she smiled. It was the most beautiful thing I had ever seen. *She* was the most beautiful thing I had ever seen, and damn if she wasn't mine.

"I never stopped loving you, too, Barrett."

Just as I rose off the concrete, she dove into my arms and our lips crashed together in a desperate kiss. After staying lip-locked for a few minutes, we pulled away to catch our breath. "I'm glad you finally believe me. I thought I might have to do something really desperate like threaten to jump off the Washington Monument or something."

With a grin, Addison replied, "You would pick a phallic object to declare your undying love from, wouldn't you?"

I laughed. "I'll have you know that thought never crossed my desperate mind. I just wanted to find a way to make you mine."

Cocking her head, Addison asked, "You're really going to belong to me and only me?"

"Yes, for the rest of my life." Taking one of her hands, I placed it over my heart. "This has never belonged to any other woman but you, and it is only yours."

After glancing around to see that no one was watching us through the windows, she cupped my dick with her free hand. "I know this has belonged to hundreds of women—is *it* only mine now?"

"Yes, for your immense pleasure only."

Addison laughed. "It sure as hell better be." After taking her hand away from my dick, she pressed herself against me, and her satisfied sigh fanned across my shirt. "I love you, Barrett."

"I love you more."

As I dipped my head to kiss her, the balcony door blew open and we whirled around to see Ty staring at us expectantly. "You guys need to get in here. They're about to start calling some major states in favor of your dad."

"Okay. We'll be right there."

Ty nodded before he headed back inside. I held out my arm for Addison to take. "Ready to go shake the hand of the president-elect?"

Addison's face lit up. "He's really going to win, isn't he?"

"He sure as hell is."

"I knew he would, especially the last few months when he was leading in the polls, but it's still surreal to believe he's actually going to be the president."

"I'd have to say it's been a pretty victorious night for the Callahan men. Dad got the country, and I got you."

Smiling up at me, Addison said, "Kiss me, First Son."

As I brought my lips to hers, I couldn't believe how lucky I was that someone like Addison could love someone like me. Just when I wrapped my arms around her to deepen the kiss, Ty banged on the door. "Cockblocker," I muttered against Addison's lips.

She giggled. "I'll make sure to make it up to the Bear tonight."

"You know, I think it's time to retire that nickname."

Her brows shot up in surprise. "You do?"

I nodded. "I'm thinking from here on out, he'll be the First Penis." Addison groaned as she started to the door. "What about the Commander in Cock?" I called to her retreating form.

"Dream on," she replied.

With a laugh, I hurried to catch up to her at the door. "Fine, we'll keep the Bear, and he'll be regulated to your cave and your cave only."

She shook her head at me. "That is both repulsive and endearing."

"That's me."

She grinned. "Yes, indeed it is."

"And you love me?"

"Yes, I do."

"And I love you."

EPILOGUE

ADDISON

THERE ARE SOME moments in life you will never, ever forget as long as you live. When you're old and grey and listening to the heave and sigh of your front porch rocking chair, you will recall those moments with a smile. I had just had just such a day, and in fact, it had been so jam-packed with memorable moments, I felt like I was on sensory overload.

Hours later, every molecule in my body continued to hum with a post-excitement buzz. Although I was physically exhausted and emotionally drained, I couldn't have slept if I'd wanted to. I wasn't sure I would ever sleep again without literally being knocked out. Besides, I never wanted today, Inauguration Day, to end. It had been far too magical.

Like a kid waiting for Christmas morning, I hadn't been able to sleep last night. Barrett seemed to be suffering from the same problem, so we ended up keeping each other occupied by making love into the wee hours of the morning. When our six AM wake-up call came, I stumbled out of bed and lurched around like a zombie.

A hair and makeup team was dispatched to our suite to get me ready. Even Barrett got some pampering as he got a shave and a haircut before being helped into his suit and tie. With the high only in the 20s, I wished to be wearing long underwear rather than pantyhose under my navy wool sheath dress, as well as knee boots instead of heels.

At precisely nine AM, we arrived at the White House to have pre-inauguration coffee and breakfast with the soon-to-be former President Mitchum. As Barrett and I followed his mom and dad down the carpeted halls, I couldn't believe that in a few hours, this would be their home for at least the next four years. When you added in the Secret Service contingency and the vast corridors of the White House, it was overwhelming. If James and Jane were nervous, they didn't show it. Instead, they sported their usual warm smiles.

Fast-forward three hours later to when I sat shivering in the inaugural boxes. Three rows down, Senator Callahan placed his left hand on the Bible Jane held and raised his right hand to take the oath of office. His voice echoed over the speakers. "I do solemnly swear that I will faithfully execute the office of President of the United States…"

Tears flooded my eyes at the enormity of the moment. On my right, Caroline sniffled and raised a tissue to dab her eyes. Glancing at Barrett, I couldn't hide my surprise that even he had tears shimmering in his blue eyes. Months ago, I would have never thought him capable of showing emotion in public, yet here he was. I reached over to take his gloved hand in mine. When

I squeezed it encouragingly, he didn't take his eyes off his father, but he did smile in acknowledgement. I loved seeing the pride in his eyes.

Once the swearing in ceremony was over, we headed back to the White House for a lunch reception in the State Dining Room. It was packed with friends, family, and supporters of James. My parents and Evan had also scored invitations, along with my sister, Amy, and her husband. It was nice having my family together again.

Then there was the parade where we marched along the Mall, waving to the cheering crowd. By the time it was over, I felt like my smile was frozen on my face, and my hand and arm ached from the exertion. After that, we headed back to the White House in time to attend yet another formal dinner where you made polite small talk with someone you'd never met and probably would never see again.

With a full stomach, I left dinner to head upstairs where my entourage waited to get me ready for my appearance at the ten official balls President Callahan and the First Lady, Vice President Smith and his wife, and their families were expected to attend.

After smoothing my white opera-gloved hands over the intricate beading of my sapphire blue dress, I glanced at the antique clock on the antique mantle. Everything in this room was old and pulsed with historical significance. For the days following the inauguration, I'd been given the Queen's Bedroom to stay in. Since Barrett and I weren't married, the White House staffers decided to preserve some decorum by having us stay in separate rooms, but I didn't know who they were kidding thinking Mr. Sex Fiend would go one night without sneaking from the family quarters into my room.

Turning slowly, I once again took in the pink painted walls and floral carpeting. I fought the urge to pinch myself for probably the thousandth time that day. I mean, I was standing in the Queen's Bedroom, which had gotten its name from the fact that so many royal queens had stayed there. American royalty had stayed in this room as well, when Jackie Kennedy had occupied the room while the family quarters were renovated back in '61. It wasn't just a bedroom—oh no, it had its own sitting room and bathroom as well.

In a dress designed by Valentino, a new pair of Jimmy Choos commissioned especially for me, and a ridiculously expensive sapphire and diamond necklace and matching encrusted earrings on loan from Tiffany's, I couldn't help feeling a little bit like royalty. Although Barrett wanted me to get used to the upscale life he was accustomed to, it was harder than I thought. I often felt like Cinderella in her rags, and I knew it was something that was going to take time. You didn't spend summers in one-room houses in poverty-stricken areas just to one day not bat an eye about having a driver or wearing designer clothes.

A knock at the door brought me out of my thoughts. "Come in," I called as I went to grab my sequined evening bag off the vanity table.

The door swung open to reveal Barrett in a jet-black tux and tails. His eyes flared as his gaze swept over me from head to toe and my skin tingled under his appraisal. Even though it'd only been a little over fourteen hours since we'd last been intimate, an ache of desire spread between my thighs, causing me to shift my legs.

"You look..." His Adam's apple bobbed as he swallowed hard. "Wow."

I grinned as I crossed the room toward him. "Why, kind sir, don't put yourself out with such a long list of compliments," I teased.

Barrett reached around to smack me on the ass. "You should feel honored that your astounding beauty rendered me speechless."

"*Momentarily* speechless." I pressed myself flush against Barrett's body while my hands encircled his neck. "I am grateful. I'm grateful that such a devastatingly handsome man with a rocking body finds me so gorgeous."

A pleased smile twitched on Barrett's lips. "I guess that means you like my white tie and tails."

With a nod, I replied, "You make that tux look good, baby."

"I'm glad to hear you like it." His eyes dropped from mine to once again take in my appearance. "Damn, that's some dress you're wearing."

"I'll make sure to give your compliments to Mr. Valentino."

"Tell him extra thanks for giving you a neckline that shows off your tits."

I tugged the strands of hair at the base of Barrett's neck in a playful warning. "Don't say tits in front of my dress."

"Oh excuse me, I didn't realize it would get so offended."

"It's very refined."

"I'd call it a prude if it didn't show off your tits so nicely."

I laughed. "You are totally hopeless."

Amusement twinkled in blue eyes. "I know. It's a good thing I have the love of an amazing woman to save me."

His words instantly melted my heart. "I love you so very much, Barrett."

Barrett's response to my declaration was to bring his lips to mine. At first, the kiss was soft and heartfelt, but like the flickers of a growing flame, it became much more passionate. Our tongues tangled together as I tugged my fingers through Barrett's hair.

When Barrett ran his hand up my ribcage to cup my breast, I momentarily froze. It wasn't that I didn't welcome his touch or that I thought it was inappropriate for him to be groping me in my ball gown; it was more about the fact that I had just remembered there was a Secret Service agent standing in the doorway. Sure, he had his back to us, but it was totally mood-killing.

Barrett abruptly ended our kiss and pulled away. "What's wrong?"

I motioned my head over his shoulder. "We have an audience," I whispered.

He grinned. "I guess that means you're not into having someone watch us have sex."

Blood rushed to my face. "No I am not!" I sputtered indignantly as I shoved Barrett away.

"Okay, okay. Voyeuristic sex goes off the list."

"It sure as hell does. Public places maybe, but never with an audience."

Barrett's hands came to cup my cheeks. "I'd be happy with just the missionary position as long as I got to have sex with you."

An unladylike snort escaped me. "Like you would ever be satisfied with just the missionary position."

"Mr. Callahan?" an unknown staffer questioned behind us.

"Yes?"

"Your parents are waiting on you in the Yellow Room."

Barrett nodded. "Tell them we'll be right there."

Once the staffer scurried off, Barrett held out his arm for me. "Come, Miss Monroe. We have balls to attend." In true Barrett fashion, he leaned over to whisper into my ear, "Of course, I would much rather you being attending to my balls."

"You're so crude."

"Like when you suck one into your warm, wet mouth while you pump my cock in your hand."

I whimpered as his words sent heat shooting between my legs. "Yellow Room, now," I murmured.

Barrett snickered. "Thinking my parents will be the cool down you need?"

I grinned at him. "It's more like I'm going to need to step outside onto the Truman Balcony to let the frigid temperatures cool me off."

After meeting up with Barrett's parents and siblings in the Yellow Room—one of the oval sitting rooms in the family residence—we made our way downstairs, where a wall of Secret Service agents closed in around us as we piled into the second bulletproof limousine behind James and Jane. Thorn and two of his Army buddies rode along with us, as did Caroline, who kept giving Ty longing looks. Who could blame her? He was gorgeous with a sexy British accent.

When we got out of the limo at the hotel, flashbulbs momentarily blinded me. Even after all my time on the campaign, I didn't think I would ever get used to the media and their cameras. As the fake fiancée/real girlfriend of the First Son, I was going to have to get used to them being an unwanted part of my life. As long as they didn't catch me accidentally flashing my boobs or my ass, I would be okay, although it did kinda suck not getting to have a say in what pictures of you were splashed across the front of newspapers and magazines.

At the banquet room door, we were momentarily held back from entering. Then the song the twelve-piece band was playing abruptly ended, and a rousing rendition of "Hail to the Chief" erupted. The doors opened wider, and James and Jane strode into the room. It was still hard to wrap my mind around the fact that whenever I heard the song now, it was for James.

After Barrett and I made our entrance, we did our best making the rounds with smiles and small talk. I found the first two balls rather stuffy and pretentious; they were made up of old money and political connections, people who had spent ridiculous amounts of money supporting James's campaign. Although my heart wasn't completely in it, Barrett and I waltzed while giving beaming smiles for the cameras.

Thankfully, the evening took a turn for the better at our next stop, which was the Texas-themed Black Tie and Boots Ball. There was just something about cowboy boots and Stetsons that made me feel welcome. The big surprise that sent me out of my mind was when I saw it was my old friend, Abby Renard, and her brothers' band, Jacob's Ladder, who struck up "Hail to the Chief" as James entered. Wide eyed, I turned to Barrett. "Did you know about this?"

He gave me his signature smirk. "I might've made a suggestion to the planners."

Squealing with delight, I threw my arms around his neck. "I love it."

"I thought you would."

After giving him a quick peck on the lips, I pulled back so we could make our entrance. When the song came to an end, Abby smiled as she took the microphone. "President Callahan, Mrs. Callahan, Vice President Smith, Mrs. Smith, I just want to say what an immense pleasure it is for my brothers and me to be here to perform for you. It truly is an honor and a career highlight to be part of such a special night."

Abby paused as applause broke out in the room. Her gaze then met mine, and she once again smiled. "In case some of you don't know, I'm an old friend of the First Son's fiancée, Addison. Our families were both part of the same missionary abroad program and after spending a few summers together as kids, we became pen pals in the pre-internet days. Thankfully, with the onset of technology, we've gotten to keep in touch over states and continents. I've loved every minute of watching her on the campaign trail in support of our newest president, and for our first song of the evening, I'd like to play one of her favorites." Abby winked. "Addison, this one is for you!"

"Where I Roam" was the song that had launched Jacob's Ladder back before Abby had taken her older brother, Micah's, place. The upbeat tempo and twangy mix of fiddle and banjo had people rushing to the dance floor.

As soon as the song ended, I made a beeline for the stage so I could say hello to Abby as soon as possible. While Eli and Gabe started up the opening chords of their latest hit, Abby hurried down the steps to hug me. "I cannot believe you're here!" I screeched over the music.

Abby laughed as she squeezed me tight. When she pulled back, she gave me a beaming smile. "I could probably say the same thing to you considering you're engaged to the First Son. That is pretty amazing, Ads," Abby gushed.

"It's more like the Second First Son since Thorn's the oldest," I teasingly said.

"Whatever. It's still pretty amazing."

"That's high praise coming from the woman who has won Grammys and CMA awards, not to mention marrying a smokin' hot rocker."

Pride and happiness radiated in Abby's eyes. "We've both come a long, long way from our missionary kid days, haven't we?"

I nodded. "We sure have."

"But I wouldn't trade those days for anything. They taught me so much."

"They sure did."

After Abby threw a glance over her shoulder, Eli jerked his chin at her. "I gotta go. Jake's at the hotel with the twins, and I'd love for you to meet them before we go home on Friday."

"I'd love to. Let's plan on lunch tomorrow."

"Okay." She waved before hurrying back up the stairs to the microphone.

When someone tapped me on the shoulder, I whirled around to see that it was Barrett.

"Ready to get your boot scootin' boogie on?"

I laughed. "I'd love to, just never use that phrase again."

Barrett grinned as we walked out onto the dance floor. We danced through two fast songs before the music changed over to a slow, smooth ballad, and I closed my eyes as Barrett drew me flush against him under the glittering lights of the ballroom. Once again, I fought the urge to pinch myself. It felt just like being in a fairytale where I was Cinderella at the ball with my handsome Prince Charming. I never wanted the moment or that feeling to end.

Inevitably, the song eventually came to an end, and Barrett's breath warmed against my ear. "I need to be alone with you, Addison."

Nervous laughter bubbled from my lips. "There are too many people, too many risks," I countered.

"Just trust me."

Against my better judgment, I let Barrett lead me off the dance floor and out onto one of the balconies. I smiled as it reminded me of election night. Barrett pulled me against his body, shielding me from the cold. "Addison?"

"Mmhmm," I murmured cautiously, waiting for him to tell me to hike my dress up and bend over the railing.

"Would you still like a wedding in the Rose Garden?"

"Wait, what?"

"Do you want to get married in the Rose Garden?"

I jerked back to stare open-mouthed at him. "What?"

"Well, from what I read in *The White House: A History*—one of the many books my mother forced on me—June is a peak month for roses, so that would probably be the best time for a wedding." He cocked his brows at me. "Do you think you could plan one in six months?"

Desperately, I tried processing what Barrett was saying. "I guess I could…" I tilted my head. "Why do you ask?"

"Because I think we should get married."

Oh. My. God. As a bundle of emotions came crashing down on me, I fought to keep myself from falling to a heap on the floor. Thankfully, Barrett had his arms around me, but that didn't last for long.

He dropped to one knee in front of me. "This is the moment when I would normally present you with a ring, but you already have one."

I glanced down at my hand. After our breakup, I hadn't taken the ring off because it would have raised suspicion. Then when we made up on election night, I still kept it on.

"I thought about buying you a different ring because this one might be tainted by our fake engagement, but when it came down to it, there wasn't another ring in the whole world I wanted you to have. This ring symbolizes the day we first became a couple, even if it wasn't for real. From that day on, my love and admiration for you began to grow. Someone who never saw himself capable of loving just one woman found the peace and contentment of monogamy. I discovered that a part of me was missing, and you were the only thing that could make me whole again. I can't imagine spending the rest of my life with anyone else but you."

My heartbeat broke into such a wild gallop, I feared it would explode right out of my chest. The range of emotions rocketing through me was seriously overwhelming. The moment I'd dreamed about was actually coming true—Barrett was down on one knee, proposing to me.

"Addison, will you marry me?"

I wasn't sure why, but at that moment, all I could whisper was, "For real?"

Barrett gave me a genuine smile full of love as he nodded his head. "For real."

"Yes, yes, YES!" I cried. I barely gave Barrett time to stand up before I leapt into his arms. After he twirled me around, he brought his lips to mine, and I poured everything I had within me into that kiss. If I had died in that moment, I would have died a very happy woman.

Even though I was freezing to death out there, I wished we could have spent the rest of the night wrapped up in each other's arms. All too soon, it was time for us to leave to make another appearance. Over the next five hours, we hit the rest of the official balls and then dropped by two private parties. As if the day hadn't already been magical enough, Barrett's proposal made me feel like I was floating on air.

By the time we got back to the White House, it was after four AM. After taking the elevator to the executive quarters, we walked hand in hand down the Center Hall to our bedrooms. When we got to the East Sitting Hall, Barrett tugged me against him. Since there was a Secret Service agent station not far from us, Barrett dipped his head to whisper in my ear, "Wanna get busy with me in Honest Abe's bed?"

I threw my head back with a laugh. "You can't be serious."

"Oh, I'm very serious." He rolled his hips against mine, and I felt that his cock was very serious as well. "I've got a proclamation to emancipate you from your panties."

"You did *not* just degrade the Emancipation Proclamation like that," I huffed indignantly.

Barrett chuckled. "I knew it would get a rise out of you, and I get so turned on by seeing you riled." He winked at me. "Besides, I'm sure Abe would forgive me—bro code and all."

Pushing him away, I wagged a finger at him. "I'm pretty sure Abe's high moral standards wouldn't stand for us sharing a room when we're unmarried, naughty boy."

"Do you know how many unmarried people have gotten busy under this roof?"

"Too many to count, I'm sure."

Nuzzling my neck, Barrett's breath singed my skin. "We're engaged now—that has to count for something."

"I know but—" With a growl, Barrett bent over, swept me off my feet, and threw me over his left shoulder. "Put me down, you caveman!"

"I'll put you down all right—down in my bed where you belong." He then smacked my ass for good measure and the sound echoed through the vacant hallway.

I let out a shriek of protest as he started marching me toward the Lincoln Bedroom. When I dared to throw a glance over my shoulder, I saw the Secret Service agent's lips twitching like he was trying very hard not to laugh.

Barrett threw open the door and then kicked it closed with his foot. My anger was momentarily forgotten as the significance of where I was washed over me—it was the bedroom of one of our greatest presidents. Sure, Lincoln had never actually slept in here, but it had been his office. This was his furniture.

Barrett was true to his word about not putting me down unless it was in his bed. After my body flopped unceremoniously down onto the mattress, I craned my neck to take in every aspect of the room—the regal gold curtains, the gold and brown patterned wallpaper, the deep mahogany furniture.

"By the expression on your face, I'm starting to think you're getting a hard-on for Abe," Barrett said as he made quick work of shedding his tux jacket.

I giggled as I propped myself up on my elbows. "I can't help it. You know what a history nerd I am."

With a grin, Barrett undid his white bow tie. "It's one of the many quirky things I love about you."

"Quirky or kooky?" I teasingly asked.

"Endearing," he diplomatically replied.

I rose up on my knees and scooted to the edge of the bed. My fingers reached out to start unbuttoning Barrett's shirt and I asked, "What else do you love about me?"

"The way your tongue pokes out when you're concentrating really hard."

Scowling at him, I replied, "Out of everything you could love about me, that's what you pick?"

"What's wrong with it?"

"Ugh, it makes me sound like a dog."

Shrugging out of his shirt, Barrett argued, "No it doesn't, it makes you cute."

"Fine. I'm cute when I stick my tongue out like a dog. What else?"

"The way you hum show tunes when you're nervous, and the light in your eyes when you see an animal of any kind."

"Yep, I'm a sappy dork."

The serious expression on Barrett's face caused my heart to accelerate. "The way you want to make the world a better place even though the cards are stacked against you, and the way you give of yourself to help others."

"That's very sweet. Thank you."

"I can be sweet."

"I know that. It's one thing that endears me to you."

A mischievous look flashed in Barrett's eyes as he unbuttoned and unzipped his pants. Standing before me in his tight black briefs, he added, "I also love the way your eyes roll back in your head when you take that first sip of morning coffee."

I jabbed my finger in his now bare chest. "It's not polite to make fun of an addict, and we both know how addicted I am to coffee."

Barrett laughed. "I'm not making fun of you, just stating the facts." He reached around me to find the zipper of my dress. After lowering it, he dipped his head so his breath warmed my ear. "I also like the way your eyes roll back in your head when my tongue or my dick is buried deep inside your pussy."

Need burned through me, causing me to shudder. His fingers came to the straps of my dress and after he eased them down my arms, I raised my hips up so he could slide the dress off. When he couldn't get me out of the dress fast enough, he started to tug on the fabric. "Hey now, you gotta be gentle with the Valentino," I urged.

"Fuck it. I'll buy you another one."

Once my dress was whisked away and unceremoniously tossed to the floor, I was left in the lacy black thigh-highs and the navy bustier that sucked me in and pushed my boobs up.

Barrett's hungry gaze caused me to lick my lips in anticipation. "I also love the way your tits look when they're cinched up like that. Makes me want to slide my dick between them."

"Why am I not surprised you found a way to make this lovefest all about sex?" I teased.

Cocking his head, Barrett suggested, "Because me being a sex fiend is something you love about me."

"That's true, just one of the many, many things." I cupped his face in my hands. "Now will you shut up and make love to your real fiancée in Lincoln's bedroom?"

"I'll shut up, but only if I can *fuck* my fiancée in Lincoln's bedroom."

"I think a compromise is in order."

"What would that entail?" Barrett questioned as he loomed over me.

"You can fuck me, but only if you promise to also make love to me."

"It's been a long day—are you sure you're up for that?"

I grinned as I eyed the bulge in his underwear. "As long as the Bear's up for it, I am."

"Trust me, he's always up for it." Barrett dipped off the mattress to open the nightstand drawer. To show his commitment to my compromise, he tossed a sheet of condoms onto the bed.

I snorted. "You just moved in here today and you already have condoms in the nightstand?"

"I thought putting them in my tux pocket would be tacky."

"Good thinking."

Opening a condom, Barrett said, "We need to get you on the pill."

"I can do that, but with only six months until the wedding, it might not make sense for me to get started now."

Barrett paused before sliding the condom on his massive length. "Why not?"

"Because I might want to have a baby right away," I teasingly replied. While I braced myself for his horror and indignation, I hadn't planned on his actual reaction.

"Why don't we start now, and we could really have tongues wagging with a shotgun wedding?" he suggested.

My eyes bulged. "You're joking."

He shook his head. "I'm ready to be a father."

"You're ready for shitty diapers, snotty noses, and bratty tantrums?" I said, repeating the line he had said to me when we had first talked about kids.

"Yep."

"Considering you didn't even want to get married, what could have possibly changed your mind about having children?"

"You did." His expression grew serious. "You changed everything, Addison."

My heartbeat accelerated, and I fought to catch my breath. "Really? I mean about babies."

"Yeah, really." With a grin, Barrett tossed the condom over his shoulder, illustrating to me that he was really in on the baby-making.

My mind felt like it was about to short-circuit with emotions, and when Barrett leaned in to kiss me, I screeched, "Wait!"

Barrett's brows shot up. Before he could ask what my problem was, I dove past him to retrieve one of condoms. At his puzzled look, I smiled. "Call me crazy, but after the unorthodox way our relationship started, I'd like to do things a little more normally, like not walk down the aisle in the Rose Garden at the White House with a baby bump."

"People do have babies first."

"I know, it's just that we've done everything untraditionally, so I'd like a little tradition in my life."

"Then I'll suit up the Bear," Barrett said before taking the condom from me. After sliding it on, he covered my body with his, pushing me down onto the mattress. When his hand came between my thighs, I gasped with pleasure.

As Barrett's fingers worked their magic on me in Lincoln's bed, I still couldn't believe this was my life, my future. Somehow I'd been chosen to fake an engagement for political gain, and as a result I'd found my running mate for life.